Hi-de-Hi!

a novel by

Paul Ableman

based on the BBC-TV series created and written by Jimmy Perry and David Croft, produced by David Croft and directed by David Croft and John Kilby

BRITISH BROADCASTING CORPORATION

Published by the
British Broadcasting Corporation
35 Marylebone High Street
London W1M 4AA

ISBN 0 563 20210 6

First published 1983

Phototypeset by
Input Typesetting Ltd, London
Printed in England by
Cox & Wyman Ltd, Reading

Contents

Stripes

It was a glorious day in mid-September. The sun was as hot as in August and the twenty ladies grouped at one end of the pool were perspiring freely. This was not surprising in view of the fact that they were engaged in physical jerks. They were being led in their exertions by an attractive yellowcoat with raven hair, a good figure and a soft Welsh accent. The twenty voluntary victims were all on the stout side. Indeed, they constituted the Maplin's Ladies Weight-Losing group. They were variously attired in bulging shorts, halters or swim-suits but the most striking impression they made was of white, massive limbs. Their moans of distress at the demands made on them by each new exercise were clearly audible above the shrill clamour arising from the toddlers' paddling pool that separated them from the deckchairs on the lawn.

The senior camper planted himself in one of these chairs, withdrew from his pocket the small square tin that held his cigarette-making equipment and began to roll himself a cigarette. He had not even reached the stage of licking the gummed rim of the paper when he was interrupted in his labours by a kind of strangled gasp from the deckchair on his left. He glanced cautiously in that direction and discovered that his neighbour was a narrow-shouldered, long-faced youth wearing white flannel trousers, none too clean, and bare above the waist. He was staring fixedly across the toddlers' pool and the senior camper followed his gaze. He saw the raven-haired yellowcoat running on the spot, her fine bosom heaving up and down, and making altogether a splendid picture of healthy womanhood. The senior camper chuckled inaudibly and returned to the manufacture of his cigarette. He had completed the task and had inserted the thin tube of tobacco between his lips when again he heard the strangled gasp. He raised his eyes across the seething pool and beheld the yellowcoat in the act of touching her toes. In truth what he beheld, since the young woman had her back to them, was a pair of fine, curved legs disappearing, only at the very last moment, into the tight little white pants which enclosed the charming bulge of her rump. He glanced again at his stricken neighbour. The youth's mouth had fallen open and his eyes were glued to the entrancing sight. The senior camper leaned towards him and said jovially:

'That's Gladys Pugh. Gets to you, does she, my son?'

A ripple of irritation at the unwanted interruption stirred the boy's narrow shoulders and hollow chest but he favoured his interlocutor with a brief look. He saw a short, dapper man with a square, friendly face and a somewhat swarthy complexion which might have derived from much sunbathing or, alternatively, from a touch of the gypsy or the Latin in his inheritance. He was wearing neatly-pressed grey-flannel trousers and a flowered shirt. He seemed somehow more poised and confident than the average camper. The boy scowled and asked:

' 'Oo are you?'

'Charley Binns,' returned the other promptly. 'I'm the senior camper.'

'So 'oo cares?' muttered the young man ungraciously.

He looked back across the pool but his quarry, with her class, were now flat on their backs and all that could be seen were limbs intermittently raised. The youth sighed and looked back at the senior camper.

'What the 'ell's the senior camper?' he asked.

Binns smiled. It was a cordial smile but very direct. It contained a hint of warning that its possessor expected to receive a measure of respect. The youth now perceived that, although small and capped with a thatch of grey hair, Mr Binns was equipped with very broad shoulders and exceedingly muscular arms. Binns asked:

'How long have you been coming to Maplin's, my son?'

The youth shrugged.

'Been here three days.'

'Your first trip?'

The other nodded.

'Well, I've been coming here for fifteen years. Three months every year for fifteen years. I know more about this place than any other camper. Come to that I know more about it than any member of the staff.'

'So why doncher write a book?' asked the other jeeringly.

Binns nodded thoughtfully.

'I might. On good manners. Yours are terrible, my son.'

The pale youth observed that Binns' right hand had knotted into a very large and horny fist. He gulped faintly.

''Ow d'yer manage it?' he asked, more politely. 'I mean, free munfs every year. Doncher work?'

'I'm self-employed, my son.'

'What, yer mean – '

'Self-employed,' affirmed Binns conclusively.

The young man nodded. His East London background had taught him not to press questions that were clearly unwelcome to his auditor, especially if the auditor was a short but stocky man who looked as if he could wrestle bulls.

''Oo'd yer say she was?' he asked, nodding across the pool to where the ladies and their leader were rising once more to a vertical posture.

'Gladys Pugh, the senior yellowcoat. Fancy her, do you, my son?'

An expression, half leer and half grin, failed to grace the youth's narrow face.

'Cor. She's got a smashin' – '

The boy's hands moulded an unmistakable part of the anatomy. Binns smiled indulgently.

'Yes, she fills her shorts very nicely now, does Gladys. But there was a time, only a few weeks ago, when she got just a bit too big for her breeches.'

Binns glanced at his watch. It was, the boy noticed, an expensive-looking gold watch. Binns said:

'Nearly an hour till they open. Care to hear about it, my son?'

The boy started to scowl and shake his head. It had been his intention to while away the rest of the afternoon playing snooker with a few mates. But there was a certain steely insistence about Binns' expression which caused his resolution to waver.

'Hear about what?' he asked finally.

Binns edged his deckchair a little closer to the other's. He leaned towards the youth, almost conspiratorially.

'About Gladys and her promotion?'

'Well – '

'Right, you shall, my son.'

Having secured his audience, Binns at last found time to light his cigarette. He took a long drag of some very pungent tobacco and exhaled slowly and contentedly. Then he began.

It all started one day when Ted Bovis and Spike Dixon had been out on the pier doing a spot of fishing. Ted's the camp host, the chubby little bloke that tells the funny stories. Spike's the one that's usually dressed as a pineapple or Old Mother Hubbard or something. He's the camp comedian. They share a chalet do Ted and Spike. Well they was strolling back towards the camp with their fishing rods over their shoulders and a couple of mackerel dangling from Ted's. After a while, Spike said:

'I hope you're not going to cook those in the chalet, Ted. When you did those kippers it took a week to get the pong out of the place.'

Ted replied irritably:

'What's the matter with you, Spike? You nag when we don't catch anything and when we do you nag about how it's going to smell. You know, your nagging will ruin our relationship. If it goes on much longer we'll have to see the marriage guidance people.'

At this point, Ted stopped dead in his tracks, gazing ahead of him with popping eyes. Then, quick as a flash, he grabbed Spike's arm and pulled him behind some bushes they were passing.

'What's up?' asked Spike crossly.

'Trouble, Joe Maplin's here,' snapped Ted.

'How do you know?'

Ted pointed ahead to where a big Rolls-Royce, with a

chauffeur behind the wheel, was parked at the side of the road.

'That's his Rolls,' said Ted.

'Is it? Well, what's it doing out here? Why isn't it in the camp?'

Ted parted two branches and peered.

'Just watch,' he urged.

At this point, a taxi, coming from the direction of the camp, drew up behind the Rolls. Ted smiled knowingly.

'That'll be Joe in that taxi. He's here visiting us. He never drives onto the camp in his Rolls because he doesn't want the campers to see he's making a fortune out of them.'

Spike gazed over Ted's shoulder. He saw a figure get out of the taxi. The figure didn't look like a millionaire to him.

'Why's he wearing that shabby old suit?' he asked.

Ted shook his head grimly.

'That's a very bad sign. He slips into the camp incognito to find out what we're all up to. It means trouble, Spike. Thank heavens it's our day off. Look out!'

As the big, impressive car began to ease towards them the two funny men pressed back into the bushes in an attempt not to be seen.

At just about this time, Jeff and Gladys were locked in conference in Jeff's office. Now Gladys is the brunette over there who's been doing things to your pulse rate. She's Welsh and she's a good sport but a little bossy with it. She's the yellowcoat in charge of sports. Jeff is a very different kind of fish. He's the entertainments manager and he's not the kind of bloke you'd expect to be running bingo in Maplin's. His full name is Jeffrey Fairbrother and before he was appointed to his place here he was a full professor at Cambridge University. But he got tired of that stuffy life and decided to throw in his lot with the people. Gladys was knocked out by him. She'd never met anyone of his class before. It wasn't long, working with him every day, before she fell for him. And Jeff took to Gladys too – but from a distance. The thing is, Jeff already has a wife. They're separated but Jeff has all the honour of his class. He wouldn't lay a finger on Gladys while he still had a wife.

But Gladys was grateful just to work with him every day. At this conference, Jeff was saying:

'I don't think discipline's as bad as you say it is, Gladys. All the yellowcoats are very popular with the campers.'

Gladys tightened her lips. She replied:

'Some of the girls don't pull their weight. It makes it very hard for me. If you're familiar with them, Jeff, it undermines my authority.'

Jeff, it has to be said, has a somewhat peculiar face. It is thin and his mouth is pulled to one side. Not everyone's idea of a smasher but perfection to Gladys. Jeff protested.

'I'm not familiar with them, Gladys.'

'Why do you allow them to call you Jeff then?'

Jeff sighed.

'I tell them to call me Jeff. I don't want to be called Mr Fairbrother. Far too formal. After all, this is a holiday camp. If we go around calling each other Mr and Miss, how can we create an atmosphere of fun?'

'We're supposed to have fun with the campers – not with each other – unless we're off duty, of course. What did your pupils call you at Cambridge?'

'My *students* called me Professor.'

'Well you could make the girls call you Professor.'

Jeff shook his head impatiently.

'Don't be ridiculous, Gladys.'

Gladys stamped her foot lightly.

'Well, something's got to change. They're getting very slack. That great, lanky one – Sylvia – she never has her hands out of her pockets. Lounging about flashing her eyes at the male campers. And then there's that Betty. All she thinks about is standing around with her hands on her hips, taking deep breaths to show her figure off.'

Jeff shook his head reproachfully.

'Oh, that's hardly fair, Gladys. She was in the pool for hours yesterday.'

Gladys nodded grimly.

'Admittedly. But was she doing the crawl? No, of course she wasn't. She was doing the back-stroke.'

Jeff blinked at her for a moment. Then he caught on.

He smiled faintly behind his hand. At this moment, Spike and Ted entered in a great state of excitement. Ted burst out:

'Bad news, Jeff. Did you see him?'

'See who?' asked Jeff wonderingly.

'Joe Maplin. He's been on the camp incognito.'

Jeff stared in astonishment.

'Surely not. He'd have made himself known to me.'

Ted shook his head positively.

'Joe doesn't work like that. He wants to see the camp functioning – warts and all. So he puts on an old suit and ferrets around.'

Jeff rose from behind his desk and went to the window which looked out over the chalet lines and the kiddies' nursery. He peered about anxiously as if assuring himself that Joe Maplin couldn't have spotted anything too terrible. He said:

'It seems a very sneaky way of operating.'

Ted sighed.

'Joe's a sneaky man. He didn't become a millionaire by following the rule book.'

Jeff nodded approvingly at the sight of a family group, encumbered with fishing rods and nets, making their way down towards the muddy fishing pond that, at the last count, had contained three frogs and a few old tyres.

'Well, I'm sure there's nothing to hide. Everything went with a swing and the campers had a great day. I hope he asked some of them.'

'Oh,' affirmed Ted, 'Joe doesn't give a monkey's about campers enjoying themselves. They'd enjoy anything.'

Spike broke in:

'So what does he do?'

Ted replied:

'Looks round for fiddles. He counts the empties from the bar. If there's twenty-four empty bottles of Scotch in the bin and only twenty have been taken from stock, he knows the manager's sold four of his own. Right? Last year he came down here and – well you know the wishing-well that the campers chuck money in and it's supposed to go to charity? He popped round there at ten o'clock at night. What did he find? Baverstock, the entertainments manager, with a shrimp net.' Ted looked meaningfully at Jeff. 'That's why you're sitting where you are today. What got me was Baverstock didn't even ask me if he could borrow the shrimp net.'

At this point, Peggy, the frustrated chalet maid, came bustling in. Peggy is frustrated not because of what you're thinking but because she wants to be a yellowcoat. Now you don't need a degree from Oxford or Cambridge to call bingo or lead the campers in chanting the good old songs but you do need a certain amount of talent and brains. Peggy is a nice, good-hearted girl but she would be mentally out of her depth running a toddlers' play-group and so she is never likely to achieve her ambition. You've probably seen Peggy staggering along with a bundle of soiled sheets. She wears glasses and a shapeless white smock during working hours but when she dresses up for an ice-cream sundae or a cocktail in the evening, takes off her glasses and puts on some colourful little outfit, she's quite presentable.

'Here,' exclaimed Peggy breathlessly, 'Joe Maplin's been on camp all day.'

'We already know that, Peggy,' Spike informed her.

Gladys rounded crossly on the new arrival.

'Why didn't you warn Mr Fairbrother, Peggy?'

Peggy, who talks a little like Donald Duck's sister, gabbled:

'Well, I wasn't sure. My suspicions were first aroused when I was sat in the Laughing Cow Milk Bar, and this man come and sat down, wearing a shabby suit with gold cufflinks, a great big diamond ring and crocodile skin shoes.'

Ted said positively:

'That's Joe. He never wears anything else.'

Peggy burbled on:

'Suddenly I remembered his picture in the brochure. You know, the one where he's got a great big toothy smile and he's saying in a big bubble coming out of his mouth, "Join the Happy Maplin Family." Then I knew it was him and so I said, "you're him, aren't you?" And he said, "Yes, I am him, and you keep your trap shut." '

Gladys said, even more crossly:

'You should have got a message to us.'

Peggy shook her head anxiously. 'I daren't. He said, "If you breathe a word to anyone before I've gone, you'll be out on your ear on Friday – and no bonus." '

Gladys sighed. 'I hope,' she remarked icily, 'you didn't bother him about making you a yellowcoat?'

'No,' declared Peggy, 'I could see he was in a bad mood and so I just followed him around and told him jokes to cheer him up. He doesn't laugh much does he?'

There was silence in the office as everyone wondered glumly about their futures. Then Jeff said:

'Where do we go from here?'

Ted enlightened him.

'You don't have to go anywhere. Tomorrow morning, at nine o'clock, there'll be a letter on your desk, telling you in plain words what action you have to take if you don't want the sack. And at three minutes past nine, we'll all be waiting outside in the staff room as you come through that door, looking rather pale and carrying that very same letter in your hand.'

Of course, Ted was right, or nearly right. The postman was a little late the following morning on account of having been bitten in the ankle by a demon toddler as he stepped out of his van and having to be rushed down to first aid for a tetanus injection before he could deliver the post. The result was that the scene, just as Ted had described it, occurred at twenty-six minutes past nine instead of three minutes past. Otherwise, it was as he'd predicted. Jeff issued wretchedly from his office bearing Joe Maplin's miserable missive in his paw. Everyone who was anyone on the entertainments staff was present and, of course, by this time everyone knew about Joe Maplin's secret swoop on the camp the previous day. While Jeff waited, letter in his hand, for Gladys to follow him out of the inner office, Ted whispered to Spike:

'Dead lucky it was my day off yesterday, Spike. Means

Joe can't have anything on me. If I'd been on camp I'd've been calling Bingo and you can bet your life Joe would have checked my bingo blower.'

Spike never ceased to be astonished by new revelations about Ted's devices for copping a little extra beer money.

'You can't fix that blower, can you?' he asked incredulously.

Ted winked.

'Well, it gets an airlock from time to time, doesn't it?'

At which point, Gladys joined Jeff and called the meeting to order.

'May we have quiet, please?'

She was immediately given a large helping of it. Everyone gazed at the menacing letter with forlorn faces. Gladys continued.

'Mr Fairbrother has a very important message from head office.'

Jeff sighed sadly and began.

'As you probably all know by now, this letter is from Joe Maplin. It's in his own words and my instructions are to read it out to you just as it stands. So here goes.'

Jeff gulped faintly because Joe Maplin's words were not the kind of words that university professors think highly of, but he had no choice. He began.

' "Right you lot, get a load of this. I come down yesterday, got up as a camper. You're a shower – you're a load of idle stinkpots. This is my dairy –" '

At this point, Jeff waved his hand helplessly and allowed himself a corrective comment.

'I think he means diary. I'll go on. "Ten-thirty – come into camp. First thing I clap eyes on is that demented jockey leading his pony trek three horses short. I don't want no empty horses!" '

At this, an expression of pain came over the face of Fred Quilly, who nurses the nags here at Maplin's. Fred is a sad case. He used to be a champion jockey but he lost his licence for some misdemeanour and has never succeeded in getting it back, although he keeps trying. So he is reduced to leading pony treks for campers along the sand on the string of antique gee-gees Joe Maplin salvages from the knacker's yard. Just to round off his misery he has to share a chalet with Partridge, the Punch-and-Judy man, who, in addition to being a habitual lush, is the worst-tempered man in the camp. Oh yes, Fred has enough on his shovel, all right. He now cried out in protest.

'The horses were sick. They weren't fit for work, Mr Fairbrother.'

Jeff nodded sympathetically at Fred but continued with Joe Maplin's words.

' "If they're not fit for work, don't give them no oats, that will teach them." '

'I can't stop giving them oats, Mr Fairbrother,' exclaimed Fred, outraged. 'That's all a horse has to look forward to.'

Jeff sighed and tapped the letter meaningfully.

'I'm afraid that's not all Fred. "They were shuffling their hoofs on the road. Make them pick their feet up. It wears out the shoes." '

This was greeted with an evil chuckle from Partridge, who then remarked:

'If I was you, Fred, I should take them off when they go to bed.'

Fred glanced reproachfully at his chalet mate.

'You're as heartless as he is.'

Jeff went on with his tricky task.

' "Ten forty-five approx. – stopped to take a gander at Punch-and-Judy show. Punch tried to hit copper three times and missed. Punch's speech was slurred. Was Punch drunk?" '

It was old Partridge's turn to look discomfited. He exclaimed:

'I never touched a drop yesterday, I swear it.'

This passionate plea was greeted by raised eyebrows and sceptical glances from all present. Jeff continued with his reading.

' "Eleven o'clock. Ballroom. Them dancers was giving a tango exhibition." '

Now, by the phrase 'them dancers' Joe Maplin was referring to Barry and Yvonne Stuart-Hargreaves who were once champion ballroom dancers of West Hartlepool or someplace. No, that's a bit unkind. They were quite well-known professionals in their day but their day was many years ago and, like most of us, Barry and Yvonne haven't been growing any younger in the interval. Like Fred's horses, their real working life is over and, like Fred's horses, they should have been put out to pasture in some comfy spot. But, being performers and probably also because they never invested their earnings soundly when they had them, they could not give up the glitter and the footlights and so they have come down to training fat campers to do the cha-cha and passy dobley or whatever it's called. They are both tall, thin and sad-looking but Yvonne, who has a way of tossing her head girlishly, is taller and thinner and sadder-looking than Barry. They are really only yellowcoats like the others but they give themselves airs and consider themselves a slice or two above the rest of the entertainments staff.

' "Tell Barry," ' Jeff was reading, ' "if that bird of his gets any thinner, I'll put her on half salary. What's he doing to her? Give her a chitty for double helpings of plum duff!" '

By this point, poor Yvonne's long, pale face had assumed an expression of refined distress and two little red points glowed in her cheeks. But Ted, whose many qualities do not include tact or consideration, chuckled and remarked:

'Tell you what, Barry, give her the oats from Fred's horses.'

Barry is not normally given to much in the way of backchat. Indeed, he *is* the silent partner in the marriage, if they are really married, and normally only opens his mouth to murmur soothingly 'yes dear' or 'no dear' but just occasionally he perks up and demonstrates that, beneath the meek exterior, a rebel is struggling to get out. He sniffed and replied:

'Yvonne doesn't look forward to oats in quite the same way.'

Yvonne directed upon him a reproachful look and exclaimed tightly:

'If anyone says one more word on this subject I shall leave the room, the camp and the town.'

Jeff continued.

' "Now about the yellowcoats – M and F." He must mean male and female. "The M's look a bit lightweight but live and let live. As for the F's, they is slack. For instance, I'd swear two of them wasn't wearing braziers." I think he means – well, you know – up above – as it were – anyway. "This is a family camp. What happens if they got knocked down and carted off to hospital wearing my yellowcoats with no braziers underneath? It would reflect on me. Apart from that they were slummocky. That Welsh bit, Gladys, threw herself into everything with gusto. She's a knockout. She's what I call a yellowcoat. Give'r another ten bob a week." '

Now, of course, Gladys had already perused the letter in Jeff's office and so was not surprised by the compliments but she nevertheless drew herself up a little higher and her whole body radiated a sense of triumph and authority. Gladys, it must be conceded, really was the senior yellowcoat in that she had been at it much longer than the other girls and boys but she had never previously had her status confirmed officially. Now she scented power. Jeff continued reading.

' "Put her in charge and tell her to sharpen up the rest." '

The other yellowcoats glanced at Gladys with eyes grown suddenly speculative and Gladys responded by surveying them one by one like a field-marshal reviewing mere generals. But Jeff hadn't reached the end of Joe Maplin's wit and wisdom.

' "Oh, and tell that potty chalet maid who kept following me around and rabbiting on to get her pocket mended. Get cracking with all these points. Joe Maplin." '

Ted nudged Spike and, grinning broadly, whispered:

'I got away with it, Spike!'

But his glee did not last long. Jeff had not quite finished.

' "PS. Tell that Ted Bovis I've changed his bingo blower and if he wants to hide from me in the hedge he'll have to take some weight off." '

You could almost hear the wind whistle out of Ted.

'Well, there it is,' said Jeff gravely. 'It's a sorry catalogue. In some measure, I think perhaps I'm to blame.'

'Oh no, you're not, Jeff,' protested Gladys loyally. 'They've let you down.'

She swept the room with her new gaze of authority and continued.

'You've all let him down. You ought to be ashamed of yourselves. I want to see all yellowcoats in here at two o'clock sharp this afternoon. That's all! And now Mr Fairbrother and I have a lot of administration to do. Come along, Mr Fairbrother.'

Even Jeff was a bit taken aback by Gladys' peremptory manner but he followed her docilely back into his own office while Ted sang softly:

' "When the Sergeant Major's on parade." '

Shortly before two, the hour specified by Gladys for beginning the great work of sharpening up the rest of the yellowcoats, Jeff was seated alone in his office, having consumed his frugal lunch of Bath Oliver biscuits, Stilton cheese and grapes, just as he had used to eat in his old study in Cambridge, when the door opened and Ted Bovis breezed in. Ted had a slip of paper in his hand and he confided to his boss:

'This is my expense chitty for the week, Jeff. It's all above board. You can check every penny – straight up.'

Jeff was, by now, not so green that he accepted this earnest assurance at face value but he was still feeling a little too bruised by Joe Maplin's harsh criticisms to embark on a searching examination of Ted's devious expense account. He waved at his in-tray and murmured:

'Just put it there. I'll check it later.'

Ted obeyed. Then he looked with concern at the entertainments manager.

'What's the matter with you?'

'Joe Maplin. Every time he criticises me all my self-confidence drains away.'

Ted chuckled knowingly.

'That's how he brainwashes people. He makes them feel

they're no good. It doesn't work on me though. I've had to develop a hide like an elephant. You shouldn't be so sensitive. You know your trouble, don't you? You never had to stand in line.'

'What do you mean?' asked Jeff curiously.

Ted shrugged.

'Well, you never had to rough it. Nanny was always there to wipe your nose for you.'

'Well, yes,' Jeff admitted. 'That was quite true until I was seven. Then I was sent away from home.'

Ted looked concerned.

'What, you mean you were nicked? Did they send you to a reformatory?'

Jeff smiled grimly.

'Something very similar – a boarding school.'

Ted was incredulous.

'What, at seven? Were you an orphan?'

'No, my mother and father sent me there. At great expense.'

'Oh, I see. Like in that film *Goodbye, Mr Chips*. Midnight feasts in the dormitory, a little cosy studio all to yourself. Tea and cakes with a lovely old teacher.'

Jeff looked thoughtful.

'That's one side of the story,' he conceded. 'But the other is bare boards, cold baths and being beaten with alarming regularity.'

Ted was shocked.

'You mean, caned?'

'Of course.'

Ted could hardly believe it. He knew that Jeff was a toff and he'd assumed that toff kids were brought up in the lap of luxury.

'They did that to you?' he asked incredulously.

'They did it to everyone. That's what your parents pay for.'

Jeff shook his head in disgust.

'If they'd done that to me my dad would have been round to the school and punched the living daylights out of the lot of them.' He stuck out his chest defiantly until it reached nearly as far as his stomach. 'No one was allowed to touch his little lad.' But then he remembered something. 'Except him, of course.'

Gladys marched in. It has to be said 'marched' because she moved with a new fierceness and swing. Her military appearance was also strengthened by the fact that she was now wearing something that she had never worn before. No, not a 'brazier'. She always wore those, being a well-brought-up Welsh girl. The new thing that Gladys was wearing was two rings of gold braid sewn round her cuffs. She had got herself up, as a result of Joe Maplin's instructions, like a lieutenant in the Royal Navy. Both Jeff and Ted spotted the adornments at first glance but, for the present, neither of them commented.

Gladys said importantly:

'Jeff, those yellowcoats will be here any minute. I expect you to back me up. I want to make it quite clear that we are going to have no more nonsense, and they've got to buck their ideas up.'

Ted could contain himself no longer. He pointed at the new fuehrer's sleeves and exclaimed:

'What's all this? How long have we had an admiral on the staff, Jeff?'

Jeff, who is not given to extravagant displays of emotion, like all the top brass at Cambridge stifled a smile.

'What is going on, Gladys?' he asked mildly.

'Well, you heard what Jo Maplin said,' Gladys exclaimed. 'I'm in charge of the yellowcoats.'

Jeff nodded.

'So you've made yourself a lieutenant? I suppose it's logical.'

'And when do your medals arrive, Gladys?' asked Ted innocently.

'Don't be silly, Ted,' Gladys rebuked him.

'But you've earned them, Gladys. Time after time. Fighting for your honour in the chalet lines after dark!'

Gladys was furious, although it has to be admitted that before Jeff arrived in the camp Gladys had never been averse to male company and lots of it.

'Ted Bovis,' stormed Gladys, 'I do not do that sort of thing, as you well know.'

'All right then,' conceded Ted, 'but how about the "no gratuities campaign" medal, for conning twenty-two boxes of chocolates and twelve pairs of nylons out of the campers in just one week?'

But Jeff, anxious to avoid a major row between two senior staff members, said soothingly:

'Now, now, Ted. It's quite a sensible idea for Gladys to wear some symbol of her authority.'

Ted shook his head sceptically and murmured:

'I bet you're the only one that thinks so.'

Outside in the staff room, the yellowcoats were assembling. Betty, a very popular yellowcoat with outstanding qualities that showed up well in a bikini, said:

'What do you think she wants us for?'

Tracey, a studious yellowcoat who spent hours studying attractive male campers, tossed her fair hair and grumbled:

'I bet she's going to give us a good talking to.'

Sylvia, the tall yellowcoat devoted to doing the backstroke, proclaimed:

'Well, if she starts to throw her weight around she'll get nowhere as far as I'm concerned.' And she plonked herself down in one of the tatty armchairs in which the staff were supposed to relax.

You probably haven't noticed because they are identical but amongst the boy yellowcoats are a pair of twins. They are called Stanley and Bruce and one of them, I think it was Bruce, now contributed:

'Well, I've done my national service so she'd better not start getting regimental.'

'The fact is,' Sylvia insisted, 'she's jealous of us because we're so popular with the campers.'

'Especially you,' said Betty spitefully.

Sylvia glared at her.

'What's that supposed to mean?'

But before Betty could make her meaning clearer, although everyone had already understood her drift, Gladys strode forcefully through the door from Jeff's office. She clapped her hands lightly for silence and, without further ado, began.

'Now, listen all of you. There's a new batch of campers arriving tomorrow so you'll have to pull your socks up or I'll want to know the reason why. I'll have no more slackness, no more slipping off for a crafty cup of coffee or a quick fag or –' and her gaze focused on Sylvia – 'anything else. You're here to work. Now stand up and let's have a look at you.'

Perhaps because Gladys really did have the bearing of a leader, all the yellowcoats obediently stood up – all, that is, except Sylvia, who defiantly continued to lounge in her chair. Gladys took a step towards her.

'I said, stand up, Sylvia.'

'I'm not standing up,' affirmed Sylvia. 'You can look at me sitting down.'

It was a direct challenge to Gladys' authority and, it has to be admitted, Gladys came off second-best.

'Very well,' she conceded, but then continued fiercely. 'Your shoelace is broken, your collar's creased, you've got a button coming off and your shorts are too short.'

Then Gladys turned her attention to Betty.

'Betty, your hair should be neater. It's flapping all over the place.'

'Of course it is,' admitted Betty. 'Because I've been running about in the open all day.'

'Then you shouldn't wear it in that silly style.'

Gladys turned to one of the boy yellowcoats.

'Gary, I don't want to see you standing around, posing all day for the girls. Talk to the old people and the plain ones. I want all these things put right by the time you meet the new campers tomorrow. And, girls, make sure you're wearing bras.'

Gladys didn't expect the response she got. All the girls promptly pulled open their blouses to demonstrate conclusively that their womanly parts were properly supported. Naturally this caused a certain amount of giggling from the boy yellowcoats. But Gladys was not in any mood for frivolity. She stormed:

'You think you're funny, don't you? But I've worked hard at my job and I've done it properly. I've earned my position on this camp and I'm not going to let anyone take it away from me. So – so – there!'

A somewhat lame conclusion, perhaps, but nonetheless the yellowcoats were impressed. Gladys turned on her heels and strode back into Jeff's office, leaving them to mutter resentfully amongst themselves.

The next morning an amazing thing happened. It happens once a week at Maplin's and I've seen it happen more times than anyone probably but it still surprises me. In the space of a few hours the whole camp empties and fills again. I mean this place is like a small town. Everyone has their little home, their chalet, and there's warehouses and storerooms, bars and shops, ballrooms and swimming pools, dining rooms and theatres and a lot more besides. Then the coaches begin to roll in and the whole population gets on them and in a trice it's a ghost town – no one left but the staff and, of course, me. A little later, a new squadron of coaches sails in, and out of it they all get, the fat mums and the henpecked dads and the squealing kids and the teenagers glancing sideways to get a load of the talent and a little later it's just as it was before, except, of course, that everyone's different, apart from me. And a couple of hours later, it's as if it had never happened. Everything's humming again and the only way you can tell what an upheaval there's been is that the new lot are as white as ghosts whereas the old lot were mostly lobster red.

The entertainments staff, having seen off the old bunch, were waiting for the new mob. Grumpy old Partridge nudged Fred Quilly and pointed slyly towards Gladys.

'Here, have you caught those rings on her arm?' he asked. 'You haven't got any rings on your arm. That's put her above you, you know?'

'I don't care,' said Fred moodily and it has to be said that Fred is an easy-going bloke with no malice in his nature. 'What difference does it make to me? She's entitled. She's in charge of the yellowcoats.'

Partridge has only two real pleasures in life: getting

smashed and stirring things. The former pleasure was barred to him on this occasion since he was already under suspicion and would not have dared to take a drink with his superiors standing around and so he had to fall back on the other pleasure. He said slyly:

'Ah, but you're in charge of the horses. You should wear some rings.'

'Horses don't care about rings.'

'That's not the point. Now how many yellowcoats is Gladys in charge of?'

'Six.'

'And how many horses have you got?'

'Twelve.'

'There you are,' exclaimed Partridge triumphantly. 'You should have one more ring.'

A little distance away, Yvonne and Barry Stuart-Hargreaves, if that's their real names, were standing trying to look dignified and superior. This was difficult for them since they were, on this occasion, wearing ordinary yellowcoats like the other yellowcoats. Suddenly Yvonne gasped and exclaimed:

'Barry!'

Barry glanced unhappily at his partner and noticed that, as he had feared, she was gazingly fixedly at Gladys' rings. He had hoped she wouldn't notice. He sighed in resignation.

'I know what you're going to say, dear.'

'I can't allow it, Barry,' said Yvonne positively. 'It makes me look ordinary.'

A tender smile appeared on Barry's face, making him look slightly like a dying pekinese.

'You could never be that, my dear,' he protested loyally.

'Well, I'm not having it, Barry. We have a position to keep up. What are you going to do about it?'

'Why don't we toss for who does the sewing?'

On another part of the camp's forecourt, just inside the main gate, Peggy and Spike were standing together.

'Cheer up, Peggy,' urged Spike. 'What are you so miserable for?'

The frustrated chalet maid really did look stricken. Her face was working convulsively and she was twisting a corner of her white smock nervously.

'I feel awful,' she admitted. 'Ever since Mr Fairbrother read out Joe Maplin's letter about me being potty. I'm destroyed.'

Spike tried to comfort her.

'Ted says that's how he brainwashes people. He makes them feel inferior. You shouldn't take any notice.'

'That's all very well for you. You've got a position. You're the camp comedian. But I felt inferior even before that letter. Now what chance have I got of being a yellowcoat?'

'Don't give up, Peggy. We didn't give up in 1940 when we stood alone against Hitler.'

But Peggy was not impressed by the encouragement.

'Oh, don't come up with that bloomin' rubbish. That was a world war. I'm Peggy Ollerenshaw. The two cases are not similar.'

'What I meant –' began Spike, but what he meant was to remain forever a secret from Peggy. Just at that moment, Gladys raised her voice and, in her lilting, but very penetrating, Welsh voice cried:

'Here they come, everyone. Stand by!'

The entertainments staff ceased their gossiping, shuffling, smoking and stared out through the wire-grill fence that surrounded the camp and down along the coast road. There they beheld the first of a train of coaches just rounding the bend. Everyone made little last-minute adjustments to their attire. Sylvia quickly undid the top button of her blouse so that Joe Maplin would have been glad, if he had been there, to be able to see that she really was wearing a bra. Barry and Yvonne smoothed down their yellow jackets as if they were evening wear and everyone moved a few paces closer to the gate. The first of the coaches rolled in and came to a halt and the door opened. Blinking in the bright sunshine, a nervous family group began first to disembark.

'Go on, yellowcoats,' cried Gladys. 'Get amongst them.'

And the yellowcoats closed in on their new guests. The family group that had first emerged suddenly started slightly and edged back as if about to leap onto the coach again. The reason for their alarm was that the hugely-amplified voice of Ted Bovis had pierced their ear-drums. The camp host bellowed:

'Hello, campers. Welcome to Maplin's. Hi-de-hi!'

From inside the coach came the answering voice of those experienced campers who had done time in Maplin's before.

'Ho-de-ho!'

'Ted can't hear you,' returned the untruthful host. 'Hi-de-hi!'

Although muffled by the body of the coach, the voices from within swelled considerably.

'Ho-de-ho!'

Ted looked pleased and the nervous family visibly relaxed once more and started again shuffling forwards towards the reception area. Ted's voice continued to boom out patter and welcome.

'I'm Ted Bovis, your camp host. If you want to know anything, don't ask me. Make your way to Reception – that building straight ahead of you – and sign in. The rest of you just make your mark. The yellowcoats will help you to your chalets but do keep an eye on your cases. Hallo, Mrs Evans, back again? The last husband didn't last, eh? And who's that? Jake Wheeler or his ghost? I thought we drowned you last year, Jake. Never mind, we'll have another go this time. Hi-de-hi, all you ladies and gentlemen – campers too. It's Maplin's time again.'

But, strangely enough, amidst all this welcoming activity the person who should have been doing most was doing nothing at all. Gladys Pugh, the newly-appointed, chief yellowcoat and self-appointed lieutenant in the Maplin Navy was not bustling about patting the kiddies and joking with the parents as she usually did on these occasions. No, she was standing frozen to the spot gazing, with an expression of horror on her face, at a small man with a rather large nose and generally drooping features, dressed in a neat but well-worn suit and carrying a battered bag, who had just disembarked from the coach.

'Oh no!' she moaned. Then she turned and fled down the walk, tastefully lined with the few remaining flowers the nippers hadn't yet pulled up, towards the sanctuary of the staff room. Spike Dixon had observed her flight and, concerned, he followed her. When he reached the ramshackle little staff room, with its few tatty armchairs and deal table, he found Gladys slumped in one of the chairs with her hands over her face.

'What's the matter, Gladys?' asked Spike anxiously. 'Are you all right?'

Gladys shook her head. Then she uncovered her face but she did not look at Spike. She stared ahead with a stricken expression and said:

'My brother's on that coach.'

'Really?' exclaimed Spike, wondering what was so tragic about that.

'He shouldn't have come. He had no business.'

Spike looked puzzled.

'Why? Don't you get on?'

'No we don't.' Gladys shook her head firmly. 'He's my half-brother actually. My mum was married before she married Dad. Gareth never fitted in. He was a bad lot. He had to leave the valley.'

Spike sat down on the chair facing Gladys.

'Sounds serious. What did he do?'

Gladys glanced moodily at Spike. Her tone became more cautious.

'Well, nothing was ever proved, mind. There was this case. He was at the cinema, you see, and he kept changing his seat.'

Spike shuddered faintly at the implications.

'Oh dear.'

Gladys hastened on.

'He got off. He said he had to move because he was behind tall people. The magistrate said there was an element of doubt, him being only five foot three – not the magistrate, Gareth. Anyway, there was an awful scandal. It's a small town.'

Spike tried to make the best of it.

'Well, that's all in the past, isn't it?'

'I don't trust him, Spike. He looks at girls in a funny way. I don't want any scandal, especially now with my position as chief yellowcoat.'

Spike spoke more reassuringly than he really felt.

'Well, we'll just have to keep an eye on him.'

Gladys' mouth set firmly.

'I'll do that all right,' she affirmed.

While this conversation had been taking place, Peggy, somewhat recovered from the dumps, was actually showing Gladys' half-brother, Gareth, to his chalet. With the little Welshman toddling behind her, Peggy tripped down the long row of identical chalets, calling out their numbers.

'84, 85 – Hi-de-hi – 86 – oh, this is it, isn't it? That's right, 86. This is yours.'

She inserted the key in the lock and threw open the door, revealing a small, oblong room with bare wooden walls and floor, a single bed and a few pieces of deal furniture. She stepped back to allow Gareth to enter and then followed him in. The little man looked about appreciatively.

'This is quite nice, isn't it?' he said.

'Oh yes. They're ever so cosy when you get settled in.'

Gareth thereupon frowned slightly and gazed at the bed with faint reproach.

'It's only got a single bed,' he pointed out.

Peggy looked surprised.

'Well, of course. It's a single chalet. What do you want a double bed for?'

'I'm a restless sleeper,' Gareth explained. Then he smiled tenderly at Peggy, his large nose and prominent teeth making him slightly resemble Mr Punch. 'You're a pretty little girl. You've got nice eyes and smooth skin.'

Peggy, like most girls, had an insatiable appetite for compliments. She suddenly perceived that Gareth, while unsuited for romantic parts in movies, was a highly-intelligent and estimable sort of bloke.

'Have I?' she purred.

'When's your day off?' asked Gareth.

'It was yesterday. But I'm around a lot. I'm to be found each night in the ballroom, at the cocktail hour, sipping an aperitif.'

Gareth patted her on the shoulder in an affectionate way.

'That's a date then,' he promised.

Just then the light darkened, signifying that someone was blocking the door. Gareth glanced in that direction and was taken aback to see his half-sister glaring at him. Gladys completed her entrance and spoke peremptorily to the maid.

'Thank you, Peggy. I'll look after this camper.'

Peggy was a little disappointed since she had been enjoying the turn the conversation had taken but Gladys was her lord and mistress.

'All right then,' said the chalet maid. And then, to Gareth, 'I'll see you later.'

Peggy tripped out. Gladys placed her hands on her hips and looked down on her little relative.

'What are you doing here?' she demanded.

Gareth smiled meekly and explained.

'Well, I need a holiday. And I knew you were here. I haven't seen you for years and so I thought I'd kill two birds with one stone.'

Gladys stamped her foot lightly.

'If you're going to stay here, you leave the birds alone, see?'

Gareth looked a trifle crestfallen. He wasn't the sort of bloke that expects welcoming committees and the red-carpet treatment but he had hoped his half-sister would be a little more friendly. He protested feebly.

'That's not fair, Gladys. I didn't do nothing.'

'Well, we'll never know that, will we?' Gladys approached her relative more closely. 'I'm head yellowcoat here. I've got a position to keep up. I don't want any scandal.'

Gareth shook his head earnestly.

'I never do nothing, honest. I only look at them. I just like looking at pretty girls.'

'You don't look,' snapped Gladys. 'You leer.'

'I don't leer either. My face leers, even when I'm thinking about something else, it leers. I was at home thinking about spaghetti once and mum said "Stop leering!" '

Gladys sighed.

'Well, don't tell anyone you're my half-brother.'

'Of course I won't,' promised Gareth. Then he added shyly, 'I'm very fond of you, Glad.'

But this tender admission failed to reach the chief yellow-coat's heart.

'Well, you watch your step because I shall be checking on you.'

Whereupon Gladys turned on her heel and strode out of the chalet leaving Gareth blinking sadly after her.

For the next twenty-four hours or so, Gareth shuffled about the camp getting into the routine. He learned where the dining-room was to be found and the bars and the pool and the other places of interest. He was a little disconcerted to find, from time to time, Gladys peering suspiciously at him through the shrubbery or from a balcony or from some other vantage point but they had no further communication. All seemed to be going well when, the following afternoon, Gladys found herself in difficulties on two fronts.

It was the day of the Holiday Princess Competition, always a favourite with the campers and especially with the young louts such as yourself who like to gawp at pretty girls in bikinis. All the prettiest girls in the camp were assembled, with sashes giving their competition numbers over their chests, around the Olympic-sized swimming pool. Also present was most of the entertainments staff. It was a superb day for the competition, a hot sun beaming down out of a cloudless sky and, at first, Gladys felt relaxed and cheerful. Then she saw a horrid sight. It had been concealed from her before because it wasn't very tall and it was behind a group of dazzling contestants in their bikinis. It was Gareth wearing a mackintosh of the kind favoured by flashers. Gladys emitted a gasp of dismay and hurried over to him.

'What are you doing standing near these girls?' she demanded furiously.

Gareth shrank a little like a snail retreating into its shell.

'Only looking, Glad,' he murmured humbly.

'Why are you wearing a mackintosh on a hot day like this?'

Gareth looked flummoxed for a moment but then inspiration came to him.

'Well, you never know. We might have a shower.'

But Gladys was far from satisfied with this explanation.

'What have you got on underneath it?' she wanted to know.

For reply, Gareth started unbuttoning the garment causing Gladys first to pale and then to flush. But these colourful exploits proved to be unnecessary for, when Gareth pulled open the coat he was seen to be adequately attired in shorts and shirt. Gladys could not restrain a gasp of relief. Then she ordered:

'Take it off. And then go and stand on the other side of the pool. Get right away from the girls.'

Removing the offending mac as he went, Gareth shuffled off as bid. But no sooner had she got rid of this affliction than Gladys was confronted by a new one. Mindful of her official duties, and especially of the fact that the potential holiday princesses were beginning to wilt a little under the burning sun, she called impatiently:

'Where are the judges?'

And then, as they appeared, she could not restrain a gasp of anger and distress. The judges this year included, as always, a few campers and three members of the entertainments staff. The selected three were Yvonne and Barry Stuart-Hargreaves and Fred Quilly. As these three subordinates came forward towards the podium Gladys saw that they were actually got up as superiors. Yvonne and Barry now sported three rings each on their yellowcoats while Fred looked ready to take on the German high-seas fleet.

His arm was banded with no fewer than four rings of gold braid.

Gladys hissed at the mutinous rabble.

'I shall have words with Mr Fairbrother about this. Now get in your places.'

Mr Fairbrother, at that moment, was not far away. He was standing a little to one side with Ted Bovis. Both of them had spotted the outbreak of gold rings and Jeff was saying glumly:

'I think this one-upmanship is getting rather out of hand.'

Ted grinned reassuringly.

'Don't worry,' he urged. 'I've already fixed it. Go on and announce me.'

'Yes, of course.'

Jeff turned to the lady organist whose heavy instrument had been lugged out into the sunlight for the occasion and called:

'Hit it, Ramona.'

He used these words because he was trying to sound like a bright and breezy entertainments manager rather than a gloomy and introspective Cambridge don. But he only succeeded, as always, in sounding like a gloomy and introspective Cambridge don making a desperate but unsuccessful attempt to sound like a bright and breezy entertainments manager. Jeff, looking a trifle embarrassed, jumped up onto the platform and seized the microphone.

'Hello, campers,' he bawled. He shuddered slightly at the demands of his position and once again uttered the ghastly words, 'Hi-de-hi!'

Dutifully, but without the kind of spirit that Ted Bovis always managed to coax from them, a few campers glumly murmured, 'Ho-de-ho!'

Jeff tried to look overwhelmed by the response.

'That's what I like to hear,' he assured them. 'Now you are all – er – cooking with gas. And now, folks, this is a very big one. You see, it's Holiday Princess time, and here to tell you all about it is your friend –'

Now, of course, the phrase that Jeff was aiming at was 'your friend and mine, Ted Bovis' but somehow he never managed to get it right. Perhaps it was just too far from the sort of greetings that Cambridge dons go in for under the dreaming spires and in their common rooms. Whatever the reason, it has to be said that Jeff regularly made a cock-up of the simple introduction and today was no different.

'Here to tell you all about it,' Jeff proclaimed, 'is your friend and indeed a very good friend of mine too because, actually, he's a most friendly person – that is, your camp host – Ted Bovis.'

Mopping his brow lightly, as Ramona struck up 'Happy Days are Here Again', Jeff slipped gratefully from the platform and went to stand beside his trusty chief yellowcoat and right-hand girl, Gladys Pugh, who immediately rounded on him angrily.

'Jeff, you've got to do something about those rings.'

For a moment Jeff wondered if Gladys might be referring, because of the huge strain he found in being jolly with the campers, to dark rings under his eyes but then he remembered the rash of gold braid and realised that she was complaining about insubordination. He whispered:

'Ted's got it in hand.'

At that precise moment, Ted entered from behind the podium, leaped up onto it and waved his arms at the campers who, as one man, gave a great cheer when they beheld him decked out with rings reaching right up to his shoulders.

'Hello, campers,' bellowed Ted. 'It's me, Ted Bovis, your camp host, who makes rings round them all. Hi-de-hi!'

At which the massed campers responded with a roar that Jeff Fairbrother would have sacrificed half his annual bonus to achieve.

'HO-DE-HO!'

But Gladys was not amused. Instead of realising that Ted was trying to cure the terrible ring plague with mockery, she concluded that he too was mocking her. She turned on her heel and stalked away.

The next and perhaps the worst moment in Gladys' ordeal began late that night in the chalet shared by the three thrilling girl yellowcoats, Betty, Sylvia and Tracey. These lovely girls were preparing for bed. They wore filmy and delightful nightgowns and negligees and were happily confiding to each other their little adventures of the day. There was a perfunctory knock at the door and Peggy, her hair done up in rag curlers which explained the seething abundance of curls she normally displayed, entered.

'Hello, girls – hi-de-hi –' she carolled loyally. 'Betty, can I borrow your night cream? I've run out.'

Betty pointed to the chest of drawers.

'There's a little bit in the bottom of that old jar,' she offered. 'You can keep it.'

'Oh thanks,' said Peggy. 'I never go to bed without it, you know. That's why I've got such a lovely skin. Gareth says it's like a peach.'

Tracey asked curiously:

'He wasn't with you in the ballroom tonight. What happened?'

Peggy giggled happily.

'Well, we've been going the pace every night and he said he wanted an evening in his chalet with a book. He's ever so well read.'

At this point, Sylvia unexpectedly gave a little scream and pointed at the window. All the others turned to see what was up and beheld a stick sticking into the room and being used to push the curtains to one side. That's all that any of the girls could see but they guessed, from events of the past few nights, what was going on.

'It's him again!' cried Sylvia, desperately pulling her negligee more protectively around her. All the other girls also made attempts to render their charms less conspicuous. At the same time, they heard faintly the sound of footsteps hastening away.

'Lock the door, quick!' urged Tracey.

'No,' protested Betty. 'Let's get after him.'

They hurried towards the chalet door where they were met by Gladys just making her way in.

'What's all the screaming about?' demanded the chief yellowcoat.

Sylvia explained.

'It's that Peeping Tom again!'

'That's three nights running.'

Spike and Jeff, also roused by the uproar, hurried in.

'Was that him again?' asked Spike.

Sylvia explained.

'Yes. He opened the curtains.'

The entertainments director nodded grimly.

'I'll go and fetch Security,' promised Jeff.

At the door he almost collided with Yvonne and Barry, peeved at having their rest disturbed.

'Could we make a little less noise, please?' asked Barry. 'Yvonne and I are trying to sleep.'

'It's him,' shrilled Peggy. 'It's the Peeping Tom.'

At this point, Gladys quietly tapped Spike's arm and whispered:

'Come with me, Spike. I might need your support.'

Spike nodded understandingly and the two of them slipped out of the chalet in the wake of Jeff Fairbrother. Meanwhile, Yvonne was wailing:

'Barry, how awful. He could have seen me in my nightdress.'

Barry rolled his eyes piteously as he murmured:

'It doesn't bear thinking about, dear.'

When Gladys and Spike burst unceremoniously into his chalet, Gareth was propped up in bed against a pillow, wearing, as far as could be seen, only his vest and panting slightly. Gladys put her hands on her hips and glared furiously at her half-brother.

'You got back into bed quick, didn't you,' she taunted him.

Gareth looked at her with seeming bewilderment. Then he looked at Spike and then back at Gladys.

'What are you talking about?' he protested. 'I've been here for hours.'

'Then why haven't you got your pyjamas on?' she challenged him.

'I don't wear pyjamas.'

Spike tried to do a Sherlock Holmes.

'If you haven't been running, why are you breathing heavily?' he asked the little Welshman.

Gareth held up the book he was reading and explained.

'It's an exciting book.'

But Gladys was having none of it.

'I don't want any argument,' she proclaimed. 'That's three nights running we've had a Peeping Tom creeping round about the camp and there's only one person it could be – and that's you! I'm not having you disgrace me. I want you out of this camp now, this minute.'

Spike felt it necessary to point out:

'There's no trains, Gladys.'

'He can walk down to the station and spend the night in the waiting room.'

Gareth whimpered faintly and protested.

'It wasn't me, Gladys, honest.'

'Shut up,' the chief yellowcoat ordered.

She went to the wardrobe and got Gareth's suitcase. She dumped it on the bed next to her cringing half-brother. She addressed Spike.

'Stay with him till he's dressed and packed.'

Spike sighed deeply. He's a tender-hearted chap with a high moral code and he hated to see this hounding of a timid, little man. But the case against Gareth looked black and Spike realised that, for everyone's sake, the camp must be purged of perverts.

'All right, Gladys,' he agreed. 'I'll walk down to the station with him.'

Gladys sniffed and turned towards the door. But before she reached it, she turned again and contemplated the little quaking jelly that Gareth had become.

'To think,' she reminisced sadly, 'you used to stand next to Morgan the Organ in Chapel, doing all those solos with a voice like an angel. And you've turned out like this.'

Then, with a hiss like a viper's, she uttered a few words of Welsh which I will not translate for you but just say that their meaning could be gathered from the look of shock and dismay that crossed Gareth's white face as he whispered reproachfully:

'There's no need to say that!'

The next morning Jeff summoned certain members of the entertainments staff to a meeting in his office. He began the proceedings by pointing out that Gladys, stationed as usual beside his desk looking haughty, was very distressed by the outbreak of rings. Why were they all behaving so childishly?

'Well, I'm sorry, Mr Fairbrother,' explained Fred Quilly stubbornly. 'But if people are having rings on their arms, I'm not going to be left out. I'm left out of quite enough things as it is.'

Yvonne was the next to contribute.

'It's a matter of principle, Mr Fairbrother. Barry and I have a position to keep up.'

Barry amplified.

'If Gladys hadn't started queening it over everyone, this wouldn't have happened in the first place.'

Jeff nodded with a faint smile. Then he squared his shoulders and announced:

'Well, I'm going to make a decision. They've all got to come off. And that's final.'

At this, Ted, who was standing back by the door, nudged Spike, and whispered:

'He's coming on. It's the iron foot in the velvet sock.'

Gladys smiled a steely smile and said softly:

'That doesn't include me, of course.'

But Jeff immediately turned to her and said firmly:

'Yes, Gladys. It does.'

The Welsh dictator thereupon gasped audibly and then counterattacked firmly.

'Well, I'm not having it. Joe Maplin put me in charge. This ring is the symbol of my authority. I'm not taking it off.'

Ted grinned and said loudly:

'There's a poser for you, Jeff. Gladys Pugh doesn't want to have it off.'

Gladys, her eyes flashing angrily at the implications of the joke, rounded on Ted. But just at that moment, the phone rang.

'Quiet, Gladys,' said Ted firmly. 'Telephone.'

Jeff, meanwhile, was answering the instrument. Everyone heard him say:

'Yes? Oh, that is good news. I'll tell the girls they can sleep safely in their beds again.'

He put down the phone and announced to the room:

'That was Security. They've caught the Peeping Tom, just before breakfast this morning. He's confessed to everything. It was that tall, red-headed camper.'

Gladys and Spike exchanged a dismal glance. Ted asked interestedly:

'Not Ginger from Sunderland?'

Jeff nodded.

'That's the one. Funny. He seemed rather a nice chap. Just shows you never can tell, can you?'

Gladys, whose chin was trembling faintly, turned on her heel and hurried out of the office, closely followed by a concerned Spike.

He caught up with Gladys in the staff room where she had seated herself in one of the sagging armchairs and had her hands over her face. Peggy was also present, dusting mechanically, and sobbing faintly. With a glance at Peggy, Spike sat down and edged close to Gladys. He whispered, so that Peggy wouldn't hear.

'Gareth kept saying all the way to the station that it wasn't him. He was ever so upset. He just couldn't understand it. I think he's very fond of you, Gladys.'

Gladys uncovered her face. Her eyes were dry but she looked drawn. She glanced at the distressed chalet maid and said:

'Peggy, you should of been finished hours ago. What are you snivelling for?'

Peggy approached Gladys and Spike. She explained.

'It's Gareth. He was ever so nice to me. He's gone and he didn't even leave a note. We were going to the pictures tonight.'

Gladys sighed deeply and said:

'Oh dear, that's a pity, isn't it. Sit down, Peggy. I'll give you a cup of coffee. It'll make you feel better.'

Peggy nodded mechanically and sat down. Gladys rose and went to the coffee-making equipment. She put on the electric kettle. Spike joined her.

'It's a bit of a mess, isn't it, Gladys?' he asked sombrely.

'Oh don't, Spike,' the chief of the yellowcoats protested. 'I feel awful. How could I be so wrong about him?'

'Well, that's life, isn't it?' asked Spike. Then he saw an opportunity. He leaned close to Gladys as she spooned out the powdered coffee and said mildly, 'You don't think you might be wrong about anything else, do you?'

Gladys frowned in incomprehension for a moment. Then she caught on. She looked down at the gold braid on her sleeve. She smiled faintly. Then she finished making the coffee and took the steaming beverage over to poor, afflicted Peggy.

'Here's your coffee, Peggy,' she said.

'Thanks, Gladys,' said Peggy, accepting it.

It was a big effort for Gladys but she was a girl of character, which was the reason why she'd been raised to her high position in the first place. She swallowed deeply and went on.

'Oh and, Peggy, when you've got a minute, do me a favour. Take these silly rings off my jacket, will you?'

The senior camper chuckled softly as he reached the conclusion of his homely tale. He lit his fifth thin cigarette, took a deep drag and blew three perfect smoke rings into the still air. He listened for a moment to the squeals and yells of the kiddies splashing in the shallow soup which, towards the end of the day, the water in the kiddies' paddling pool tended to resemble. The Maplin's Ladies Weight-Losing class had long since dispersed, taking the energetic Gladys Pugh with them.

'What do you think of that, my son?' asked the senior camper, confident of the applause he always received at the conclusion of one of his expertly-narrated and gripping stories of camp life.

'Cor, that's smashing,' said the thin, pale youth in the next deckchair.

'You think so, do you?' asked the senior camper complacently.

'I never seen no one do three before.'

The senior camper frowned in momentary puzzlement.

'Three what?'

'Them smoke rings. You do them better'n my uncle Arfer. Couldyer teach me?'

The senior camper sighed.

'Not likely, my son. To learn anything you have to have a brain. Did you misplace yours or weren't you never issued with one?'

' 'Ow d'yer mean?'

'Have you no comment on my story?'

A trapped look came over the youth's face causing him to squint hideously.

'Dunno,' he murmured sullenly.

'Let's take it step by step. Did you understand it?'

'Fink so.'

'What did you understand?'

'It was abaht this tart, warn't it? And she had these rings on 'er arm. I didn't understand that bit? Was they growing there or what?'

The senior camper glanced at his watch. He stretched elegantly and stood up.

'Come along, my son,' he urged. 'I'll buy you a pint of lubricating oil. Might get the wheels going.'

The pale youth stood up eagerly.

'I like brahn ale,' he announced.

'You shall have it. But, as we walk, just a few more tests to see if you own even a pinch of grey matter. In my story there was a character called Spike. Do you remember?'

'Fink so.'

'Good. Excellent. Spike is the camp comedian. You must have seen him about. He gets big laughs, does Spike. And do you know how he gets the biggest laughs of all?'

'Nah.'

'You don't? It's when they push him into the pool. Like this.'

And leaving the shriek and the splash fastidiously behind him, the senior camper strolled away through the balmy air towards his favourite bar.

Eruptions

It was a wet, cold, grey afternoon but, as he made his way along a wind-swept path towards the Kon Tiki tea-rooms, the senior camper was in excellent spirits. A few minutes before, he had met, by appointment, an acquaintance of his from South London. Perhaps 'acquaintance' is not the right word. The bullet-headed, brawny man with the thin scar running from left ear to mid-cheek, was really more of a colleague or perhaps associate would be closer to the mark. The two had, on various former occasions, participated in little business enterprises together, sometimes in the company of other sturdy men. They had met, as if by chance, on the banks of the campers' fishing-pond, deserted apart from themselves. They had stood and gazed speculatively at the murky water from which the skeleton of a push-chair and some tyres protruded forlornly, and exchanged a few cordial remarks. They parted less than five minutes later, the bullet-headed man to make his way swiftly back to London in a very fast car and the senior camper to amble through the drizzle towards the Kon Tiki, content with the knowledge that a substantial sum of money had been deposited in his name in a certain South London bank.

Arriving at the Kon Tiki, the senior camper removed his smart mac and carefully dried his face and hair with a large, emerald-green handkerchief which he then tucked into one pocket of the mac. Restored to something like the spruce and dapper appearance he was careful to maintain at all times during the long season he spent annually at Maplin's, he moved on from the foyer into the spacious tea area. This was decorated, in deference to its name, with an abundance of items suggestive of the Pacific Islands. There were several huge stone heads, made out of plastic, as indeed were all the decorations, with protruding lips. There were plastic parrots and plastic totem poles. The totem poles were not, strictly speaking, geographically authentic since they derived from the plains Indians of North America but they blended very nicely with the plastic palms and plastic bunches of bananas and coconuts.

The senior camper gazed about, a slight frown displacing his amiable expression of a moment before. The place was crowded. This was not surprising in view of the weather. It was no day for outdoor pursuits and hence most of the campers were gathered in the various playrooms and leisure activity centres. The senior camper had, of course, known that the weather would keep people indoors but he had never seen the Kon Tiki so crowded. He was about to turn and make his way to the Laughing Cow Milk Bar, which also served tea, when he spotted an empty place. It was just beneath the centrepiece of the tea-rooms, which was a large, plastic model of the Kon Tiki raft tilting precariously on blue plastic waves. With a sigh of relief that he would not immediately have to brave the weather again, the senior camper made his way over to the one empty seat and sat down.

There was only one other person at the small table. It was a bearded man of about thirty, clad in a decent lightweight grey suit, engrossed in a paperback book. In front of him was an empty teacup and a plate with a few crumbs remaining in it.

The senior camper favoured the Kon Tiki tea-rooms because, although the tariff was slightly higher than in the other places of refreshment in the camp there was waitress service. There was not, however, much of it and by the time the senior camper had managed to catch the eye of one of the few overworked waitresses, beckon her to his table, give his order and then endure another tedious wait until his cup of tea and toasted teacake had been deposited on the table in front of him he was gasping with thirst. He was not, however, the man to forget his manners no matter how urgent his need and so he refrained himself from seizing his cup until he had exchanged a pleasantry with Diana, the delightful waitress with whom he always enjoyed a nod and a wink, although nothing of a disreputable nature ever passed between them.

'Ta ra then, my daughter,' he called cheerfully to her retreating, and ample, rump and then turned his attention to his refreshments.

He received a shock. The teacake, uninvitingly decked with congealed butter, lay on its little dish but his tea had disappeared. He glanced crossly from side to side and immediately saw it, just approaching the lips of the bearded bloke on his left who, as he prepared to sample the fruits of his bare-faced theft, still had his eyes glued to his book. Never one to tolerate dishonest practices, in others at least, the senior camper shot out his massive left hand and seized the other by the wrist. The effect was dramatic. As the senior camper began to say firmly: 'Do you mind, my son!' the culprit gave a little scream of horror and shook himself free with violence, sending the tea cascading over the table and both of their trousers. The senior camper exclaimed and jumped in his seat from the impact of the hot fluid and the other did likewise. Then, order somewhat restored, they stared at each other with, for the moment, intense mutual dislike.

'What the hell did you do that for?' asked the senior camper reproachfully. 'My best pair of bags and all.'

A contrite look appeared on the other's face, as he glanced down and beheld the damage he had wrought.

'Why did you grab my wrist?' he asked.

'You was about to guzzle my tea.'

'Was I? I thought it was mine. Sorry.'

'You didn't have to squeal like that and jump about.'

'I thought you were the snake.'

'Snake? What snake?'

In spite of his sturdy common sense, the senior camper glanced up involuntarily at the boughs of the plastic palm which overhung them, half-expecting to see a serpent slithering down the trunk.

'In my book. You just caught me at the passage where Dan Champion is locked in an attic in the dark with a deadly mamba and is feeling his way about to strangle the snake before the snake bites him. I thought it had got him – me. See what I mean?'

'I see you have a very vivid imagination,' suggested the senior camper. Then he began to perceive possibilities in the situation. 'Fond of a good story, are you?'

'Yes, I am. Look, I'm sorry about your trousers. Have them cleaned and pressed and send me the bill. And I'll get you another cup of tea.'

The senior camper smiled benevolently. He knew a gent when he met one. He waved his hand dismissively.

'Forget the pants, but I'll accept the tea with pleasure. Incidentally, I'm Charley Binns, the senior camper.'

'Oh really? I've heard of you.'

The senior camper felt a distinct pulse of affection. He had always been a good judge of character. This bloke was one of the best, no doubt about it.

'What have you heard, my son?'

'You must be the crackpot who spends all his time here. How do you stay sane?'

The senior camper's affectionate smile wavered slightly but then he made an effort and restored it. His neighbour had just experienced a severe shock and was doubtless still a little incoherent from it.

'My patch, Maplin's. Only home I've got. Rest of the year, I travel about.'

'Really? So do I. In hosiery. What are you in?'

'Oh – different lines.'

'But you are a salesman?'

'Not exactly. But I deal in – all kinds of items. Enough about me. You haven't told me your name yet, my son?'

'Blast. I thought I'd caught that waitress's eye. But she got away.' The bearded chap held out his hand. 'Dank – Elmer Dank. Pleased to meet you and thank you for being such a good sport.'

'No sweat, my son,' affirmed the senior camper, heartily wringing the other's hand, 'but do I gather you have reservations about Maplin's? That you're not having non-stop fun?'

'Ghastly place,' said Dank, with a shudder. 'Oh, I'm sorry. You obviously like it.'

'What I don't understand, my son, is why you're here if you find it such a trial.'

'Wife and children. They love it. They're at the junior ballroom final now. My little girl, Annabelle, is probably just receiving the gold medal for the junior tango. If she's not the chalet will be hell tonight.'

'So where would you go for a holiday? If you had the choice?' pursued the senior camper, gratified to see that a waitress had finally responded to his companion's increasingly desperate semaphore.

'Africa. Brazil – the jungle – love to be in the jungle. Might give the poles a spin – the old way with dogs. None of your effete airdrops and Sno-Cats.'

'Do I detect a craving for adventure?'

'God, yes. That's what I crave. Adventure. But all I get is the haberdashery departments and Maplin's.'

'And Dan Champion,' added the senior camper, tapping the volume which now lay on the table in front of them.

'Keeps me sane,' nodded the other ruefully. 'Read up to ten books a week – all adventure.'

'Well, you've come to the right place for it, my son.'

The other regarded him suspiciously, under the impression that he might be being had. But the senior camper pressed on urgently.

'Straight up. Maplin's is a hotbed of adventure – if you know where to look. Why just last month there was thrilling stuff – sabotage, pursuit, incarceration. Care to hear about it?'

'Well –'

'If you insist, my son. Just keep signalling, she'll get here in the end.'

It all started when old Partridge got drunk again. Now you may not have seen Mr Partridge on account of he is usually togged up in a big upright box. The fact is he is Maplin's much-loved Punch-and-Judy man and has probably already provided your kiddies with hours of fun. Sometimes he puzzles the kiddies just a bit because his, or rather Mr Punch's, speech gets slurred and the kiddies sometimes wonder what a pint of foaming ale is doing on the ledge where Mr Punch is supposed to fight the crocodile and duff up Judy. Usually these little hiccups in his performance pass without causing much stir amongst the nippers but on the occasion I am referring to Mr Partridge overdid the bevvy with the result that his whole Punch-and-Judy theatre crashed down amongst the kiddies. Fortunately none of them was hurt and Mr Partridge finally crawled unscathed from the wreckage. But tidings of the incident reached Jeffrey Fairbrother, the incorruptible entertainments manager who was once a Cambridge professor but decided that there was more fun to be had at Maplin's. So naturally he invited Mr Partridge to a conference in his little office. Gladys Pugh, his right-hand girl and chief yellowcoat, was also there. Gladys, between ourselves, has a very soft spot for Jeff but Jeff is married and a very upright sort of bloke although he is separated from his wife. You must have heard Gladys. She has the delightful Welsh voice we hear all day long on Radio Maplin. Anyway, on this melancholy occasion, poor Mr Partridge was stammering:

'I – I don't know how it happened, Mr Fairbrother. I must apologise. I don't know what came over me.'

Old Partridge has a chunky, wedge-shaped face beneath iron-grey hair and he wears spectacles. His bulky figure, like his ruby complexion, betrays his hobby which, as I have suggested, is boozing.

'Nothing came over you,' snapped Gladys unkindly. 'You were drunk.'

Partridge's eyes narrowed. He is a bad-tempered old man who hates kiddies, which is probably, considering his profession, what drives him to drink. He turned on Gladys, ready with a biting retort, but then he remembered the delicacy of his situation and only said humbly:

'I can only say I'm sorry and assure you it will not happen again.'

Jeff Fairbrother shook his head sadly and sighed.

'I'm afraid it's happened once too often, Mr Partridge,'

he said firmly. 'Some of the parents have complained and it will have to go in my Thursday report.'

At this, Partridge started to gnaw his lower lip. He knew that a bad report would mean the sack. He had been caught drunk too often before for Joe Maplin to excuse him. On the other hand, he had a fairly clean record this year. This was not because he had stopped getting drunk but because Jeff, a very decent bloke, had not yet put in a bad report about him in spite of much provocation. But last year, when there was a different entertainments manager, Partridge was booked several times.

'Can't you overlook it for once?' asked Partridge.

Jeff was troubled. True, Partridge was a backbiting old reprobate without many redeeming features but just now he looked simply like an old man near the end of his tether. Jeff had to do his job, nonetheless. He said:

'I've been overlooking it regularly twice a week since I came here.'

Partridge smote his right hand into his left and exclaimed bitterly:

'It's the kids that cause all the trouble. They're the ones that make me drink. If it wasn't for those little perishers, I'd be as right as rain.'

'But unfortunately,' Jeff pointed out, 'you are engaged as a children's entertainer.'

Partridge bared his teeth in a grimace of anxiety and then opened his mouth to reply. But just at that moment there was a sharp rap at the door and, without any pause, Ted Bovis strode in. You must love Ted. We all do. He's our jovial camp host, short, fat and with a head like a pumpkin.

'Can you spare a moment, Jeff?' he asked with a certain weary insistence in his homely voice.

Jeff nodded.

'Mr Partridge is just leaving.'

Taking his cue, Partridge rose and shuffled towards the door. When he reached Ted, he paused and confided:

'You know what he's done, Ted? He's put his finger right on my problem. If I wasn't a children's entertainer I wouldn't get drunk.'

'Thank you, Mr Partridge,' said Jeff firmly.

'That's all right,' said Partridge and ambled on to the door. But instead of passing through it, he stopped again, turned and then said passionately:

'You won't put that report in, will you, Mr Fairbrother? You're not only a man of great intellect but you've got a soft heart.'

Then, with a suspicious sniff, Partridge turned again and finally departed. Ted Bovis looked after him.

'Been at the sauce again, has he?' he asked.

'I'm afraid so,' agreed Jeff, 'and I just can't let it pass this time.'

Ted approached the entertainments manager's desk and tapped lightly on it with his knuckles.

'I think you've been very tolerant with him,' he observed. 'I'm sorry to increase your burdens but here's another problem. Did you see my act last night, in the ballroom?'

'Yes. I thought you went awfully well.

Ted shook his head gloomily.

'You're just being kind. Not only that but you don't know what you're talking about. I'm looking you straight in the eye, Jeff, and telling you I've never worked under such appalling conditions in my entire career. I'd sooner play the monkey house at the Zoo.'

Gladys clucked audibly and said icily:

'You're exaggerating as usual, Ted.'

Ted turned on her and said bitterly:

'It's all right for you. All you have to do is sit there at the mike in Radio Maplin and say –' Here Ted made an attempt at mimicking Gladys' soft, and much-loved, Welsh lilt, ' "Hello, campers – Hi-de-hi".'

'I don't speak like that,' maintained Gladys. 'I'm not an Indian.'

Ted blinked and turned to Jeff again.

'Look, I have to grab that audience and make 'em listen. Answer me a question, when you're giving a lecture on mummies –' Ted was here referring to the fact that Jeff, in the old days at Cambridge, used to spend his time unwrapping ancient Egyptians to see what he could find out about them – 'have you got a ruddy great ball of little mirrors going round just above your head and dazzling all your pupils?'

'Students!' interjected Jeff firmly.

'Whoever – dazzling them with multicoloured lights?'

'Not at Cambridge,' admitted Jeff. Then he smiled and made one of his little jokes that his colleagues never laughed at. 'I'm not sure what they do at Oxford.'

He sniggered slightly but Ted glared at him and continued.

'It's no laughing matter, Jeff. Last night I was just coming to the punchline of my story about the pouff helping the bishop to button up his gaiters and Sylvia flashes a sign saying there's a baby crying in chalet number forty-six.'

Gladys, who is the senior yellowcoat, commented:

'No manners, that girl.'

'Then to top it all,' Ted continued. 'I was in the middle of my last song which is "I Believe" and which is a really lovely song, Jeff, all about God –'

'Yes, I've heard it, Ted,' the entertainments manager assured the earnest camp host.

'Well, I'd got 'em right there in the palm of my hand, when the silly bitch of a barmaid walked right in front of me, tripped up and spilled two Bloody Marys, a dry Martini and a lager and lime right where I'm about to kneel down, raise my arms and call on the good Lord above.'

Jeff tried to soothe the troubled singer.

'It was an accident, Ted. It doesn't happen every night.'

But Ted pressed on remorselessly.

'Then finally I was doing my sincere "thank you from the bottom of my heart" speech just before "Good night, Campers" and the doors were flung open and all them workmen started chucking planks of wood in the corner.'

'Ah, that won't happen again,' Jeff reassured him. 'They've been working all night on the Mighty Mountain of Pitzpalu.'

'The what?'

'It's the new display. It's called "The Mighty Mountain of Pitzpalu".'

Ted sighed.

'I know about the displays. Joe Maplin is crazy about them.'

'Well, this one's got to be finished by five o'clock this evening, so you won't be bothered by the builders any more.'

'The thing is this, Jeff,' said Ted severely, 'while I'm doing my act, I'm having the ball switched off, no waitresses on the floor and no flashing from yellowcoats.'

Gladys looked outraged. She said:

'You can't start laying down the law like that.'

Jeff held up his hands as if to separate the two. Then he gave his decision.

'I'll watch your act tonight, Ted, so that I can see what your problems are and then we can discuss it tomorrow.'

That night happened to be Hawaiian night which all the girls love because it gives them a chance to wear grass skirts and show off their legs. There was a great variety of grass skirts on display in the ballroom, varying from those made out of real grass that the girls had picked to one or two sad efforts made out of strips of newspaper. But the general effect was very pretty and if you had a strong imagination you could easily have believed you'd suddenly been transported to the South Seas. The only false note was Peggy, the frustrated chalet maid, who was wearing an ordinary skirt and blouse and, instead of swaying and waving her arms softly, was jitterbugging wildly with a teddy boy camper that had picked her up.

At one end of the mighty ballroom stood the Mighty Mountain of Pitzpalu. This was actually a five-foot-high wooden model of a volcano with palm trees on its slopes and at its base and clouds on wires drifting past it. Ted was standing in front of it, surveying it critically. With him was Fred Quilly, the unfrocked jockey, a nice man who loves horses and takes campers for rides on his string of them. Ted finally shook his head in disgust.

'I don't know why Joe Maplin's wasted his money on it,' he said sternly. 'It's paltry.'

'There's nothing happening, Ted,' commented Fred.

'You're right, it's inanimate. I'm always telling Spike, to hold the public's interest a thing must be animate.'

Spike is, as you may know, the camp comedian and he is learning his trade under Ted's patient and expert supervision.

'They should have a racetrack going round the bottom of that mountain,' averred Fred, whose mind seldom canters far from horses, 'with little ponies that people could bet on.'

Spike joined them. He was wearing a large cooking pot and holding a big container marked 'salt'. An important part of Spike's job is dressing up in funny clothes and I have seen him dressed as everything from the Eiffel Tower to a pint of beer.

'What do you think, Ted?' he asked anxiously.

Ted studied the costume.

'It's better, but you should be red all over.'

'Why?'

Ted shook his head impatiently. He sometimes despaired of Spike who seemed to lack any real instinct for the comic.

'Because if you'd been cooked you'd be red. You must have reality, Spike.'

Meanwhile Gladys was seated some distance away at the bar, wearing a very attractive Hawaiian costume with two leis, that's garlands of hibiscus flowers, round her neck. She was glancing about as if expecting someone. In fact, she was hoping that Jeff Fairbrother would join her. Gladys has a very soft spot for Jeff Fairbrother as the rest of this story will make plain. In due course, Jeff arrived, not dressed Hawaiian-style exactly but sporting a colourful blazer and a panama hat. He sat down on the bar stool next to Gladys.

'I like your panama hat, Jeff,' purred the chief yellow-coat. 'You look like Bing Crosby in the road to somewhere or other.'

Jeff smiled faintly.

'Well, I thought I'd show willing. Don't want to be too standoffish,'

'Oh, you could never be that,' insisted Gladys. 'Why

don't you wear one of these?' she asked, removing one of the leis from her neck. 'They're a symbol of everlasting love and affection.'

She thereupon started to hang the plastic garland round her boss's neck but Jeff restrained her.

'No, I'd rather not. I'm allergic to flowers.'

'Oh, don't be silly. They're only plastic.'

But before she could pursue the point, Gladys suddenly noticed her three junior girl yellowcoats, in Hawaiian dress, clustered a little way down the bar. As she watched, the barman deposited three lagers on the bar for them. Gladys immediately approached the group, Jeff following her.

'You're not going to stand there boozing, are you?' Gladys demanded. 'You've got work to do.' She looked her subordinate up and down and gasped in distress. 'And what have you done with your grass skirts? They're too short and too thin. You've been pruning them.'

Sylvia, a tall, blonde yellowcoat, made a wry face.

'They were sticking out to here,' she said defensively. 'My backside looked enormous.'

Jeff raised a hand to his mouth to conceal a smile. He came to their rescue.

'I think they're very flattering.' He turned to his right-hand girl. 'After all, Gladys, they have got lovely legs.'

Gladys sniffed, unwilling as ever to credit her yellowcoats with anything but lechery and lethargy.

'Well, before you three start swigging beer, you can finish giving out the leis.'

'What about you?' asked Tracey cheekily.

'I'm management,' snapped Gladys. 'It's not my place to give out leis.'

As the girls departed, muttering subversively, a new problem for Gladys and Jeff hove into sight. This was Yvonne and Barry Stuart-Hargreaves, the haughty ballroom dancing instructors and demonstrators. In fact, Yvonne and Barry constitute a permanent problem for Jeff because they give themselves airs and consider themselves much too up-market for a place like Maplin's. As a result they are always moaning and refusing to do things they consider beneath their dignity. Their arrival is never an occasion for delight to Jeff. But this time they represented an additional problem in that they were dressed not in grass skirts and sarongs but in Dutch costumes. They looked as if they had come straight from some dike that they had been strengthening with their fingers. Reaching Jeff and Gladys, Yvonne broke out petulantly:

'Mr Fairbrother, may I ask why everyone is wearing Hawaiian costumes?'

Jeff sighed and explained:

'Well, believe it or not, Yvonne, it's Hawaiian Night.'

Barry, who, if anything, is more like a refined spinster than Yvonne, sniffed and commented:

'That's charming, isn't it? Nobody told us.'

Yvonne went on.

'Hawaiian Night is always on Thursday. Tonight is Wednesday – which is Dutch Night.'

'I'm afraid we had to change it,' explained Jeff, 'to celebrate the arrival of the Mighty Mountain of Pitzpalu.'

Barry glanced at the offending volcano and shuddered fastidiously.

'What, that dreadful common thing over there?' he queried.

Gladys broke in.

'I announced the change on Radio Maplin at half-past five. You should have heard it.'

Yvonne haughtily explained.

'For your information, at five-thirty Barry and I have our plugs in.'

'We have a little siesta,' Barry amplified, 'to give us strength for our performance and you can't zizz in this lunatic asylum without earplugs.'

A little later, Yvonne and Barry, with martyred expressions, turned and stalked off to their chalet to change into Hawaiian costume. Meanwhile Ted and Spike were standing under the volcano of Pitzpalu, careless of the possibility of an eruption, chatting gloomily.

'Just look at that ball of mirrors, Spike,' Ted was complaining. 'How can I compete against it?'

'You're absolutely right, Ted,' Spike sympathised, 'they should switch it off when you're on.'

'I'm not having it. Now, listen, Spike, while I'm doing my act you go and stand near to Jeff and point out every distraction I have to bear.'

'That I will, Ted.'

And he was as good as his word. Half an hour later, while Ted was gushing forth his usual stream of exceedingly filthy jokes, and the whole audience was rocking with laughter every time he mentioned lavatories or actresses, Ted hovered at Jeff Fairbrother's elbow making sure he missed none of Ted's ordeal.

'Aren't you going to make notes, Mr Fairbrother?' he asked anxiously.

'I think,' Jeff remonstrated gently, 'I'm capable of remembering the salient points.'

'Well, you must admit that ball is very distracting.'

'But he's going awfully well, Spike.'

'That's not the point. Ted's creative artist – a very sensitive man.'

At just that moment, the 'sensitive man' was holding up two fingers and making a very rude noise, which duly brought the house down. Ted joined in with a wicked chuckle. Then, as the delight began to subside, his bawdy expression changed to one of piety. He made his eyes round and little wrinkles appeared on his brow. He hunched his shoulders slightly as if in deference to the Almightly. He said:

'It's good to have a laugh, ladies and gentlemen, but there is a more serious side to life. The next number is dedicated to the book that we all love and hold dear, the Bible.'

Whereupon, with a gesture to the band leader who promptly started his band, Ted began singing a mournful religious song. Eight bars into it and a waitress, burdened with a tray full of drinks, crossed directly in front of him. Ted's pious expression momentarily gave way to one of fury, but he hastily reassembled the meek look and went on singing.

'Did you see that, Mr Fairbrother?' Spike eagerly asked Jeff.

Jeff nodded soberly.

'Yes, it is distracting. She could at least go behind him.'

But the waitress was soon totally outclassed as a distraction. A moment later, the Mighty Mountain of Pitzpalu began to come to life. It started with a thunderstorm, deep rumbles of thunder and flashes of lightning. At the first rumble, Ted looked stricken and glanced over his shoulder. But he was too much of a trouper to stop the performance. He went on singing as campers, attracted by the flashes of light and the sound of the thunder, first gazed at the display and then began to exchange comments on it and finally to rise and move towards it. Ted went on singing even while campers streamed past him like stampeding cattle. He went on while, to the delight and astonishment of the campers, the God of Pitzpalu, a foot-high plastic head, rose slowly from behind the mountain and the God's voice boomed out:

'I am the mighty God of Pitzpalu. You have sinned against my laws. Let the mountain erupt and the lava flow.'

Ted even went on singing as clouds of smoke began to belch from the mouth of the volcano, while the God descended again, and as porridge-like lava also began to issue from the crater. He only finally gave up the struggle when smoke from the fearsome eruption began to make visibility difficult and also to choke him. Then, and only then, did he, after coughing spasmodically a little, raise his hands for the band to stop and announce wearily:

'Ladies and Gentlemen, Maplin's proudly present your star ballroom champions, Yvonne and Barry Stuart-Hargreaves.'

And this, of course, compelled the luckless display dancers, shooting furious looks at Ted, to come cha-chaing onto the floor in the smog.

At half-past ten the following morning, the conspiracy was brought into being. Yvonne and Barry knocked at the door of the chalet that Ted and Spike shared and Ted opened the door. Spike and Peggy were seated on the bed. Before Ted had uttered a word, Yvonne was in full cry.

'I presume, Ted, that you have called us here to apologise for throwing us into that dreadful situation last night.'

'Belt up, Yvonne,' remarked Ted gloomily. 'You and Barry take a pew and I'll tell you why I've called you in here.'

Seating themselves with every sign of reproach, the two dancers fixed Ted with beady eyes.

'Well?' asked Barry.

'What I have to say concerns us all,' announced Ted. 'At ten thirty last night I instructed Jeff to tell Joe Maplin that he had to switch off the ball, stop the bar service and elbow the Mighty Mountain of Pitzpalu or I wouldn't do my act.'

Barry looked sceptical.

'How did that go down with Joe Maplin?' he purred.

Spike, revealing more of a comedian's instinct than Ted normally credited him with, offered:

'He told him not to do his act.'

Ted darted a reproachful look at his chalet mate and disciple.

'That's not quite right, Spike. We can't be sure that Jeff put it to him properly.'

'All the same,' said Spike, 'Joe Maplin's refused to do all that stuff you wanted.'

At this point Ted received some welcome support from Yvonne who declared shrilly:

'Well, some action will have to be taken. Otherwise Barry and I will definitely get on to our agent.'

'And what will she do?' asked Ted pointedly. 'Nothing.'

At this Peggy burst into a long speech. Peggy is very excitable and she tends to gabble. She sounded a little like a speeded-up gramophone record.

'Well, I think it's dangerous,' she exclaimed vehemently. 'They shouldn't have a volcano in the ballroom. Supposing it got out of hand? Look what happened at Pompeii. All the people were covered in lather –' She gets words wrong too sometimes, does Peggy. '– the whole town was wiped out and it killed a little dog in its basket as well.'

Spike shook his head pityingly and pointed out:

'It's only a five-foot-high model, Peggy.'

'All right,' agreed Peggy, 'but if that little God got really cross you never know what might happen.'

'Peggy –' began Ted, but Peggy had reached the unstoppable stage.

'He was punishing the people for their sins and there's plenty of that goes on round here.'

Peggy became aware that everyone was gazing at her reproachfully. She blushed and stammered:

'Sorry, I get carried away. It's my imagination. It just takes flight. I can't control it.'

Spike said thoughtfully:

'Peggy could be on to something. I mean it was dangerous the way everyone rushed across the ballroom and knocked the chairs over. If the Fire Chief had seen that he wouldn't have liked it.'

Barry took up the theme.

'The fireman comes round every night. Why not draw his attention to the danger?'

Spike added:

'It would help if it smoked a lot. You know how firemen hate smoke.'

'That's it,' said Yvonne decisively. 'Make it smoke a lot.'

'How?' asked Ted sarcastically. 'By offering the God a Woodbine?'

Yvonne clucked at this boorish retort. She said haughtily:

'It must have some mechanism that carries out the sequence. Well, you could alter it in some way.'

'Oh yes,' enthused Ted. 'I'm a fully-qualified atomic scientist. Einstein used to ring me up twice a week for advice. Talk sense, Yvonne.'

'Wait a minute,' said Spike, frowning thoughtfully. 'Fred Quilly was an instrument mechanic in the RAF.'

'Ooh yes,' squealed Peggy. 'One of our washing machines was playing up and he put it right in ten minutes.'

Ted glanced from Peggy to Spike with a look of intense interest.

Spike shook his head sadly.

'But you'd never persuade him to do it, Ted.'

'Never persuade him?' asked Ted indignantly. 'If it came to protecting my act I could persuade Kruschev to join the Conservative Party.'

No one ever found out what arguments Ted used on Fred Quilly but he achieved his goal. Perhaps all he had to do was ask because Fred is a nice bloke with a strong instinct for friendship which is why having to share a chalet with an evil-tempered old lush like Mr Partridge is such a burden to him. Anyway, that night, in the early hours of the morning, Partridge was awakened by the sound of his chalet-mate thumping about in the little room.

'What are you doing?' asked Partridge irritably. 'It's one o'clock.'

'Go back to sleep,' urged Fred. 'I'm just going to help Ted out. That Mighty Mountain of Pitzpalu is ruining his act and I'm going to make a few precision adjustments to it.'

Partridge guffawed coarsely.

'Like what? Chop it up with an axe?'

'Mind your own business,' urged Fred. 'Get some sleep.'

'How can I?' complained Partridge. 'With what I've got on my mind. Fairbrother's written about me in his report. Once that goes in I've had it.'

'I don't blame him,' said Fred mildly. 'I reckon he's been very tolerant considering you spend half your life legless.'

'Ah, shut your face!' snarled Partridge.

He turned over onto his side and watched as Fred, clad in old trousers and a roll-neck sweater, tiptoed to the chalet door and out. Then Partridge turned onto his back again and closed his eyes. A moment later he opened his eyes and sat bolt-upright. He gazed after the departed Quilly with a frown revealing (not a pretty sight) that he slept in far from spotless long johns, climbed out of bed and made his way to the deal wardrobe for his clothes.

A few minutes, later, Partridge was tiptoeing along the lines of staff chalets towards Jeff Fairbrother's. Reaching it, he raised his hand to knock, paused, reflecting that a number of the staff were known to be light sleepers, and then quietly turned the handle and entered. Once inside he crept to the bed and switched on Jeff's bedside lamp.

'Mr Fairbrother?' he said hoarsely. 'Wake up, Mr Fairbrother.'

There was an upheaval amongst the blankets and Jeff's anxious face appeared.

'What?' asked the entertainments manager. 'What are you doing here?'

'I've got a little proposition to put to you, Mr Fairbrother,' said Partridge with what he hoped was an ingratiating smile.

Its effect was to cause Jeff to draw back sharply and pull the blankets up around his chin.

'What do you mean?'

Partridge leaned towards his boss and a smell such as might be caused by an overflow in a brewery engulfed the latter.

'If I was to give you information concerning the sabotaging of certain equipment,' purred Partridge, 'would you be prepared to take my name off that report?'

Jeff contemplated him unenthusiastically for a moment.

'What information?' he asked.

'Like I said, would you be –'

'I can't promise anything,' said Jeff decisively.

Partridge was silent for a moment, gnawing his lower lip.

'All right,' he said finally, 'but don't forget that what I'm about to tell you could save the good name of your department and let you keep your job. Fair's fair.'

And Partridge launched into an account of what he knew. When he'd finished, Jeff rose from his bed and began to don his dressing gown which had been hanging over the side of a chair.

'I'd better tell Gladys,' he said, 'just in case any of the yellowcoats are in on this.'

'I don't want you to think I'm a grass, Mr Fairbrother,' whined Partridge, 'but you've been good to me and I wouldn't want to see you lose your job.'

Jeff shot him a contemptuous glance and then left the chalet, Partridge shuffling after him.

A few chalets along, Gladys Pugh was having a lovely dream. Naturally I cannot tell you what it was about but I can say with confidence that it was probably about Jeff Fairbrother since Gladys has a yearning for his attentions. A moment later dream and reality blended into one. Gladys heard a voice in her ear, saying:

'Gladys, wake up.'

She promptly opened her eyes, every nerve thrilling at the arrival of the moment she had feared would never come. She breathed:

'I'm not asleep.'

'It's Jeffrey,' whispered her boss.

'I know it is,' returned Gladys, trying not to sound too eager.

'We haven't got much time.'

'Of course we have,' exclaimed Gladys fervently. 'It's only one o'clock.'

'Shall I switch the light on?' asked Jeff.

'Oh no,' gasped Gladys, 'I prefer the dark.'

At which precise moment, Gladys' dream of romance was brutally shattered. The light flooded on and, silhouetted in the doorway, Gladys beheld the repellent figure of Mr Partridge. She gave a little squeal of dismay.

'What's he doing here?'

'He's come to help us,' Jeff explained, puzzled at the look of horror that momentarily came over his trusty assistant's face. 'You see, Ted's persuaded Fred Quilly to chop up the Mighty Mountain of Pitzpalu to stop it interfering with his act.'

Gladys tossed her head angrily.

'Well, why don't you inform Security?' she asked.

'If I do that,' Jeff explained, 'everyone will get the sack. Get dressed, Gladys, we're going down to the ballroom to stop them.'

Whereupon Jeff turned and left the chalet, urging Partridge ahead of him. A little later, Gladys, wearing a mackintosh buttoned up to the neck, joined them. She said:

'I've been thinking, we're wasting our time. Fred can't get into that ballroom. It's got burglar alarms.'

Jeff looked at her and nodded.

'That's a point,' he agreed.

But Partridge made an angry sound.

'He probably got in the same way I'm going to show you, through the Three Bears' Cottage in the kiddies' playground. Are you coming or not? I can't stay up all night at my age.'

He set off along the chalet lines and, after a moment's pause, Jeff and Gladys followed him.

Old Partridge was wrong. Ted didn't know about the entrance through the Three Bears' Cottage. He did, however, know about the burglar alarms. So he had decided on a very tricky and adventurous method of gaining access. He intended to go in through a skylight on the roof, just as, so I've heard, burglars do sometimes. In order to get up onto the roof he needed a great big ladder and a long rope and a lot of help. For this reason, a large party, something like a commando unit about to land in France and blow up a secret German radar station, slipped through the shrubs and trees towards the ballroom. It was made up of Peggy and Fred Quilly who were, you might say, the operational spearhead. It was their job to actually penetrate the ballroom and make the necessary adjustments to the Mighty Mountain of Pitzpalu. The assault party consisted of them plus Ted and Spike who were to wait on the roof while the spearhead did its terrible work and then assist them up again. In addition, there was the back-up party. This consisted of the Stuart-Hargreaves whose assignment was to wait on the ground beside the ballroom, keeping themselves and the ladder out of sight of any prowling security men, and then, when the assault party was ready to return to base, to attach the ladder to the rope that Ted would throw down, so that the assault party could haul it up and then use it to descend with the operation completed. Thrilling stuff.

And it all went smooth as clockwork most of the way. The roof was scaled, Peggy and Fred were lowered into the ballroom. Fred changed the mechanism on the Mighty Mountain so that the smoke worked off of the rain switch.

Since the rain went on all the time this meant that the Mighty Mountain should now belch out clouds of smoke perpetually. It was only when Peggy and Fred, having cleared up all signs of their raid, reached the rope once more that things began to go wrong. To realise how and why, we must go back a little in time and follow the track of what we should now call the pursuit force, consisting of old Partridge, Jeff and Gladys, although, as you will shortly discover, it was soon reduced to only Jeff and Gladys.

Led by Partridge, the pursuit force made its speedy way to the Three Bears' Cottage. This was a very small structure, designed for the exclusive occupancy, under normal circumstances, of infants and then only for brief periods of time. The rear wall of the Three Bears' Cottage in fact consisted of the outer wall of the ballroom but on the other side of the building from the one where Ted's commando was even then engaged upon its mission of sabotage.

When the pursuit force reached the Three Bears' Cottage, Jeff was dismayed to note that it was secured by a hefty padlock on a hasp. The whole building was only four foot high and Jeff crouched down to inspect the tiny door and its fastening.

'What do we do now?' he asked, finding the padlock was strong.

He stood up and confronted Partridge. The latter, to his astonishment, fished out of his pocket a large bunch of keys and started checking through them.

'I'll just find the right one,' he announced.

Gladys Pugh glanced about nervously and pulled the collar of her mac more closely around her pretty neck.

'What are we going to say if Security spots us?' she asked in her attractive Welsh lilt.

'I haven't got the faintest idea,' Jeff admitted. Then, hearing what he took to be the patter of footsteps from somewhere out in the moonless night, he urged, 'Do hurry up, Mr Partridge.'

'I think this is the one,' exclaimed Partridge. He stooped down and inserted it into the padlock. 'Yeah – that's it. Good.'

He unlocked the padlock, opened it and and removed it from its hasp. He then opened the little door. The three pursuers then got down on all fours and inched their way into the tiny room. It contained very little furniture but there were, naturally, three beds for the three bears. On their footboards were stencilled 'Father Bear', 'Mother Bear' and 'Baby Bear'. The first was four foot long, the second three and little baby bear's bed was only two foot long. The fake windows were painted with nice little scenes showing the forest surrounding the cottage and on a shelf were three porridge bowls, also in graded sizes, and also credited as the property of father, mother and baby bear.

'Close the door,' hissed Partridge over his shoulder to Jeff, who was bringing up the rear. 'I want to put the light on.'

'Right you are,' said Jeff.

He closed the little door and Partridge switched on the dim electric light. Jeff looked about with approval.

'I've been in here before,' he remarked. 'It's rather sweet.'

'This way,' said Partridge, unneccessarily since there was only one narrow route possible to them.

The three crawled across the floor to a little three-foot-high door that had a yale lock securing it. Above it was written 'Tom Thumb's Cottage'.

'Why are we going into Tom Thumb's Cottage?' asked Jeff. 'We'll have to slither.'

'It's not Tom Thumb's Cottage,' explained Partridge. 'It's the back of the bar. It's the emergency exit from the ballroom.'

He once more fished out his massive bunch of keys and sorted through them.

'Why have you got all those keys, Mr Partridge?' asked Jeff pointedly.

Still searching through his collection, Partridge snapped: 'I don't ask questions about your private life. Let's have some manners, please.'

He thereupon inserted a yale key into the lock and opened the door leading into the ballroom. He then backed up past Jeff and Gladys, saying, 'I'm going back to bed. If Fred catches me with you he'll kill me. Now when you've finished, don't forget to close this door. And when you've left the cottage, put the padlock back on the outside door. How do you feel about that report now, Mr Fairbrother?'

Jeff said stiffly:

'We'll discuss it tomorrow.'

'I see,' said Partridge bitterly. 'Well then, put the light out while I leave.'

Jeff did so, switching it on again after Partridge had crawled out through the little front door and shut it behind him. Then he pulled the 'Tom Thumb' door open and, pressing a finger to his lips to Gladys for silence, he crawled through it into the space behind the ballroom bar. Gladys followed. The two of them then stood up and, barely able to see in the gloom, began to feel their way in the general direction of the Mighty Mountain of Pitzpalu. Jeff had taken no more than three steps when his foot touched something. He felt whatever he had touched wobble and then begin to collapse. He made a desperate attempt to grab at whatever it was but he failed. With a tremendous crash a crate full of empty bottles collapsed onto the floor. Jeff and Gladys froze.

Now they weren't the only ones who froze. The spearhead had just regained the roof when Jeff had his mishap. The sound was deafening.

'What was that?' asked Peggy fearfully, peering down through the hole in the ballroom's ceiling through which Fred's head was now appearing.

Ted remarked grimly:

'It's either a ruddy great mouse or Security. Hurry up, Fred.'

He reached down and helped Fred up through the hole. He snapped to Spike:

'Get that rope out of the way and shut the ceiling trap. Time we were out of here.'

'Right,' said Spike. He hastily untied the rope and then, without thinking what he was doing, dropped it down into the ballroom. He replaced the ceiling panel.

Some twenty feet beneath him, Jeff and Gladys, satisfied that they were alone in the ballroom, had made their way to the Mighty Mountain of Pitzpalu and were inspecting it by the light of a pocket torch that Jeff had wisely brought with him.

'Nobody's touched it,' said Jeff wonderingly.

Gladys sniffed.

'Old Partridge made it up.'

'Why would he do that, Gladys?'

'I expect he was drunk.'

Jeff shook his head positively.

'He wasn't drunk. Couldn't have been. When he's drunk he falls over a lot.'

Gladys shivered.

Let's get back,' she urged. 'I'm cold. I've only got my nightie on underneath this.'

Jeff stared.

'Why didn't you put some clothes on?' he asked in astonishment.

'You were in a hurry. I didn't expect to be prowling around half the night. Come on.'

She led the way back to the little door giving onto the Three Bears' Cottage. They both crouched down and made their way into the minute chamber. Jeff pulled the door shut behind him, making sure the yale lock clicked, and then they both crawled towards the outer door. Little did they know it but the trap had already been sprung.

And not only on them.

Twenty feet above their heads, Ted Bovis was calling, softly but urgently, down into the darkness surrounding the ballroom:

'Barry? Yvonne? Are you there?'

He was relieved when, almost at once, he received an answering call. It came in the refined and sulky tones of Barry Stuart-Hargreaves.

'You've been ages. We're both perished down here.'

'Quick. Let's have the ladder. Somebody's poking about in the ballroom.'

This time it was Yvonne's ladylike voice which floated up out of the gloom.

'Throw down the rope.'

'Throw down the rope, Spike,' ordered Ted.

'The rope?' said Spike, gazing at him with anguished eyes.

'Get on with it. Only one end, mind. So we can haul the ladder up.'

'You said to get rid of it,' protested Spike.

'Get rid of what?'

'The rope.'

'What are you talking about?'

'I got rid of it. I dropped it down into the ballroom.'

A shudder of apprehension went through the assault party and Peggy uttered a low moan and looked up at where scudding rain clouds obscured the moon. Ted took off his hat and beat Spike about the face with it which did not improve the situation but relieved his feelings somewhat. Then he leaned over the parapet and called down:

'Barry, we've lost the rope. You'll just have to walk the ladder up to us.'

Now you will have noticed that both the factions in this gripping and elemental tale of adventure were worried about the same hazard. This was the camp's corps of security men. You will also have noticed that, thus far, none of these worthies had appeared to trouble either group. You may have concluded that the Maplin's security force were just a bunch of untrustworthy layabouts who were swigging beer and playing poker in their chalet, cynically disregarding their duties. Nothing could have been further from the truth. The patrols were out, keenly ensuring that the campers slept soundly in their beds and that no intruders threatened their persons or their property. Their keenness, in fact, was about to become evident to Jeff and Gladys in a most unfortunate way. The two senior members of the management staff had crawled through the Cottage of the Three Bears and reached the outer door. Jeff gave it a push but the door failed to open. The reason why was that, only minutes before, a security patrol had passed by, spotted the open padlock, glanced into the little edifice and seen that no one was inside (but failed to note 'Tom Thumb's' door slightly ajar) and carefully re-padlocked the door.

'My God!' exclaimed Jeff, pushing the door harder and finding it immovable.

'What's the matter?' asked Gladys.

'It's locked.'

'It can't be.'

'Well, it is. You don't think – Partridge double-crossed us?'

Gladys backed up and sat down on Little Bear's bed.

'Not in his interest. He's not suicidal. It must have been Security. They saw the open padlock.'

Jeff backed up and sat on Father Bear's bed.

'What are we going to do?'

Gladys glanced around at the little chamber. She perceived that there was no place in it where Jeff could get very far from her. She smiled.

'It's quite cosy,' she pointed out.

Jeff ignored this irrelevant comment.

'How's this? We shout for Security and when they arrive we simply say we'd been working late in the office and we decided to go for a walk to clear our heads. We noticed that the door was open so we came in here to see if everything was all right. While we were inside someone locked the door. What's wrong with that?'

'Just one little detail,' said Gladys dryly, opening her mac and revealing her pretty pink nightgown. 'What was I doing in the office dressed like this?'

'Keep it buttoned.'

'All right. I'm sure Security will accept that we both crawled in here to inspect the place. They won't think anything else. Rumours won't fly about the camp.'

Jeff stared at her in dismay. She was right. It was a ridiculous tale. The security men wouldn't even bother to conceal their grins of delight.

'Oh Lord, this is awful,' he exclaimed.

'We can easily slip out when they unlock it in the morning.'

But that won't be for six hours!'

'I'm sure we can make ourselves comfortable.'

Something in her tone made Jeff turn and contemplate her. Gladys was leaning back with a soft smile playing about her lips.

'Oh God!' said Jeff.

'I know,' said Gladys, 'why don't we put all three beds together and snuggle up?'

Jeff jumped visibly and edged away from her.

'No, I – I don't think so, Gladys.'

In one sense, the pursuit force was luckier than the assault party. They were at least dry. But up on the roof Ted, Spike, Peggy and Fred were standing in a downpour, miserably pulling their coats tighter about them to try to ward off the elements. They had small hope of rescue. Barry and Yvonne had laboured for a while to raise the heavy ladder but they were both frail creatures and the task proved beyond them. Finally, when the rain started, the lure of their snug chalet had proved irresistible and, calling good-bye to the incredulous group above them, they had strode away home.

Everyone was trapped, the assault party on the roof and the pursuit force in the Cottage of the Three Bears and a long and desperate night was endured by everyone.

Early the next morning, two hefty male campers, despatched by the Stuart-Hargreaves, arrived at the ballroom, effortlessly threw up the ladder and enabled the drenched and sneezing assault party to make good their escape. A little later, Security unpadlocked the Cottage of the Three Bears and, after a discreet interval, Jeff and Gladys stole away into the rising sun. And that night, as usual, the entire entertainments staff were present in the ballroom for another night of fun and frolic. As the campers began to straggle in, the Fire Chief arrived for his nightly inspection. Spike and Ted were downing a couple at the bar. Spike nudged Ted.

'There he is now.'

Ted put down his glass.

'Come on. Let's sow the first seeds of doubt in his mind.'

As they ambled up to him, the Fire Chief was trying to light one of the palm trees with his cigarette lighter, gratified to discover that it wouldn't ignite.

'What's the matter?' asked Ted. 'Want to keep warm? Try the volcano.'

The Fire Chief, a short, fierce man with a black moustache, turned on the camp host.

'It's my job to make sure everything in here is fireproof. You wouldn't laugh if this place went up.'

Ted shook his head innocently.

'I was only saying to Spike the other day,' he affirmed, 'it takes so little to create panic amongst these campers. Didn't I say that, Spike?'

'Something like that, Ted,' his oppo confirmed.

Ted continued.

'Smell of burning, or a wisp of smoke, and pandemonium could run through this mob like water off a duck's back.'

'Where are the buckets?' asked the Fire Chief nervously, glancing about for them.

Jeff and Gladys were at the bar, having a refreshing cocktail. Jeff looked a little like the Hunchback of Notre Dame with his head bent to one side. This was a result of the awkward posture in which he had finally fallen asleep on Father Bear's bed. Peggy joined them and said to the barmaid:

'Can I have a Whisky Mac, please?'

She thereupon burst into a bout of sneezing. Jeff looked solicitous.

'Got a cold, Peggy?' he asked.

'Oh no,' protested Peggy quickly. 'It's just my hay fever. I'm a martyr to it. What are you holding your head like that for, Jeff? Have you got a stiff neck?'

'Mind your own business, Peggy,' snapped Gladys.

Further down the bar, the three delightful girl yellowcoats, statuesque Sylvia, charming Betty and pert Tracey, were fortifying themselves for the evening's capers. Betty had noticed something strange in the air.

'What's going on, Sylvia?' she asked. 'Why's everybody whispering in corners?'

Sylvia glanced about to make sure no one was listening before confiding, with a giggle, 'Well, I was on my way for an early-morning swim and I saw Jeff and Gladys sneaking out of the Three Bears' Cottage.'

Tracey cocked her head and suggested:

'Well, maybe they were looking for something.'

Sylvia sniggered.

'It was seven in the morning and Gladys was in her nightdress.'

Tracey shrugged.

'Perhaps they found something.'

Betty contributed:

'It's funny. At six thirty this morning I saw Fred, Ted, Spike and Peggy all sneaking back to their chalets.'

'Do you think they'd been to an orgy?' asked Sylvia.

Betty said:

'If they had it was a flop. I heard Peggy say it was the wettest night she'd ever spent.'

Sylvia eyed Betty narrowly.

'What were you doing out at six thirty this morning?'

'Let's change the subject,' suggested Betty.

Peggy had left the company of Jeff and Gladys and joined Fred for a conspiratorial chat. Fred said glumly:

'My body aches more than when I fell off at the first fence in the Cheltenham Gold Cup. Seven horses went over me. How do you feel, Peg?'

'Ever so nervous,' returned Peggy, stuttering a bit and, when she wasn't doing that, sneezing. 'Ted's given me a big dramatic part. When the Mighty Mountain of Pitzpalu erupts, he wants me to be overcome by smoke and fumes in close proximity to the Fire Officer. In front of all these people. It's like playing Lady Hamlet or some other part from Shakespeare in a great big –'

'Shut up, Peg,' cautioned Fred. 'Ted's on.'

'Hi-de-hi!' bellowed the irrepressible camp host from his customary place under the band.

'Ho-de-ho!' roared the campers in reply.

Ted cocked a hand to his ear and gazed up at the ball,

gratified to see that it was no longer flashing or revolving, as he returned untruthfully:

'Ted can't hear you. Hi-de-hi!'

'HO-DE-HO,' bawled the campers in a truly impressive response.

Ted nodded satisfaction and announced:

'And as the first treat of a packed evening, I want to present our resident ballroom champions, Yvonne and Barry Stuart-Hargreaves, in a South American extravaganza, the Mexican Hat Dance.'

Whereupon Yvonne and Barry, dressed in dashing Spanish attire, pranced out onto the floor, looking about as Iberian as Brown Windsor soup. For all that, they soon had the campers shouting 'Olé', as Barry stamped and Yvonne swirled, but only for about thirty seconds. At that point, with a sinister rumble and a good deal of flashing suggestive of a fluorescent tube packing up, the Mighty Mountain of Pitzpalu began to erupt.

Jeff frowned at the spectacle and confided to Gladys:

'I do agree with Ted. That thing is awfully distracting for the artists. I'm sure, given time, I'd have found an opportunity to do something about it.'

He was surprised when Gladys, recalling the long night they had passed together in the Three Bears' Cottage, turned on him crossly and snapped:

'Opportunity! You wouldn't recognise an opportunity if it had flaming red lights and bells on it.'

By now, Fred Quilly's precision adjustment was beginning to make itself noticed. The Mighty Mountain was belching out smoke in great gusts which were beginning to swirl around the two dancers, who were casting it furious glances, and to cause the seated campers nearest to it to clear their throats and wipe their eyes.

Ted and Spike had made a point of staying near the Fire Chief as he continued his rounds. Now Ted said enthusiastically to Spike:

'By gum, look at all the smoke? Isn't that a wonderful effect?'

Spike, as agreed, retorted anxiously:

'I just hope people don't think it's a real fire.'

'That's a point,' said Ted earnestly. 'They're simple folk. They just might.'

'It does look a bit like a fire,' insisted Spike.

The Fire Chief said 'shh' urgently and glanced about in dismay.

'Never use the word "fire" in a public place,' he cautioned. 'It could cause a panic.'

'You heard what he said, Spike,' Ted urged. 'Don't keep saying "fire".'

Right on cue, Peggy staggered onto the floor with one hand clutched to her throat. She cried:

'Stop that thing smoking! I'm choking. My eyes are burning. I can't stand it. I can't stand it.'

'Quick, Spike,' ordered Ted. 'Get her out of here before there's a stampede.'

The Fire Chief shook his head and said firmly:

'I'm putting in a report about this. If that contraption isn't out of here by tomorrow, I'm closing the place down.'

'Oh dear,' said Ted. 'The campers will be disappointed.'

The following morning Jeff Fairbrother put in a long-distance call to Joe Maplin in London. While he did so, Gladys prepared his morning coffee for him in the staff room. She brought in the steaming cup just as he was hanging up and she placed it on his desk. Then she started to leave the room. Jeff said brightly:

'All fixed up.'

Gladys turned and faced him.

'Really?'

'Yes, Joe Maplin was most understanding. He said the insurance company would be very cross if the ballroom burned down. He's sending another display but I told him it mustn't be too distracting.'

'I see,' said Gladys and turned to depart.

'Gladys,' said Jeff earnestly.

She turned again.

'What?'

'You've been very – distant this morning.'

'No, I haven't. I've been in the staff room.'

'You know what I mean. Gladys, we have to work together and I don't like atmospheres. I feel it only fair to make my position quite clear. I'm just surfacing from a deep emotional involvement and I'm not anxious to dive into another.'

Gladys tossed her head slightly.

'I don't want you to do no diving,' she affirmed. 'But you won't even put your toe in the water.'

'What you don't –'

But at that moment, there was a brusque tap at the door and Ted waddled in.

'Jeff, you've missed a treat,' he chuckled. 'I've just been watching them load the Mighty Mountain of Pitzpalu on to a lorry.'

Jeff smiled.

'Yes, Mr Maplin's replacing it with something that doesn't smoke and belch fire and brimstone. It's a sort of a great big ape thing.'

Gladys stared coldly at the camp host.

'How did you do it, Ted?' she asked.

Ted contrived to look astonished and innocent at the same time.

'I never put a finger on it. That's the truth.'

'Anyway,' said Jeff in a conciliatory way, 'the ball won't be lit either. It seems you've got your own way, Ted.'

'What about the waitresses?' asked Ted cannily.

'I've told them not to cross the floor during your act.'

Ted beamed.

'You're a pal, Jeff.'

'Well, I was on your side, Ted. You can't have all those distractions. I'd hate it if I was giving a performance.'

'I expect the audience would and all,' said Ted softly, as he turned to depart.

Ted strode into the ballroom that night feeling better than he had done for ages. He was a sensitive artiste who, given half a chance, could wow any audience in England. But you couldn't call it even half a chance if he had to sing with coloured lights flashing in his eyes and volcanoes erupting behind him. But tonight, all distractions had been banished. Tonight he would give the performance of his life. Tonight he would make show-business history at Maplin's.

He spied Spike and Peggy standing in front of a large cage holding an eight-foot-tall gorilla. For a moment, the smile faded from his lips. He hadn't realised the new display would be here so soon. Then he shrugged in resignation. Joe Maplin was mad about displays. There was no way they could be permanently kept at bay. But, ugly and distracting though the big ape undoubtedly was, Ted felt he was a match for it. He could hold an audience against any still display ever made. It was only when they started acting up that they became a threat. By the time he reached his colleagues, Ted felt almost benevolent about the overgrown monkey.

'What is it?' he asked.

Peggy pointed to a sign on the front of the cage.

'It's King Kong in captivity. He looks ever so sad. I don't think they should keep wild animals in cages.'

Spike shook his head and pointed out:

'Stuffed ones don't really suffer, Peggy.'

Ted walked round the cage and back to the other two.

'Pathetic,' he commented. '*King Kong* was an old film. The kids won't even know what it is. Nowadays everything's television. They should have Dixon of Dock Green in here.'

Sylvia, the tall, statuesque yellowcoat, approached Ted and asked him:

'Ready to go on?'

Ted nodded and said sternly:

'And don't forget what I told you. I want a big build-up tonight.'

'Don't worry. We've been rehearsing. You won't be disappointed.'

'Nor will the audience,' promised Ted. He turned to the camp comedian. 'I'm going to paralyse 'em tonight, Spike. You watch.'

Spike grinned affectionately.

'Good luck,' he said.

The lights dimmed and the band struck up with a fanfare. The three girl yellowcoats pranced onto the floor and said in unison:

'And now, the one you've been waiting for, your friend and ours, Mr Cuddles himself, Ted Bovis.'

This was it – triumph time. His body swelling still more with self-confidence as a spotlight picked him out, Ted spread his arms and strode out onto the floor, singing, in his throaty tenor, 'Today I love Everybody' while the audience, sensing his mood, cheered wildly.

Jeff and Gladys, friends again, were watching enthusiastically from the bar when Mr Partridge edged up to them. Tapping Jeff lightly on the arm, he whispered:

'Have you decided what you're going to do about that report, Mr Fairbrother?'

Jeff sighed and shook his head.

'Not yet, Mr Partridge,' he admitted.

Partridge smiled benevolently. His face was not used to it and he looked slightly as if he was suffering from excessive wind. He said indulgently:

'I expect you had a nanny when you was a little nipper.'

Jeff frowned, failing to catch his drift.

'As a matter of fact I did. Why do you ask?'

'Well I expect she told you the story of Goldilocks and the Three Bears.'

'Yes, of course,' said Jeff, recalling childhood days in the nursery.

'Ah,' said Mr Partridge meaningfully, 'but did she tell you the version where Goldilocks had short black hair and a Welsh accent, and when dawn came she crept out of the cottage in her nightdress?'

And before Jeff could think of an appropriate retort, he turned to the barmaid and ordered a large whisky and a beer chaser.

Meanwhile, Ted was reaching the high point of his act. It had all gone like a dream thus far. Every joke had been a belter and every song a winner. Ted knew that he could do anything he wanted with these people. And it was time to prove it by getting serious.

'You can't help laughing, can you?' he asked rhetorically, while the audience wiped the tears streaming from their eyes. 'But just to be serious for a moment. You know, ladies and gentlemen, sometimes when I'm taking a stroll along the beach, and I look at the sea and the sky, I think about the man who created it all. They wrote a book about him and they called it – The Bible. And this is Ted's tribute to it. Thank you, professor.'

In obedience to his wave, the band started on the doleful opening bars of 'The Book'. Ted took up the lyric and, as his voice swelled out to the furthest reaches of the vast ballroom, he knew that he was uplifting hearts, that every single camper there would lay his or her head on their pillows that night a better human being than they had been before his song. He was reaching now the great, soaring passage when – there was a hideous roar from behind him. Involuntarily, Ted paused with open mouth as the music played on. What on earth – or come to that in heaven or hell – and then he grasped the awful truth. King Kong was coming to life. No, thought Ted, I'm not going to be beaten this time. A volcano may be a match for Ted Bovis but not a mangy stuffed ape. He issued once more into song and hastened to catch up with the band. From behind him came a jangle that sounded like an earthquake in a hardware shop and Ted noticed that the campers' eyes were no longer glued to him but were gazing over his shoulder. Still singing, and unable to resist the impulse, he half-turned and glanced over his shoulder. In spite of himself, he recoiled. King Kong was shaking the bars of his cage. His eyes had lit up and shone like horrible green lamps and the cage was jittering about on the floor. Ted's response was to sing louder. But now the campers were rising and beginning to close in on him. Ted held out his arms to ward them off but as King Kong began to scream and bellow with rage and the cage to shake even more wildly, Ted, still singing, was borne backwards and pinned against it. He stopped singing at last. He turned. He grasped the bars and, rivalling King Kong himself, he shook them and roared with uncontrollable fury.

The senior camper chuckled reminiscently as he reached for his cup of tea. He had become so involved in telling his tale, that he had forgotten how thirsty he was. He took a welcome sip, welcome in spite of the fact that the brown fluid was now cold.

'What do you think of that?' he asked his bearded companion.

'Of what?' asked the other with a slight frown.

'Of all that adventure?'

'You call that adventure?'

'Well yes – don't you?'

'I call it piffle.'

'Piffle?'

'Pure piffle. You must lead a very sheltered life.'

'I suppose I do – from time to time.'

'You have no idea of adventure. Good Lord, I know we're both commercial travellers but you astonish me. I've been here and there. I've seen some things and I've done some things in my time. You really call that adventure?'

'Well, the security guards and being stuck on the roof and –'

'Pathetic, as your Ted would say. If that's your idea of adventure, I hope you never get out of your rut. Because you'd be in trouble. I don't get much chance at adventure but I read about it. I read all the Dan Champion books and many more. I'm at least ready for adventure. If the opportunity ever arose, I could look after myself. I could meet it boldly and fearlessly. I wouldn't quail or cringe – my God!'

'What is it?' asked the senior camper anxiously.

His companion didn't answer. He was staring through the window as if at a distant smoke signal. The senior camper followed his gaze and saw, outside, a hard-faced young woman flanked by a hard-faced girl of about thirteen and a hard-faced boy of about nine.

'She didn't win,' muttered the bearded man and his teacake fell from nerveless hands.

'Didn't win? Who didn't win?'

'Annabelle. She didn't win the Junior Tango. She's not

wearing the medal. It's going to be hell – pure hell – tonight.'

'But surely, my son,' said the senior camper, 'you can face it boldly and fearlessly?'

'Hm? Oh that. Indians, yes. Black mambas, certainly. Assassins with guns firing pellets of nerve gas – piece of cake. Bombs, earthquakes, jungle treks – pure routine. But this –! You'll have to excuse me.'

And the bearded young man rose to his feet and, in response to the sternly beckoning finger of the hard-faced young woman outside, stalked, as if he had been turned into a zombie by the fearsome voodoo of Haiti, out of the Kon Tiki. He had taken only a few steps before the senior camper noticed that he had left his Dan Champion book on the table. He rose to his feet.

'Hoy,' he called, 'your adventure book.'

But the hypnotic trance cast on the unfortunate by the sinister agent of Smoosh locked him into its spell and the unfortunate strode on towards his grim fate.

'Oh well,' reflected Charley Binns, the senior camper, and he sat down again and rolled himself an elegant little cigarette with equipment he kept in a square tin. When it was finished he lit it and took a deep, satisfying drag. Then he reached out and grasped the Dan Champion book and opened it. He read for a few minutes in silence. Then he snapped the book shut.

'Piffle,' he murmured softly.

He looked about at the flanking tables, hoping he might see someone who looked bored and alone and in need of cheering up with a thrilling tale of high adventure at Maplin's.

Co-respondent's Course

The ballroom was about two-thirds full. Considering that it was a fine, if windy, day in early autumn and that the event was the Happy Families Competition, this was not bad. The Happy Families Competition never packed them in like the Guess Whose Bum (all time high ratings) or the Holiday Princess competitions did. But it was steadily popular with the more sentimental campers at Maplin's.

Ted Bovis, the jovial, pumpkin-shaped camp host was just concluding his interview with the head of the last family to be paraded. The three families who had already displayed their happiness to the admiring applause of the audience waited to one side. Facing the camp host and his family group consisting of mum, dad, a girl of fourteen and two boys of nine and seven, was a row of four chairs which held the judges. These were Sylvia, the charming yellowcoat with the tall, shapely figure, Yvonne Stuart-Hargreaves, the ballroom dancing instructor who simply had a tall figure, Jeff Fairbrother, the entertainments manager, who didn't usually judge competitions but was filling in for Spike Dixon, the camp comedian who had a cold possibly from repeated immersion in the camp pool, and the senior camper, Charley Binns. Charley Binns had a privileged position at Maplin's because he had been coming there steadily, summer after summer, for fifteen years and, what's more, spending three whole months each year in the establishment. He knew more about Maplin's than most of the staff and he was head of the Campers' Council, a nebulous body that met only infrequently and, when it did, hardly ever decided anything at all. But Charley Binns was called upon regularly to judge competitions in collaboration with staff members. He was so accustomed to judging the Happy Families Competition that he could tell the winner from a single glance at the contestants upon entering the ballroom. In this case, he knew that the present family, the Dixons, were the clear winners and his mind was hardly involved with Ted's irrelevant patter.

'All right then, Bob,' Ted was saying to the head of the family, 'you're a milkman and you live in Huddersfield and you met Lois here when you were both larking about in a haystack –'

Roar of laughter from the campers as Ted hastily corrected his deliberate mistake.

'Sorry, watching larks from the cover of a haystack. You're both keen bird-watchers. A bit like some of the blokes who come here. Nuff said. Now, Bob, I want you to tell me – and don't hold back – you're amongst friends – what was the most embarrassing thing Lois ever did to you? Come on, think hard. What did she do that turned your face as red as a tomato? Eh?'

Bob was a lanky man with a long pointed nose that was multiplied, with eerie precision, by his children. Lois, on the other hand, was a plump girl with a snub nose. She had a dimple on her chin and this mark was faithfully reproduced in the three youngsters.

'There must be something, Bob,' Ted urged with a hint of desperation. The happy families were not normally a very articulate lot but this Bob was in a class of his own. Getting a word out of him was like trying to catch trout in a bathtub. 'Did she ever do something that –'

Ted paused expectantly as Bob, who had been rocking back and forth on his heels with a sheepish grin, suddenly moved his lips slightly. Ted leaned forwards.

'Yes?' he pleaded.

'Was soomthin' –' Bob admitted with a shy glance at the audience.

'And what was it, Bob? Made you want the earth to swallow you up, did it?'

'Aye, 'appen –'

'We're all agog to hear it. Some of us are two or three gogs. Let's have it.'

The taciturn milkman issued into speech, only it was speech so faint that Ted, who leaned towards him, could not catch the gist of it.

'Well, she mumble, mumble, mumble, mumble.'

Ted abandoned the quest and, with the skill borne of long practice, burst into enthusiastic applause accompanied by a loud chuckle.

'She didn't? And your mother-in-law was in the next room? Get on, I don't believe it. Is that true, Lois?'

'Nay, it waren't –' the infuriating milkman started to protest at this misrepresentation of his tale but Ted felt he'd had his chance. He turned to the audience and confided:

'Lois admits that it really happened. All I can say is I wouldn't do that in front of my mother-in-law. Any road not before I'd checked to see that her chain was secure. She's a lovely woman my mother-in-law, a retired actress. Straight up. You can see her in a lot of old films. Not always in the starring part, mind you. She was stand-in for King Kong. I'm always telling the wife I don't mind having her live with us now that she's too old to work but the expense of feeding her two keepers is crippling. Anyway, that concludes this week's Maplin's Happy Families Competition. Now, while the judges are deliberating, I'll sing you one of my favourite numbers. It's a lovely, old –'

As Ted's voice swelled out in an emotional rendering of 'All the old familiar Places', the senior camper turned to Sylvia on his left and murmured: 'The Dixons?' Sylvia nodded. The senior camper repeated the performance with Yvonne on his right and received the same affirmative. He then rose and went round Yvonne's chair to that of Jeffrey Fairbrother. He leaned over the entertainments manager and whispered:

'The Dixons.'

To his astonishment, Fairbrother frowned and asked:

'Why?'

'What's that, my son?' asked Charley Binns, gaping.

'Why the Dixons? They didn't seem particularly happy to me. I thought the second family – what were they called –?'

Jeff glanced at the list he had made in his notebook and continued, 'Oh Yes, the Bellamys. Of course, it's impossible to reach a genuine appraisal on a matter that is intrinsically so imponderable but –'

'It's got to be the Dixons,' said the senior camper positively.

'I'm afraid I don't see that.'

'They've got the same nose and chin.'

'I beg your pardon?' Jeff gazed at him in blank incomprehension.

'They look alike. Therefore they're the winners.'

Jeff shook his head.

'I haven't the faintest –'

'Hang on. I know you're new this season but I'd have thought you knew the rules of the game by now. If they look alike it proves they're a family. That's all that counts. The others – you don't know whose they are. Mum or dad could have been up to something on the side. No, the campers don't give a toss if they're happy. Who's happy anyway? What they want to be sure of is that they really is a family. That means the Dixons.'

'Yes, but –'

'They're getting impatient, my son. Do you want to stand up and enrage your audience by giving it to some family with different noses?'

'But this is ludicrous – oh, very well.'

The senior camper returned to his place and, a moment later, when Ted had finished belting out his number, the entertainments manager stood up and awarded the prize (an electric blanket) to the Dixons.

'The Dixons are obviously a very happy family. They have exactly the same – er – interests and sympathy and – I think you'll all agree that they are this week's happy winners.'

The applause was loud and prolonged and the Dixons shuffled off with the prize. Jeff Fairbrother hastened away to his office and Yvonne to change her frock in preparation for a dancing session. Sylvia offered to buy Charley Binns a coffee but he hadn't yet had a chance to read his newspaper and was anxious to check the winners at Sandown so he refused politely. The audience began to rise and move out of the ballroom, Charley Binns amongst them. But as he neared the door, the senior camper noticed a chunky woman, clad in a red dress and a yellow hat, who had not risen from her place. In fact, she had her hands over her face and her shoulders were heaving suspiciously. Charley Binns was torn. He felt pretty sure that he might have a winner in the four-ten steeplechase but he was a good-hearted man who hated to see his fellow mortals suffer. He hung behind and watched the distressed lady. Then, when the great ballroom had virtually cleared, he approached her.

'What's up, luv?' he asked sympathetically.

'Clear orff and mind yer own business,' came the choked rebuke.

'It is my business. I'm the senior camper. Everything that happens in Maplin's is my business. You don't look as if you're fully participating in the endless fun and games.'

'What do you care?'

Charley Binns sat down on the vacant seat beside her.

'Is it the happy families? Are you touched to the bottom of your heart by so much happiness?'

The chunky woman moved her hands apart an inch or two and peeked at the senior camper. Reassured, apparently, by Charley Binns' frank, honest countenance and manly thatch of grey hair, she fumbled with one hand in her bag for a handkerchief while keeping the other over her face. When she had found the linen square she turned away and dabbed at her face and eyes. When she finally turned to confront the senior camper she was restored to the appearance of quite a good-looking woman of about forty. Her face was a trifle square but handsome. The only thing that marred her appearance was the little lines of her brow, which spoke of anxiety.

'It's the happy families, all right,' she sniffed. 'I hates them.'

'Why is that, my daughter?' asked Charley Binns, faintly shocked by the admission.

'Do you want to know? I'll show you. Come along with me.'

And the chunky woman rose and started towards the exit. Charley Binns accompanied her.

'Where are we going?' he asked.

'To the Laughing Cow. Even the bloody cows laugh around here.'

Abashed by the bitterness in her voice, the senior camper remained silent. Together they trudged along the asphalt walk amongst happy campers, who were squealing as skirts blew up and hats blew off in the stiff breeze, towards the Laughing Cow Milk Bar. Arrived there, the chunky woman gazed about the room for a moment or two and then led the senior camper to a vacant table. She sat down and he sat down facing her. After a while, he asked:

'Well, my daughter?'

'That's it,' she said harshly. 'Facing you.'

Charley Binns looked ahead. There was nothing facing him but a man drinking a fruit drink of some kind two tables away. The man was about the same age as his companion and had big ears and a face a little like a donkey's.

'Nothing's facing me,' he confided.

'Oh yes, there is,' the chunky woman said positively. She turned and pointed at the donkey-faced man who gazed back at her steadfastly. ' 'im. 'e's facing you.'

'So who is he?' asked the senior camper, embarrassed by the situation.

'All these happy families. 'e's why I 'ate them. That's my miserable family.'

'Your –'

'My old man. My 'usband.'

'I see. Perhaps we should join him?'

The senior camper had once or twice in the past had unpleasant encounters with jealous husbands and saw no reason to tempt providence. The donkey-faced man seemed supremely indifferent to the presence of his wife with a strange man at a nearby table but he might be working himself up for a scene. Charley Binns had no reservations about his ability to handle any situation that might arise but he hated violence. It spoiled his image.

'If we do, we'll only row,' said the chunky woman. 'That's all we ever do is row.'

'What do you row about?' asked the senior camper earnestly.

'Everything. If he says it's white, I say it's black. If I say it's hot, he says it's cold. We never talk like other people. We just row.'

'Do you have any children?' asked the senior camper solicitously.

'Four. All grown up. All married. They never come to see us no more because they can't stand the rowing. Now do you see why I hate the happy families? Because I've got the most blooming miserable family that ever existed.'

'You don't believe that, do you?'

' 'Course I do. Around here, everyone's happy the whole time. We're miserable.'

'But you don't want to be so gullible.'

'What?'

'You don't want to believe everything you see. Didn't you never hear it said that appearances can be very deceiving?'

'You trying to tell me those families – what we just saw in the ballroom – ain't happy?'

The senior camper shrugged eloquently.

'Who's to say? They stand there grinning all over their faces. But do you see them at home? Do you see them in the struggle of everyday life? If you did you might be surprised. You might find some of their so-called happy homes are pure hell.'

The woman shook her head doubtfully.

'Someone 'ud only have to spend ten minutes in the company of 'arry and me to be put off marriage for life. Oh, I don't know why we come here. We belong on some great lonely 'eath where there's no one to see our misery.'

'Have you tried having fun?'

'Fun?' the woman laughed a hollow laugh. 'Could you have fun with 'arry? Or come to that with me? It's asking too much. That's why I 'ate it 'ere.'

'Shhh,' cautioned the senior camper, shocked by the heretical utterance. He glanced around to make sure that none of the happy campers had been contaminated and was relieved to find none within earshot. Harry, he noticed, was gazing stolidly in his direction and munching steadily on a chocolate biscuit. He looked more than ever like a donkey.

'My daughter, people put on a brave face. Take my word for it, the ones around here has problems too. It's only human.'

'Not like us, they don't. Oh, I know you're just trying to cheer me up. But I've got eyes. The campers and the staff – they're all oozing happiness.'

'You might be surprised.'

'Go on. Take the yellowcoats. Those girls and boys – I never saw such a happy bunch. That Gladys – the Welsh one – she must be the happiest person in the world.'

'If you only knew.'

'And there's that lovely man – the entertainments manager – who was one of the judges just now – what's 'is name?'

'Jeffrey Fairbrother.'

'I can just imagine his marriage. He's a toff and I bet he leads a lovely, gracious and happy life with his loving wife.'

The senior camper sighed.

'I don't like doing it,' he said, 'I don't like telling intimate stories about people who have taken me into their confidence but the truth is the truth and what you need, my daughter, is a big dose of the truth. I'll tell you a story about Jeff Fairbrother and his marriage and about Gladys and then you judge for yourself if they are happy or not.'

'I don't need no stories. I can tell just by –'

'Please, my daughter,' urged the senior camper. 'Just listen.'

Withdrawing a small, square tin from his lively checked sports jacket, opening it and beginning to roll himself a cigarette, the senior camper began.

Today, my daughter, you have witnessed the Happy Families Competition. Delightful and entertaining though it was, it is only one of the numerous exciting competitions that the entertainments staff at Maplin's run practically non-stop for the amusement and fun of the campers. Amongst the others, and ever-popular, is the Ladies Custard Eating Competition and the events you are about to hear occurred little more than a month ago and had their roots in the Ladies Custard Eating Competition. A hefty lady called, if my memory serves me, Irene Hazlehurst had just won it in record time. Ted Bovis, whom you just heard introducing the Happy Families, also presided over this sporting event. At its conclusion, and after Irene had demonstrated an ability to consume custard which might have made her valuable as an auxiliary pump on a leaking ship, Ted Bovis stepped forwards and addressed the happy campers.

'And now, ladies and gentlemen,' he proclaimed, 'the winner of the Ladies Custard Eating Competition. She has consumed no fewer than eight pints of thick custard in just three minutes and forty-two seconds. Here she is – the astounding Irene Hazlehurst. Give her a big hand.'

And the champion, lathered in custard from hair to midriff, came beaming forwards to receive her prize. As she approached the entertainments manager, who was smiling bravely and holding in his hands a handsome plaster Alsation which was the prize, she threw out her arms and cried:

'Give us a kiss, Jeff.'

The entertainments manager, as you have correctly noticed, is a toff. He used to be a professor at Cambridge University and I suppose he rarely found a student approaching him who resembled a walking mound of custard. Little wonder that he recoiled from Irene's proffered embrace in apparent alarm. The prize-winner only giggled at this display of diffidence but the next moment she laughed out of the other side of her custard-spattered face. In recoiling, Jeff stumbled slightly and dropped the plaster Absatian which shattered on the flagstones surrounding the outdoor pool where the event is held.

'I say, I'm awfully sorry,' Jeff apologised.

He looked around at the trestle table on which were arrayed numerous prizes for the winners of other bizarre events and saw, to his dismay, that it contained no more plaster Alsatians. Trying to make light of the mishap, however, he grasped a plaster statue of a small boy holding up an umbrella and tendered this to the prize-winner.

'I tell you what,' he urged. 'Have one of these instead.'

Irene shook her head firmly. When asked what prize she would like if she won (and she had known that she was unbeatable) she had specified the Alsatian which, she knew, would enhance a small niche beside the fireplace in her front parlour.

'I don't want that,' she said firmly. 'I want the Alsatian.'

Jeff wretchedly replaced the boy and umbrella and scanned the table's bounty.

'I'm awfully sorry,' he repeated, 'but we simply haven't got any more Alsatians. How about a greyhound?'

Irene licked at some custard which was threatening to ooze down into her mouth and repeated firmly:

'I want an Alsatian!'

Jeff's face began twitching miserably, which it does sometimes when he is under stress, and an ugly situation was averted only by the experienced and diplomatic Ted Bovis grabbing things off the table and thrusting them at Irene with the words:

'Here, take the boy, the greyhound *and* a box of chocolates.' And then, to forestall another dismal repetition of the winner's demand, he shouted, 'Give her a big hand, campers. Hi-de-hi!'

Drowning out the plaintive protest of Irene came the campers' answering roar of: 'HO-DE-HO!'

Ted turned to Jeff.

'That could have been nasty. If I hadn't been here they'd have mobbed you,' he whispered. Then he turned to the audience again. 'And our next fabulous attraction is Joe Maplin's famous window-dressing competition. All right, let's have the window dressers, please.'

Ted looked towards his left and out from the hut where they had been changing minced three campers dressed in artists' smocks and berets.

'That's it, lads,' Ted enthused. 'Now what you have to do is to take the clothes off these models,' and he indicated the three lovely girl yellowcoats who stepped up onto tubs placed on the small stage. The girls were wearing crinolines and bonnets, all carefully made so that they could be removed by releasing a few catches. '– And put them on these models.'

Ted pointed to the other side of the stage where Fred, the man who looks after the horses, miserable old Partridge, the bad-tempered Punch-and-Judy man, and Barry Stuart-Hargreaves, one of the champion ballroom dancers, were standing on similar tubs clad only in long johns and long-sleeved vests. Ted explained: 'The first one to get his model dressed is the winner.'

At this point the camp comedian, Spike Dixon, who has the same name as the family that won the Happy Families and whom you have probably seen about the place dressed as a turnip or a wall or something, pranced out onto the stage, also dressed like a window dresser, and said, with a phoney French accent:

'Excuse, please. I am the one who should dress the models. Let me get my hands on them.'

And Spike reached lecherously towards the three girls. That's his chief laugh line, pretending to be chasing the girls the whole time. In actual fact, as I know well, Spike is a very well-brought-up and reticent lad but he is learning his trade as comedian under Ted and there's no doubt he's got the makings of a top comic.

Ted naturally played up to Spike. With a howl of mock anger, he bellowed:

'Why it's Monsieur Plaster of Paris. The touch-up artist.' And, to Spike: 'You're not going near any of those girls.'

'Oh yes, I am!' insisted Spike, making fake lunges towards them.

'Oh no, you're not!'

'Oh yes, I am.'

Here Ted turned to the audience and held out his hands in supplication.

'You hear what he says? What shall we do with him?'

This was a familiar ritual and the campers all knew the answer to the question. They roared:

'Chuck him in the pool!'

Ted looked doubtful.

'Shall we?'

'Yes!'

'Really?'

'Yes!'

'Go on then, lads!' ordered Ted.

Whereupon the three boy yellowcoats grabbed Spike and, with a one, two, three, swung him far out into the pool. Although they had seen the moist spectacle many times before, the campers howled with merriment. Ted turned to the window dressers.

'All right, you, window dressers,' he instructed them. 'Now's the moment. Go!'

And as Ramona, our versatile organist, started playing fast games music on the organ which had been specially lugged out into the open, the three male campers dressed as artist/window dressers made a dive for the girls.

'Here they come,' whispered blonde Tracey fearfully.

Sylvia closed her eyes to block out the spectacle of the three avid males bearing down on them and returned:

'Just grit your teeth and think of Maplin's!'

And then pandemonium reigned. Within minutes the clothes had been torn from the backs of the girls and draped higgledy-piggledy over the men. The girls were left wearing nothing but tiny bikinis in which, it has to be said, they looked very fetching indeed.

Watching this gripping contest from the wings were Jeff Fairbrother, Gladys, the senior yellowcoat, and Yvonne Stuart-Hargreaves who has the same name as her dancing partner, Barry Stuart-Hargreaves, but some have questioned her legal right to use it. Still, they are very genteel, the Stuart-Hargreaves, and consider themselves several cuts above everyone else on Maplin's territory. Yvonne was saying:

'The truth is, Mr Fairbrother, the girls find this whole procedure most undignified.'

Gladys Pugh sniffed impatiently.

'They're making a lot of fuss over nothing,' she pronounced. 'It's only a bit of fun!'

The entertainments manager sighed deeply.

'I must say I do sympathise with them. I'm sure some of the campers try to take advantage of the situation.'

Yvonne pressed her advantage.

'And, as you may imagine, it's absolute torture for someone of Barry's sensitivity.'

Gladys said sarcastically:

'They don't take advantage of *him*, do they?'

Yvonne glanced at her distantly but continued to address the entertainments manager.

'I think it only fair to say that we've been discussing it and Barry and I intend to complain to Mr Glover, the new director of entertainments at Head Office, when he comes down here tomorrow.'

With which, Yvonne turned daintily on her heel and, with a shudder at the glimpse she obtained of her dancing partner dressed in a crinoline and poke bonnet and looking as if he would, on the whole, prefer martyrdom at the stake, she strode away from the scene of fun and frolic.

The visit of Mr Glover, the new director of entertainments, was, of course, an important even to the whole entertainments staff. A commendation from him could result in a rise or even a promotion. On the other hand, a thumbs down might see the unhappy recipient banished from the Maplin's empire and, although a good deal of grumbling went on all through the season, each and every one of them would have been dismayed by such a contingency. In order to present, so far as possible, a common front to Mr Glover, whom no one yet knew by sight, Jeff Fairbrother called a conference of those most closely concerned with the Window Dressing Competition in his officc the next morning. Present were the three lovely girl yellowcoats, Gladys, Barry and Yvonne, miserable old Partridge, Fred, Spike and Ted. After Jeff had invited views from all present, Barry spoke first.

'Honestly, Mr Fairbrother,' he whined, 'I'm not one to complain but to have some hairy camper dress me in Betty's warm corset and poke bonnet seems more suitable for Hamburg than Maplin's.'

'Not complain?' snorted Ted. 'You do more moaning than a foghorn.'

'I wasn't addressing you,' said Barry primly.

'What about you, Fred?' asked Jeff, turning to the unfrocked jockey.

'I look at it this way, Mr Fairbrother,' announced Fred. 'If they find out I've been dressing up in women's clothes, will it go against me at the Jockey Club when I try to get my licence back?'

Partridge, the bad-tempered Punch-and-Judy man, now had his say.

'I've been here fifteen years, Mr Fairbrother, and the humour's always the same. Toilet rolls, lavatory seats, jerries and men dressing up in women's clothes. I appeal to you as an intellectual and a man of letters – can't you lead a crusade to get us out of the bog?'

Jeff nodded thoughtfully.

'You're all preaching to the converted,' he said. 'I think the competition is degrading and vulgar and I mean to put a stop to it.'

Ted snorted more loudly.

'You'll never change it,' he said moodily. 'It's the British sense of humour. It's seaside postcards. Fat ladies with big charlies and little men.'

'But surely –' began Jeff only he was interrupted by Peggy knocking on the door and immediately entering. In her hand she held a bunch of letters.

'I've brought the mail over,' announced the frustrated chalet maid. 'Sorry I'm late with it. I had to go and see Miss Cathcart, my supervisor. Guess what? I've been given a rise. Two and six a week. Miss Cathcart said she was very pleased with my work and that my basins were the best in the whole camp because I'm the only maid that bothers to polish the bit round the plug-hole. She says it's the little things that count in this world.'

While Peggy had been gushing on like this in her customary way she had been passing out the mail. Everyone was now concentrated on their letters since mail to the staff of Maplin's Camp is a little like it was to plantation managers in Malaya and India in the old days when all they saw was the natives for month after month and they craved for letters from home. Of course, the campers are not exactly like the natives in that they do not squat on their haunches and eat rice with their fingers but they do whoop and yell quite a lot so the comparison is fair. Jeff, amongst others, had received a letter and he was contemplating the envelope earnestly. As he did so, he murmured:

'Jolly good, Peggy. I'm glad about your plug-holes. Well, thank you, everybody. That will be all for now.'

Whereupon the junior members of the entertainments staff all rose and shuffled out, leaving Jeff with Gladys, Ted, Spike and Peggy. Peggy is, of course, very junior but she is not a member of the entertainments staff at all although she longs to be made a yellowcoat but probably never will because her wits are somewhat disordered. She now approached Jeff's desk and, collecting them as much as she could, said earnestly:

'Mr Fairbrother, when Mr Glover comes down today, you will remind him about my application for employment as a yellowcoat, won't you?'

Jeff nodded absently as he began to open his letter.

'Yes, of course, Peggy.'

'Ooh, thanks ever so!'

Smiling happily, Peggy left the company. Ted was the next one to seek Jeff's attention.

'Jeff, er Spike won't ask you himself,' he said with the tremulous sincerity he could get into his voice when he tried, 'but he needs some cash for this new costume of his.'

'Oh yes?' muttered Jeff, who was now reading his letter which, the others noticed, seemed to have a clipping from a newspaper or magazine attached to it. Ted pressed on.

'It's a funny Windsor Castle with a turret for his hat, a drawbridge round the back with a "No Entry" sign on it and a gargoyle on the front that squirts real water. It's a knockout, Jeff, but it needs three quid to complete it.'

Jeff, who had finished reading his letter, looked at Ted with unseeing eyes.

'I'm sorry,' he murmured, 'what were you saying?'

Ted sighed wearily. Gladys said to him sharply:

'There's thirty bob in the petty cash from last week. That's all you can have.'

'Yes, but –' began Ted. Then he fell silent as Jeff rose from his seat looking a trifle dazed.

'I have to make a private phone call,' Jeff said softly.

'Do you want us to go?' asked Ted grumpily.

Jeff shook his head.

'No, I'll use the box in the corridor. I don't want this call to go through the switchboard.'

Under the astonished eyes of all present, and first placing his letter in his desk drawer, Jeff hurried out of his office.

'What's happened?' asked Spike. 'He looks really upset.'

Gladys said sagely:

'It must have been something in that letter.'

Ted pointed firmly at the drawer.

'Well, go on,' he urged. 'Find out what it is.'

'Certainly not,' exclaimed Gladys, outraged. 'Mr Fairbrother's private business is nothing to do with me.'

Ted shook his head impatiently.

'You have a look, Spike,' he incited the camp comedian.

Spike shook his head decisively.

'I'm not reading somebody's personal letter.'

'Lily-livered lot,' muttered Ted and he himself went round to the drawer and obtained the letter.'

'Ted Bovis,' ordered Gladys, stamping her foot, 'put that down!'

'Gladys,' said Ted soothingly, 'if he's in trouble, how can we help him if we don't know what the trouble is? Let's see. It's from his mother. I'll read it out loud. "My dear Jeffrey, I found this in *The Tatler*. She's making a fool of you, but if you neglect her, what do you expect? Come home at once and put your house in order. Love, Mother." '

'What's all that mean?' asked Spike wonderingly.

Ted detached the cutting which was clipped to the letter and examined it. Then he read the caption.

' "Davinia Wentworth's coming out ball. Mrs Jeffrey Fairbrother enjoys a good joke on the stairs with her escort, the Honourable Max Tewkesbury".' Ted waved the clipping at the others and remarked sarcastically, 'Look at 'em, enjoying a good joke – I bet it was a belter.'

'Is that really his wife?' asked Gladys tremulously. 'What does she look like?' Ted held the clipping where she could see it. 'I thought so,' said Gladys with a sniff of disapproval. 'Horsey and stuck up.'

Ted guffawed coarsely.

'That dress isn't stuck up! If she raised her arms we'd all enjoy a good joke on the stairs.'

Gladys took out her dainty handkerchief and sniffed into it a little. She was deeply affected by the development because – and it was an open secret amongst the entertainments staff – she had long nourished a tender feeling for Jeff Fairbrother.

'Poor Jeff,' she said, with a catch in her throat, 'it's not fair. There she is gadding about in society and he's in this place trying to broaden his horizons so he can be less boring. It's just not fair. She doesn't give tuppence about him and I'd do anything for him – anything!'

Ted shook his head and frowned.

'I can't understand why he doesn't get shot of her.'

'If you ask me,' Spike gave his opinion, 'I think he's still in love with her.'

Considering the admission that Gladys had just made this was not the most tactful observation Spike could have produced. But that's Spike, for you, a decent, well-meaning young fellow but about as tactful as brass knuckles. It was too much for Gladys who, first making a valiant effort to maintain her composure, relapsed slowly into gulps and sobs and finally, with a wail of despair, rose and rushed out of the room.

'Spike,' Ted rebuked his student in mirth, 'what did you want to say that for?'

'Well, it's true,' maintained Spike doggedly.

Ted sighed philosophically.

'What's that got to do with it? This world would be a far better place if only people stopped going round telling the truth. We're none of us ready for it. The best thing that could happen to Jeffrey Fairbrother would be to marry Gladys Pugh. She'd be the making of him, but it's no good telling him.'

'He doesn't love her,' observed Spike.

Ted clucked impatiently.

'What difference does that make? In the first place, she'd be the making of him because she's got a bit of guts and go about her. The trouble with these artistocratic families is they're all interbred. There's no stuffing in them. That's why all them dukes became stage-door johnnies and married chorus girls with big thighs. She's a real woman is Gladys. You wouldn't be joking on the stairs with her. You'd be up them.'

'You're probably right, Ted,' Spike conceded. 'But it's not our place to go interfering with other people's lives.'

'There you go again. You come out with them one after the other. Gladys is our friend. I'd like to see her happy. She deserves him – and he deserves her.'

And Ted slapped Spike on the back and winked broadly.

Later that morning Peggy opened the staff room door and peeped in. She had been doing this at regular intervals for some time. The reason was that she was determined not to miss the chance of having a word with the new entertainments director, Mr Glover, who was expected to arrive from London at any time. Peggy trusted Jeff to put in a good word for her but she felt, against all the evidence, that if Mr Glover had a chance to be exposed to her scintillating personality he would be disposed to recommend her promotion to yellowcoat.

However, on this occasion the only person she found in the staff room was Fred Quilly. She was about to withdraw again with a friendly word when she noticed that Fred seemed a little sheepish or guilty in his manner. He was standing near the coffee tray where the coffee things were laid out so that the staff could have refreshments when they wanted them. Peggy opened the door again and entered the staff room.

'Hello, Fred,' she carolled. 'What are you up to?'

'Nothing,' protested Fred, but Peggy noticed that he kept his hands concealed in his coat.

'Come on,' coaxed Peggy. 'What have you got under your coat?'

Fred brought out his hands and opened them. They were full of sugar lumps.

'Just a few lumps of sugar,' he pleaded.

Peggy, a frugal soul, was shocked.

'There's nearly half a pound there!' she exclaimed.

'It's for me horses, Peggy,' Fred explained. 'They don't get much out of life. They get up in the morning – well, they're already up. That's because they sleep standing up. Then they're out trekking all day with great heavy campers on top of them, and all they see is the backside of the horse in front of them. How would you like to spend your life plodding along looking at the backside of a horse?'

Peggy is a very soft-hearted girl who has been known to feel sorry for stuffed gorillas.

'Oh, poor things!' she said feelingly. Then she grabbed the sugar bowl and emptied it into Fred's hands. 'Take the rest for them. I can get some more.'

'Thanks, Peggy,' said Fred gratefully. 'I'll go and give them a nibble straight away.'

He moved towards the door but, as he neared it, it opened and a man entered. He was a tall, mustachioed man who had evidently been outfitted by a very good tailor. There was something haughty and even aristocratic about him. Peggy, who is no judge of character at all, jumped to the conclusion that it was Mr Glover, the new entertainments director. In actual fact, it was the very same Max Tewkesbury whom we last met having a good joke on the staircase with Jeff's wife in the clipping from *The Tatler*.

Max glanced from Fred to Peggy and back, wondering which was the most suitable one to address. He settled for Peggy, although far from confident in his choice.

'I wonder,' he asked politely. 'Can you tell me where I can find Jeffrey Fairbrother?'

He had a beautiful accent, polished in one of our great public schools and probably Oxford as well, but it never occurred to Peggy that this was not the sort of accent you would expect from Mr Glover. She immediately started simpering and being very helpful and trying to make herself noticed so that she would get to be a yellowcoat. She pointed to the door leading to the adjoining office and explained, with a dazzling smile:

'That's his office. He'll be back in a minute. I'm sure it'll be all right if you go in and wait.'

Max nodded civilly and said: 'Oh, thanks.'

He then opened the door to Jeff's office and entered it. As he turned to close the door after him, he found that Peggy had followed him and was standing in the doorway looking as if she might be about to curtsy.

'I'm Peggy Ollerenshaw,' she gabbled quickly. 'I'm working as a chalet maid. I get on well with campers. I tell jokes and do impressions. Who do you think this is?'

Whereupon, to the faint alarm of Max Tewkesbury, she pouted her lips and smiled seductively while curving her body and placing her hands on her hips. Stepping back a pace, Max guessed.

'A goldfish?'

Peggy smiled waggishly and shook her head.

'No. It's Marilyn Monroe. Mind you, it's better without my glasses.'

Max nodded sagely.

'I'm sure it is.

Peggy glanced about and lowered her voice confidentially.

'I'm telling you so that if Mr Fairbrother mentions my name, you'll know what I look like. I'd give anything to be a yellowcoat.'

Max concluded that Peggy was round the twist. Not knowing anything about Maplin's, or its staff, he reacted just as if she'd said: 'I'd like to be a pink skirt' or a black suspender belt or any other item of clothing. After he'd been in the camp a while and seen some of the yellowcoats he realised what she'd been talking about but, for the moment, he took a step backwards so that, if necessary, he could keep the desk between him and Peggy.

'I see,' he said judiciously.

Peggy beamed him another big smile and then retreated back into the staff room where Fred, mystified by these proceedings, was still standing with his hands full of sugar.

'What was all that about?' he asked.

Peggy moved up close to him and confided:

'That's Mr Glover, the new entertainments director.'

At which point, Jeff walked moodily into the staff room. Peggy immediately cautioned him.

'Oh, Mr Fairbrother, Mr Glover's in your office. Don't forget to mention about me being a yellowcoat.'

Jeff nodded abstractedly.

'Yes, of course. Thank you, Peggy.'

Jeff went on into his office and Fred took off to sweeten the lives of his horses. Peggy glanced about, shut the outer door to the staff room and then went and listened at the keyhole of Jeff's office.

When he entered, Jeff thought there was something familiar about Max Tewkesbury but he had only seen a smudged likeness of him in *The Tatler* clipping and simply concluded that he was confusing him with someone he'd known somewhere. He said:

'Hallo, Mr Glover, nice to see you. I'm Jeffrey Fairbrother.'

Max shook his head, smiling somewhat grimly.

'My name's not Glover.'

'Oh?' said Jeff, puzzled. 'I was told that you were Glover, the entertainments director.'

Max again shook his head.

'My name's Max Tewkesbury.'

This immediately clicked with Jeff. His long, sad face with the slightly twisted mouth set in a defiant expression.

'Is it indeed,' he said harshly.

'You know about me?' Max asked dubiously.

'Yes, you tell jokes on staircases.'

Max nodded.

'You've seen *The Tatler* photograph.'

'Oh yes,' jeered Jeff. 'We all read *The Tatler* at Maplin's. It passes the time while we're waiting for the Ugly Face

Competition to start. Incidentally I feel you might do very well in that.'

Max ignored the gibe.

'I've been seeing rather a lot of your wife,' he admitted, having decided that manly candour was the best approach to take.

'How very delicately put,' said Jeff.

'And I would like to marry her.'

Jeff stared at this cool customer with intense dislike.

'A pity,' he sympathised. 'She's already married to me.'

Max sighed and lightly brushed his neat moustache.

'You're not making this very easy,' he pointed out. 'Now, we're both civilised people. I was hoping we could settle this in a civilised way.'

'I see,' Jeff nodded, making an effort to restrain an impulse towards violence. 'Are you going to offer me large sums of money if I divorce her?'

'It's not quite as simple as that,' Max confided. 'I want you to give her grounds so that she can divorce you.'

Jeff frowned in incomprehension.

'Don't tell me that Daphne is suddenly concerned to protect her good name?'

For the first time, Max looked distinctly embarrassed.

'Well no, not exactly. I am the fly in the ointment. I move in rather straight circles.'

Jeff smiled wolfishly.

'And would you describe yourself as a mathematician or a contortionist?'

Max waved a fastidious hand in dismissal.

'It would help this discussion if you would stop talking like some second-rate Oscar Wilde. You know as well as I do that there is a certain social stigma in being the guilty party in a divorce. There's the Royal Enclosure at Ascot. I'd have to resign from my club and I'm the sole heir to an extremely wealthy aunt who's still so incensed about Mrs Simpson that she won't touch Brown Windsor soup. Now what are we going to do?'

Jeff closed his eyes for a moment. Jeff is, of course, a

gentleman and a scholar. He found the situation trying. But he did his best.

'I find you and your values totally repugnant,' he said firmly. 'I happen to believe in marriage and I regard our present separation as a temporary setback. It can very likely be attributed to my own shortcomings but it is undoubtedly none of your damn business. Now as Oscar Wilde would so wittily put it: if you're not out of here in one minute, I shall punch your ugly face in.'

Now Max Tewkesbury was in no way intimidated by this threat. He was a polo player and had won a blue for boxing at Oxford. He could take care of himself. But a punch-up, he knew, was not going to help him achieve his object. Quite the contrary. It might have the effect of making Jeff dig his heels in and Max still thought that, unless he achieved Jeff's co-operation, he would never succeed in his design. He was about to discover that there might be another way.

He nodded politely at his rival and said:

'Very well. I hope you'll think the situation over. None of us gains anything from this intransigence.'

He then turned and left the entertainments manager's office. Jeff gazed after him angrily and then, when he sank into his chair, found that he was trembling slightly from the stress.

Max made his way to one of the public telephones dotted about Maplin's and dialled the operator. He asked her to connect him, long distance, to a London number and some time later, after the usual clanks and groans and crossed lines, he found himself talking to his solicitor.

'Hello, Clive?' he said hopefully. 'It's Max here. I'm at that Holiday Camp place.'

'Oh good,' came his solicitor's juicy voice. 'How did you get on with Daphne's husband?'

'He won't co-operate. He refuses point blank.'

'Oh dear, that is bad news.'

'It's absolute deadlock. What do we do next?'

'Well, you're a man of the world. He must have been up to something while he's been staying up there. Ferret around. See if he's had a relationship with anyone. Mind you when it comes to the crunch, tittle-tattle's no good. We must have hard facts.'

Max didn't fancy snooping about like some down-at-heel private eye but he did want that divorce.

'How do I get hard facts?' he asked distastefully.

Clive was unabashed.

'Chambermaids usually give us the best evidence. What you need is a signed statement from somebody who's seen him in a situation where – well, where intimacy can be inferred.'

Max thought for a moment.

'There's a potty chalet maid here. I suppose she might come up with something. I could make it worth her while.'

A sanctimonious note immediately came into Clive's voice.

'As a solicitor, I could never be party to that sort of thing, Max. But off the record I can tell you that what you'd need is –'

And Clive outlined for Max the sort of evidence that would stand up in court.

At that very moment the 'potty chalet maid' was in the camp coffee bar, confiding secretly, to anyone who would listen, what she had heard through the keyhole to Jeff's office. Her audience, quite prepared to listen, consisted of the three gorgeous yellowcoats, Fred and miserable old Partridge. Yvonne and Barry Stuart-Hargreaves were watching this scene. They had already been the recipient of Peggy's eager confidences. Yvonne shuddered fastidiously and said to her consort:

'There goes Peggy telling her sordid little story for the umpteenth time.'

'That's the awful thing about this place,' drawled Barry. 'Nothing is private.'

Yvonne agreed.

'The chalet walls are like paper. You can hear absolutely everything.'

'Look at that night we had the ouija board out,' Barry reminded her, 'and we'd just got through to your Aunt

Alice on the other side who said she had a message for you. You said in quite a low voice "give it to me; give it to me" and a moment later Ted was knocking on the wall offering to do so.'

Yvonne, who thought the reminiscence in dubious taste, gave her partner a cold look. Meanwhile Peggy was in full flight and the tale was already acquiring embellishments.

'Then Jeffrey Fairbrother,' she said dramatically, 'drew himself up to his full height, and with a disdainful look on his clean-cut features, set his lantern jaw and said "How dare you besmirch the good name of my lady wife". Then he slapped that Max across the face with a glove and challenged him to a duel.'

'Go on,' said Betty sceptically. 'You're making it up, Peggy.'

'It's true,' insisted the potty one. 'I heard every word. I had my ear glued to the keyhole.'

Sylvia perceived a flaw in her account.

'In that case,' she asked, 'how did you see him draw himself up to his full height and set his lantern jaw?'

Peggy looked nonplussed for a moment but then found the answer.

'Well, I changed from ear to eye and eye to ear.'

Tracey, the poshest of the yellowcoats, actually subscribed to *The Tatler*. As soon as she had learned of the situation, she had gone to her chalet and fetched the relevant issue. She now laid it on the table with the famous staircase picture in view. She contemplated it and said:

'Jeff's wife's not a bad-looking woman. I wonder why she left him?'

Fred leaned over and inspected the picture.

'Nice stair carpet,' was his only comment.

Partridge cleared his throat, a process that took a little while because of all the boozing and smoking he did, and then regaled them with his views.

'When I was top of the bill,' he explained, 'we used to go to places like that doing cabaret. While the photographers were around you'd think butter wouldn't melt in their mouths. Then they'd have a few bottles of champagne and they're at it like mice in the gunroom. Believe me, promiscuity is the privilege of the upper classes.'

Fred snorted like one of his more turbulent horses and said:

'Common people do it as well. Otherwise you wouldn't be here.'

'That's him!' hissed Peggy urgently.

Her audience all understood what she meant. Max had entered the coffee bar. As discreetly as they could, they all had a butcher's at Jeff's rival.

'Not bad,' murmured Betty appreciatively.

'If I was Jeff's wife,' contributed Sylvia, 'I'd grab that quick.'

Tracey was more reserved.

'He looks a bit supercilious. I don't suppose he's got Jeff's brains.'

Sylvia giggled.

'Yes, but what happens when the talking stops?'

Partridge hoisted himself to his feet with a grunt.

'Your generations's all the same,' he sneered. 'Sex is no more important to you than a game of ping-pong.'

Fred laughed softly and commented:

'You're just jealous because you're too old to grip the bat.'

'Shut your face,' snarled Partridge. 'And come along with me. You're going to do your share of tidying the chalet for once.'

Fred muttered under his breath but rose obediently and accompanied grumpy Partridge out of the coffee bar.

'If you really want my view,' began Tracey, but just then three amplified notes on a xylophone indicated that one of Radio Maplin's announcements was about to be transmitted. They all fell silent and listened. Gladys' charming Welsh lilt filled the room.

'Hello, campers! The single girls' versus bachelors' water polo is due to start in a few minutes' time. Will the teams please assemble by the diving board of the Olympic-sized swimming pool.'

Betty sighed and rose to her feet.

'Come on, Sylvia, and this time I'm going to captain the bachelors.'

'You're welcome,' returned Sylvia. 'They're all pimples this week.'

She and Tracey also rose, the latter cautioning:

'Watch out for that ginger-haired one who bites his nails. Good-bye, Peggy.'

'Ta ra!' called Peggy cheerfully. 'And hi-de-hi!'

Then she started as a soft, insinuating voice spoke in her left ear.

'Thank you for looking after me this morning.'

Peggy looked to her left and saw the distinguished figure of Max Tewkesbury beside her.

'Oh, that's all right,' she returned nervously.

Max seated himself at her table.

'Do you mind if I join you?'

'Feel free,' offered Peggy.

'Can I get you anything?'

Peggy's first impulse was to refuse. After all, by now she had Max placed as a sinister moustache-twirling villain, but then she reflected that accepting a little refreshment from him wouldn't make him any more villainous.

'Thank you,' she said and then called to the girl behind the bar. 'Edna, my special, please.' Then she leaned towards Max and explained: 'It's a knickerbocker glory with a side serving of pistachio nuts with a double fudge sauce. You ought to try it.'

'Perhaps later,' said Max smoothly. 'Tell me, is that the chalet maid's uniform you're wearing?'

Peggy made a rueful face.

'Awful, isn't it? But you should see me in the ballroom when I'm off duty. It's a magic transformation.'

'I'm sure it is,' purred Max. 'You're a very attractive girl.'

In spite of her better judgement, Peggy felt her heart go out a little to this dashing man. Compliments were a thing she had no power to resist.

'And clearly very intelligent,' Max gilded the lily. 'I

suppose that as a chalet maid you get to know what's going on in this camp?'

'Oh yes,' agreed Peggy. 'I could tell you things that would make your hair stand on end.'

'Good heavens,' said Max, shaking his head in apparent disbelief. 'And are you responsible for the staff chalet lines as well?'

'Yes. They're the worst of the lot.'

'You astonish me. In that case it's just possible you might be able to help me. If I could get certain information about Mr Fairbrother I would be prepared to pay very well for it.'

'Oh? What information?' asked Peggy, wide-eyed.

'Well, if you could –' began Max, but at that moment, Edna, the bar-girl, deposited in front of Peggy a large mass of gooey material which made Max feel a little unwell just contemplating it. Nevertheless, when Edna had departed he once more leaned towards Peggy.

'The thing is –' he began with a friendly smile as Peggy plunged her spoon into her knickerbocker glory.

At just about this moment, Gladys was looking through some files in Jeff Fairbrother's office. There was a tap at the door and Gladys said 'come in' whereupon a large lemon walked in and said:

'Hello, Gladys, I wanted to have a word with you.'

'Did you, Spike?' asked Gladys without warmth.

'Yes, I did.'

Two hands sticking out of the sides of the lemon then pushed at the top part which rose like a hat and revealed Spike's face sticking up from the body of the lemon. He continued:

'Glad, I'm sorry if I said anything to upset you. I mean, I'm sure Jeff's not still in love with his wife.'

Gladys could tell that Spike was only trying to be nice and didn't really believe what he was saying. It made her cross in spite of herself. She snapped:

'I don't care who he's in love with.'

Spike tried to shake his head but the lemon made it difficult.

'No,' he continued, 'it's got nothing to do with us really, has it?'

'Nothing at all,' hissed Gladys.

'I mean,' continued Spike, and because he was feeling confused about the situation his words of comfort also emerged a little confused, 'we all have our own lives to live, and we can't judge each other, because we don't know what goes on inside each other. But things do go on and then if people make vows and promises to each other I think they ought to keep them and not give way to every passing whim. I may be old-fashioned but that's the way I see things because that's the way I was brought up. You were probably brought up differently and, then again, Jeff perhaps was brought up even more differently. If you see what I mean.'

'Oh, shut up,' said Gladys ungraciously. 'If you want to know, I'm madly in love with him. I think about him day and night. I can't sleep because my whole body yearns for him. It's like some awful ache. It won't go away and I'd do anything to get him – anything.'

'Oh, I see,' said Spike, feeling he hadn't struck the right note. 'Well, I'd better be running along then.'

And he pulled the top part of the lemon back down over his face, turned round and fell over a chair.

Just about then, in the chalet that Ted and Spike shared, Ted was practising one of his more lucrative fiddles. He spun a raffle drum mounted on Spike's bed, stuck his hand into the hole and pulled out a raffle ticket. Without looking at it, he said aloud:

'And the winning ticket is –' whereupon he glanced at the ticket, 'number 24.'

Ted then put the 'winning ticket' back in the drum, spun it again, drew out a ticket and repeated:

'And the winning ticket is –' he glanced at it, grinned and said again, 'number 24.'

He tried it a third time.

'And the winning ticket is –' he glanced at it, shrugged and muttered, 'number 79. Oh well, two out of three. Not so bad.'

The door of the chalet opened and a giant lemon entered. Ted addressed it.

'Hello, Spike. How did your funny lemon go down?'

'Knockout,' said the camp comic, starting to change from being a citrus fruit. 'I don't think I'll bother about the funny Windsor Castle.'

Ted shook his head reproachfully.

'Spike, you can't stand still,' he rebuked his pupil. 'You mustn't get complacent. Look what happened to Terry Noble.'

'Who,' asked Spike as he stashed his lemon outfit in a corner of the chalet, 'is Terry Noble?'

'Precisely,' grinned Ted.

There was a knock at the chalet door and Ted grunted, 'Come in.' The door opened and the potty chalet maid tottered in looking distraught.

'Ted, Spike,' she addressed them, 'can you spare a moment? I need some advice. I'm stuck on the horns of a dilemma.'

'What's your problem?' asked Ted solicitously.

'Well,' said Peggy, seating herself on Spike's bed. 'You know this man Max Tewkesbury that's in love with Mr Fairbrother's wife? He asked me to sign this paper saying that I've seen Mr Fairbrother in a compromising position with Gladys Pugh and if I sign it, he's going to give me two hundred pounds.'

'And you want to know if you should hold out for three hundred?'

'Ted!' said Spike, deeply shocked.

Peggy shook his head.

'It's not that, Ted. It's that I haven't seen Jeff in any sort of position with Gladys.'

'All right,' said Ted, 'let's have a look at the paper.'

He could see it, clutched tightly in Peggy's left hand. He held out his own hand for it and Peggy relinquished it, saying wistfully:

'I could do with the two hundred pounds. It's more than I earn in a whole season, but that paper's a pack of lies.'

'Are you sure about that?' asked Ted sagely. 'Let's go

through it slowly. It begins: "the twelfth of July, 1959." Is that right?'

Peggy looked exasperated.

'Of course it is. It's just the date.'

'It goes on: "I, Peggy Ollerenshaw." Is that right?'

'Of course.'

Ted waved the paper triumphantly.

'Well, there you are. I've read all that and there's not a single lie so far. I'll continue. "I, Peggy Ollerenshaw, on the night of the eighth of June at 12.45 a.m." Well, 12.45 a.m. has to be at night so that's true. "At 12.45 a.m. had occasion to pass chalet E7, and noticed that the door was ajar. I observed Mr Jeffrey Fairbrother in his pyjamas and Miss Gladys Pugh in her nightdress, in bed." '

'There you are, Ted,' burst out Peggy. 'That's not true.'

'Not true? What are you talking about? Peggy, you must go to the chalets at all hours and so you must have seen Jeffrey in bed in his pyjamas.'

'Well, yes.'

'And you must have seen Gladys in bed in her nightie.'

'Yes, I have – but not in the same bed!'

Ted looked at her in feigned surprise.

'Peggy, it doesn't say the same bed. Look, it just says "in bed".'

Peggy glanced over his shoulder at the paper. It was her turn to look surprised.

'You're right,' she admitted.

Ted continued with his reading.

' "Shortly afterwards, the door closed and the light was extinguished." Well, you must have seen a door closed before?'

'Oh yes, hundreds of times.'

'And lights go out?'

'Of course, I have.'

Ted rested his case.

'Well, there you are. Sign it. You'll get your two hundred quid and I'll only charge you fifty pounds for legal advice. Here's a pen.'

But even as Peggy reached for the ball-point that Ted held out to her, a hollow voice spoke from the other bed.

'That's not right, Ted.'

Ted looked around as if mystified.

'Wait a minute, I heard a voice. Where did it come from? Oh, it's Dan, Dan the conscience man.'

Spike got off his bed and joined the other two. He looked earnest.

'You can make fun as much as you like,' he urged, 'but it's still not right.'

Ted contemplated his awkward chalet mate for a moment. Then he broke into speech.

'What do you mean "not right"? Is it right for Jeff's wife to go playing around, cuckolding him all over the place and making him look a fool? Is it right that this geezer's got plenty of money but can't take her off Jeff's hands unless he gets evidence? Is it right that Gladys would make Jeff a wonderful wife, but he won't look at her because he's being an honourable public school twit so she's going round crying all day? Only one thing's right: it's right for our Peggy to sign that paper.'

Spike shook his head sombrely.

'You're just thinking of your fifty quid.'

Ted arranged his face into an expression of wounded innocence.

'You can be very hurtful, you know, Spike. Did I or did I not say yesterday, in these very socks, that the best thing in the world for Jeffrey Fairbrother would be to marry Gladys Pugh?'

Spike pounced.

'In that case don't charge for the advice.'

But he was no match for Ted. Looking even more offended by an unjust world, Ted asked:

'Should a man be branded because he wants a fair wage for a fair day's work?'

Spike was outraged.

'Fair day's work?' he exploded. 'She's only been here two minutes.'

'You cannot put a price on expertise, Spike. I defy you to find fault with my analysis of the situation.'

'Perhaps I can't,' admitted Spike. 'It's true that Jeff would be better off without that wife of his. It's true that Gladys is a wonderful girl and would devote her life to him. But if Peggy signs that paper, she'll be telling lies. Telling lies is wrong!'

It was clear that both sides had now summed up and the two barristers, Spike and Ted, looked earnestly at the defendant, or witness, or client or whatever, Peggy, the potty chalet maid, who sat with the pen in her hand looking from one to the other with an agonised expression. For a long time, or so it seemed, she remained locked into her dilemma. Then she made her decision. She uttered the nearest thing to a strong oath that good-hearted Peggy ever gave voice to.

'Oh, bum!' she exclaimed fiercely.

And with a quick gesture she tore the paper in half.

When Peggy told him of her decision, and handed him back his torn and unsigned statement, Max Tewkesbury may well have been seething with inner rage and vowing a terrible vengeance on those who had thwarted him but outwardly his manner remained calm and courteous.

'Very well,' he said to Peggy. 'Naturally, I wouldn't have wanted you to make a false declaration. Where can I get a taxi?'

Peggy directed him to the office at the main gate and a little later, peeping from a vantage point just inside the main building, and concealed by the two potted plants outside the Maplin's Ladies Coiffeur and Manicure Booth, she had the satisfaction of seeing a worsted Max chug away from Maplin's. But had she done right? Peggy didn't know. The money apart, she could perhaps have smoothed the path for Jeff and Gladys to achieve romance. But that would have meant telling lies. Ted said that telling lies was good. Spike said it was bad and somehow, whatever the outcome might have been, Peggy knew that Spike was right. She sighed and went to get her bucket and mop for it was time to clean the latrines.

Late that afternoon, Ted was sorting through the funny costumes in the cupboard in the staff room. Spike had been letting the side down recently. His funny lemon was fine but most of his outfits were showing signs of age and wear. As Ted pulled out the funny policeman costume and contemplated it ruefully, Spike himself entered the staff room.

'What are you about?' he asked.

'You'll have to smarten up, Spike,' returned Ted. 'Look at this funny policeman costume. It's had twenty-five custard pies on it and it won't take no more. It will have to go to the cleaners. First rule of comedy, Spike, you must look dapper. No mucky props.'

'I agree but it'll have to keep. Gladys has just blown a fuse. We were about to start the Ugly Face Competition when she burst into tears and ran off. You'd better go and talk to her, Ted.'

'Bit late now. You had a chance to do something about it earlier. But your high and mighty attitude stopped Peggy doing the right thing.'

'Please, Ted.'

'What can I say to her? She's fallen in love with an iceberg.' Ted nodded towards the closed door to Jeff's office. 'It's him in there that should be doing the talking.'

'Yes but if he –'

Spike bit off his speech for at that moment the door to Jeff's office opened and a spruce man wearing stockbroker's pin-stripes came out.

'Hullo, Mr Glover,' Ted addressed him. 'We haven't met. I'm Ted Bovis, the camp host. I expect Joe Maplin's told you all about me.'

Glover shook his head.

'No, he hasn't actually. But I've only been with the organisation for a week.'

Ted indicated Spike.

'This is our new camp comic, Spike Dixon.'

Glover shot out an accusing finger and pointed to the Funny Policeman outfit that Ted had laid over the back of a chair.

'Are you going to wear that uniform?' he asked Spike.

Spike nodded.

'Yes, it's my funny policeman.'

Glover peered more closely at the offending garments.

'Well, for heaven's sake get it cleaned,' he instructed. 'I can't stand dirty costumes.'

'That's what I keep telling him, Mr Glover,' Ted agreed earnestly. 'I'll see that he does it.'

Ted smiled in a winning way at Glover and Spike felt a little nauseated watching him. Glover nodded curtly and moved on out of the office. Ted turned to Spike and said sadly:

'You just won't be told, will you, Spike?'

'I'll get it cleaned. Anyway, what are you going to do about Gladys?'

'Have a chat with someone.'

Ted ambled towards the door of Jeff's office, knocked perfunctorily and marched in. He was surprised to see Jeff wearing the tweed suit he normally reserved for his days off. But the entertainments manager was engaged on checking a list of events for the next session. He glanced up when Ted entered and asked:

'Did you see Glover?'

'Oh yes,' said Ted earnestly. 'He knows all about me. Joe Maplin has apparently been singing my praises.'

'Well, he seems a reasonable sort of chap,' said Jeff thoughtfully. I think we'll get on well together. What can I do for you, Ted?'

'You've upset Gladys,' said Ted bluntly.

Jeff laid down his pencil and leaned back in his chair.

'What on earth makes you say that?' he asked quietly.

Ted approached the desk and sat on a corner of it.

'Don't you realise she's head over heels in love with you?'

Jeff sighed. He rose and went over to his little window. He looked out on the unending stream of campers having fun all over the place. Everyone out there was happy, or so it seemed. But were they really? The staff probably all seemed happy to the campers and Jeff knew what a mess some of them made of their lives. He turned back to confront Ted.

'I can hardly be responsible for that, Ted,' he urged. 'I've given her no encouragement.'

Ted stood up from the corner of the desk and sat down in the swivel-chair opposite Jeff's. He asked:

'What have you got running through those veins, cold tea?'

Jeff sat down on his own swivel-chair once more. He spoke tightly. He didn't really consider the subject to be any of Ted's business but informality seemed to be the rule here at Maplin's.

'I can assure you, Ted,' he said evenly, 'if the conditions are right, my blood can be very hot indeed. And I'm well aware that physically Gladys is a very attractive woman.'

'Then what are you waiting for?' cried Ted, exasperated.

Jeff continued in the same cool, even tone.

'Mentally we have nothing in common whatsoever.'

Ted shook his head helplessly. He simply could not understand Jeff's attitude.

'Couldn't you force yourself? You know, pretend?'

'And where would that lead, Ted?'

'It would lead to Gladys going round with a contented smile instead of bursting into tears every five minutes. Go and talk to her – say something warm and nice.'

'It's my day off, Ted, although I've been working till now. I was planning to go for a walk along the sea-front.'

'Well, take Gladys with you. It's as simple as this, Jeff, if you're both going to go on working together, you'll have to do something.' Ted rose from the chair and headed for the door. When he reached it he turned to deliver his parting shot. 'You don't know how lucky you are. I'd give up my bingo fiddle to have a girl like that in love with me.'

After Ted had departed, Jeff sat for a long time in thought. Finally, he sighed and rose. He left his office, walked through the staff room and made his way to the staff chalet lines. He knocked on the door of Gladys' chalet. There was no answer. He knocked again. From within came the request, delivered in a charming Welsh lilt.

'Go away.'

'Gladys,' called Jeff winningly. 'It's me.'

There was an even longer pause. And then Gladys called: 'What do you want?'

Jeff glanced up and down the lines. He didn't want to attract a lot of attention.

'May I come in? I don't like shouting.'

The next moment, Gladys was opening the door. Jeff noted that there were unmistakable signs of tears, hastily brushed away, on her face. She was an attractive girl. No doubt about that and yet Jeff found her as strange as a country he had never visited. He smiled and said:

'I'm going for a walk along the beach. I thought perhaps you might like to join me?'

'I don't mind,' said Gladys quickly. Then she added. 'Are you sure?'

'Quite sure. We could get some bread from the kitchen and feed the gulls.'

Quarter of an hour later, they were in a quiet cove out of sight of the camp. It was a grey day but dry. The shingle stretched down to a calm grey sea and up above gulls were wheeling and mewing. As they walked, Jeff had done his utmost to start a conversation but for the life of him he couldn't think of a thing to say. They had virtually nothing in common. Nor had Gladys helped. She had just walked quietly by his side and Jeff had sensed uneasily that she was perfectly content just to be with him.

He opened the bag of stale bread the kitchens had provided and began throwing pieces to the gulls. Within moments, the air was full of the greedy but beautiful birds.

'Would you like to throw some?' he asked Gladys.

'I don't mind,' she returned without any noticeable enthusiasm.

He held out the bag to her and she dutifully took a few pieces and aimed them at the circling gulls.

'Incidentally,' said Jeff. 'I spoke to Glover. He's agreed about the window-dressing competition.'

'Oh good,' said Gladys. 'Are you going home to put your house in order like your mother said?'

Jeff felt a little shiver go through him. He both wanted and didn't want to confide in her. Part of him said: it's none of her business. She has no place in my life. But another part said: she's a kind, considerate girl who has the misfortune to be in love with me. She has a right to know. He sighed and said:

'No, I'm not.'

He could almost feel the girl go rigid.

'Don't you want your wife back then?' she asked.

'I honestly don't know.'

'You don't know much, do you?' she asked scornfully. Now she sounded like the old Gladys again and Jeff was both sorry and glad that she could look after herself so efficiently. She went on. 'All you know about is dead things. Fossils, mummies.'

Jeff nodded sadly.

'Yes, you're probably right. Oh dear, I've run out of bread.'

'So have I.'

Jeff gazed at the birds which were still darting about hopefully above their heads.

'Funny how they hang around,' he observed, 'hoping to get something.'

'That's life, isn't it?' returned Gladys and the bitterness in her voice was not wasted on Jeff.

He turned to her and looked into her eyes. She looked back at him and he saw what big, dark, lovely eyes she had. It would be the easiest thing in the world to reach forwards, to slip his hands onto her waist, to pull her towards him –

He said:

'Let's go and chuck some stones in the water.'

He turned and ambled down towards the water's edge. He picked up a few flat stones and skimmed them along the sea's calm surface. Out of the corner of his eye he noted that Gladys hadn't moved. He skimmed another stone and, over his shoulder, he called:

'Aren't you coming?'

Her reply was so faint that he barely heard it but he saw her start down the beach towards him.

'You only have to raise a little finger don't you?' was what she said.

There was a long silence after the senior camper had finished his melancholy tale. It was broken by his companion saying urgently:

'Well, get on with it!'

'Get on with what, my daughter?' asked the senior camper, puzzled.

'The story. What 'appened? Did they get together? Is they going to be married?'

'Is they indeed?' echoed Charley Binns rhetorically. 'Who can say? Much as I appreciate your natural craving for a happy ending all I can tell you is that the situation is unchanged.'

'Unchanged? You mean 'e's still married to that 'ard, unfeeling woman what jokes on staircases with smooth villains and that lovely yellowcoat is still eating 'er 'eart out for 'im?'

'He still is. She still is. Nothing has changed.'

'And they 'aven't – I mean they don't –'

The senior camper held up his hand to ward off this line of inquiry.

'Jeffrey Fairbrother remains the soul of honour.'

'Shyme.'

'Two lonely people. But you'd never guess it, would you?'

'Never in this world. They always seem so – so blooming 'appy!'

'They try. Don't you think, my daughter, you should try?'

'Oh, I do!'

The lady with the square, but pleasant, face suddenly turned quickly in her chair and contemplated for a moment her donkey-faced husband who was doing nothing at all. Then she turned back eagerly to Charley Binns.

'You've made me so ashamed! Look at 'im, sitting there, so alone.'

'Tragic.'

'And we 'ave so much, compared to them. I thought they 'ad everything. I was filled with bitter envy and really 'Arry and I could 'ave so much more. We've got each other. Why can't we be 'appy?'

'Why not, my daughter?'

'Will you come with me? Just to break the ice? I want to try.'

'My privilege,' said Charley Binns cordially.

The lady rose and the senior camper did the same. They then moved towards the table where the lady's husband was keeping his solitary vigil. When they got there, the lady said.

' 'Arry, I want you to meet Mr Charley Binns, the senior camper.'

'What for?' returned the donkey-faced man without apparent enthusiasm.

' 'e can 'elp us. 'e already 'as. Sit down, Mr Binns.' The senior camper, discreetly sizing up Harry in case the latter showed any impulse towards aggression, sat down at the table. The woman said to her husband, ' 'Arry, can I get you something? A nice cup of tea or some other drink? Something to eat, perhaps?'

Harry's jaw dropped and for an instant Charley Binns was convinced he was going to bray. But he gazed at his wife in stupefied silence. Finally he found tongue.

'Do what?' he asked incredulously.

'I want to be nice to you.'

'Since when?'

'Since hearing Mr Binns' story. Oh, 'e does tell a lovely tale, 'Arry. 'Arry, do you think we could turn over a new leaf?'

Harry looked from his wife to Charley Binns and back again. He was clearly baffled by this turn of events.

'Do what?' he asked finally.

'Turn over a new leaf. Be kind and considerate to each

other. Talk about things – you know, have conversations. Not just row all the time.'

The novelty was clearly too much for Harry. He simply gazed in perplexity at his wife. She went on eloquently.

'Oh, 'Arry, it's worth trying. We 'ave so much – compared to some. Mr Binns has told me. All these 'appy people. Underneath they 'as terrible problems. We 'aven't. It's just us. We make ourselves miserable. But we don't 'ave to. What abaht it, 'Arry? Shall we 'ave a go?'

Harry swallowed and said simply:

' 'ow?'

' 'ow?' repeated his good woman. 'Well simply by – just by – well all we 'ave to do is –'

And she fell silent. She glanced at the senior camper imploringly and Charley Binns, as always, rose to the occasion.

'I think, Mr – er – Mr –'

The woman leaned towards her spouse.

'Our name, 'Arry. Tell him our name.'

'Oh – yuh. It's Bilkins, 'Arry and Wanda Bilkins.'

'Well, Mr Bilkins,' resumed the senior camper smoothly. 'It's simply a matter of seeing the other person's point of view, in a word, of sharing. Share things and you'll enjoy them twice as much. Life is not made for strife.'

'Oh, ain't that true, 'Arry,' enthused Mrs Bilkins. 'Life ain't made for strife. Oh, 'Arry, shall we try?'

The other shrugged.

'All right. You'll 'ave to start, mind.'

'Oh, I will. I will right now. 'Arry, 'asn't it been a beautiful day?'

'Bloody nip in the –'

' 'Arry!' cautioned Mrs Bilkins.

'Oh, yuh. Yuh, it's been a beautiful day. Very beautiful. Best day I seen.' Harry blinked a few times as if at some new but not disagreeable experience. A moment later and Charley Binns was quietly gratified to find Harry trying to make the running himself. 'Uh, Wanda, I like your dress,' he offered shyly.

'Do you, 'Arry? I'm so glad. And I've been meaning to

tell you. You don't 'alf look smart in your new suit. Smartest camper about, in my opinion.'

'You fink so? That's good, Wanda. That's very good. And now can I offer to fetch you somethink to eat?'

'In a minute, 'Arry. What shall we do this evening? Do you want to go to the camp concert or would you rather go to the bar?'

'Bleedin' concert!' snorted Harry, having a momentary relapse, but he quickly saw the error of his ways and amended. 'I mean, if you is keen on the concert, Wanda, that's what we'll do. For myself, I am always partial to a pint of ale in the bar.'

'I know, 'Arry, we'll go to the bar first and you can 'ave a pint of ale and I'll 'ave a Bloody Mary which I'm particularly fond of and then praps we'll go on to the concert. 'ow does that strike you?'

'That's a very good programme, Wanda. I'm very grateful to you for suggesting it. I been meaning to tell you – uh – my dear, that you is a good wife to me.'

'Oh 'Arry, you can be the best of 'usbands when you tries. And from now on –'

At about this point, Charley Binns rose quietly to his feet and, without even being noticed by the affectionate pair, so intent were they on themselves, stole out of the Laughing Cow Milk Bar.

All the rest of the day and into the evening, Charley Binns felt conscious of a warm feeling of satisfaction. Sometimes, as he toiled over his pools coupons or wrote brief business notes to associates in various parts of the land, and especially those parts which were the site of Her Majesty's Penal Establishments, he would cease in his labours to wonder at his underlying glow of contentment. And then he would remember how he had brought happiness to the Bilkins and a fraternal smile would crease his rugged but attractive features.

Because he was rather behind with his correspondence, it was later than usual, that night, when he arrived in his favourite bar. It was modestly crowded but he had not penetrated far into room when he saw, together at a small, circular table, under a plastic palm tree, Harry and Wanda Bilkins. Deviating in his course to the bar he made eagerly towards them. As he got nearer he saw that their glasses were nearly empty and, on a generous impulse, he headed back to the bar and bought two pints of ale, one for himself and one for Harry, and a Bloody Mary for Wanda. Then he returned to their table. As he neared it, the couple seated at the table on the opposite side of the plastic palm from the Bilkins' rose to depart and Charley Binns, overcome by an impulse to eavesdrop a little on his good work, slipped into one of the chairs they had vacated and placed the drinks on the table in front of him. In a moment, he would surprise the Bilkins with them but, for the present, he just wanted to bask in their new-found happiness. As he sat down, he heard Harry say:

'That was a very nice supper, we 'ad, Wanda.'

'Wasn't it just, 'Arry?' returned Wanda enthusiastically. 'And I did so enjoy talking to you abaht – oh, what a muddle-'ead I am, 'Arry. I've forgotten what we talked about at supper.'

' 'Ave you, my dear luvey? So 'ave I.'

'Think 'ard, 'Arry. Remind me,' pleaded Wanda.

The senior camper reached for the glasses, imagining the look of pleasure that would come over the Bilkins' faces when he appeared at their table with his tribute. But before he could make a further move, a remark of Harry's caused him to freeze in his seat.

'What does it bleeding matter, my precious pet?' asked Harry and the senior camper detected a note of petulance in his voice.

' 'ow do you mean, 'Arry?' asked Wanda, puzzled.

'What do I mean? I mean, my little lump of custard, 'oo cares what we talked abaht at supper?'

'You don't sound very considerate, 'Arry,' returned Wanda, and there was a distinct edge to her voice.

'Maybe that's because I'm sick to the eye teeth of being considerate. It's boring, being considerate. It don't make me 'appy. It makes me even more miserable than I was before.'

'But, 'Arry,' remonstrated Wanda. ' 'Ave we given it a fair chance?'

'I 'ave. I prefer 'aving rows.'

'Oh, you do, do yer? So you would, you stupid gorilla. You aren't capable of 'aving a decent conversation because you're so thick.'

'Now 'oo doesn't sound considerate?'

'I can't be considerate on my own. Anyway, it's not natural with a hulk like you. All you're fit for is rows.'

'That's better,' said Harry, and there was enthusiasm in his voice. 'More natural, ain't it?'

'If you must know, yes. I was goin' round the twist trying to be considerate. 'e didn't tell me that, that nosey, interfering senior camper – 'e didn't tell me what a strain it was. Finish your beer and let's go to the concert.'

'Bloody rubbish, the concert.'

'You're bloody rubbish. Just want to sit there and swill evening after evening. Don't know why I stay with you. Next year, we'll go our separate ways. Never goin' on 'oliday with you again, you miserable –'

The senior camper put down the empty Bloody Mary glass, the contents of which he had just drained at a gulp although he loathed the concoction. He grasped a beer mug in each hand, rose and tiptoed away to the most distant part of the room where, concealed behind several plastic shrubs, he drank both pints and brooded on the perversity of human nature.

Trouble and Strife

'Mind if I join you?' asked the tall, distinguished-looking man in the good-quality lightweight suit.

'Delighted,' said the senior camper.

The other thereupon joined him at the table in the Laughing Cow Milk Bar. Another might have been surprised by the distinguished-looking man's request since the room was practically empty. This was because it was a glorious late-summer day and almost the entire camp was either in or around the Olympic-sized swimming pool, waiting for the Holiday Princess Competition to begin. The senior camper, however, was not surprised. Since the distinguished-looking man's arrival, by taxi rather than the more customary charabanc, the previous Saturday the senior camper had several times felt himself under observation by him.

'We've met before, haven't we?' said the distinguished-looking man cordially.

'Not that I recollect,' returned the senior camper, withdrawing from his pocket a small tin from the contents of which he began to roll himself a thin cigarette.

'Really? You seem most familiar to me. Yes, I have it. The Isle of Wight. Surely we met on the Isle of Wight?'

'Impossible,' said Charley Binns, shaking his head firmly. 'Never been there.'

'Some four – no, five years ago? I was only there for a couple of months. July, it would have been, or August.'

'Settles it,' said Charley Binns. 'I spend my summers here, have done for fifteen years.'

'Really?'

'Absolutely.'

'Cardew's my name,' said the other. 'Walter Cardew.'

'Nice name,' the senior camper complimented him.

'And yours?'

'Binns. Charley Binns.'

'Oh well, you were right.'

'I often am.'

'Yes. The chap I was thinking of – the one on the Isle of Wight – had a different name. Quite different it was.'

'Glad you're convinced.'

'Uncanny resemblance, though. I never spoke to him but I used to see him around quite a lot. It was a small community. Everyone knew everyone else – at least by sight.'

'How interesting.'

Charley Binns lit his cigarette and took a deep drag of the strong, pungent tobacco. The other withdrew a gold cigarette case and extracted from it a black cigarette with a gold rim which he also lit. The two smoked in silence for a while. Then Walter Cardew remarked:

'You must know this place very well.'

'That's right. Inside out.'

'Interesting. If you had been the other man – the one I used to see on the Isle of Wight – I might have approached you with a proposition.'

'Is that so?'

'Oh yes. Would you care to hear the kind of proposition?'

'Not much point, is there? Since I'm not the geezer.'

'Probably not, no.'

There was renewed silence for a while. Then Walter Cardew resumed:

'On the other hand, you might be interested yourself. Who knows? Shall I tell you about my proposition?'

'I wouldn't bother.'

'No bother. We both, it seems, have an idle hour. You see I'm not down here for a holiday.'

'You're not?'

'No. I'm a businessman. I came down here because I had an idea there might be business opportunities.'

'What kind of opportunities?'

'Who's to say? I'm very flexible in my approach. Have you noticed the bingo?'

'Don't play it myself.'

'Quite considerable sums are wagered over the course of

the week. Maplin's is supposed to cater to – how shall I put it? – the lower-income bracket but I have an idea there might be quite a lot of spare money floating about.'

'Just floating, eh?'

'Exactly. I can't help feeling that with the right approach one might set up a successful enterprise here in the camp. Or perhaps a multiplicity of enterprises.'

'Lets me right out. I'm just here for a holiday, same as every year.'

Cardew sighed deeply.

'Pity. You see the sort of undertakings I had in mind would require a partner. Someone who knew the ropes. Who knew where things were and who was around at what hours. That sort of thing.'

'Don't know anyone like that.'

Cardew laughed ruefully.

'Great pity. I have reason to think the other chap – the one who looks so uncannily like you – was good at that sort of thing.'

'But he's not here.'

'Apparently not. Mark you, I don't mind telling you that if he were here I'd do my level best to persuade him to go into partnership with me. I wouldn't scruple to put pressure on him.'

'What kind of pressure?'

'Oh, one hears rumours, you know. There are things about all of us we'd rather were kept quiet. Now suppose you were that chap and you came here every summer masquerading as an ordinary camper, you'd be very reluctant to have some of the things I know – about the other chap, I mean – come out. Wouldn't you?'

'It's quite possible. But since I'm not him, it doesn't apply, does it?'

The other laughed heartily.

'Of course not. There's no way I could put pressure on you, is there?'

'Absolutely not.'

'Charley! Hi-de-hi!' came a piercing call from somewhere in the vicinity of the counter.

The two men looked in that direction and Charley Binns recognised Peggy, the frustrated chalet maid, just collecting a knickerbocker glory with a side order of pistachio nuts and double fudge sauce from Edna, the serving girl. He waved amiably. Peggy yelled:

'Can I get you something? A knickerbocker glory? And your friend?'

'No thanks, Peggy,' called the senior camper.

'Who's that charming creature?' asked Cardew in a low voice.

'That's Peggy, the chalet maid,' admitted the senior camper. 'Light on brains, but strong on heart.'

'Chalet maid, hm?' mused the other. 'I should imagine she's a mine of useful information.'

'She's kind-hearted.'

'So I gather. So you come here every year – Mr Binns, I think you said?'

'That's right, Charley Binns. Every year, regular as clockwork.'

'May I ask why?'

'For the endless fun and games. Also I'm a student of human nature.'

'Really? Find much of it around here?'

'If you know where to look.'

Peggy bore down on them, bearing her knickerbocker glory and side dish.

'Mind if I join you, Charley?' she asked, doing so. 'Who's your friend?'

'This is Mr Walter Cardew.'

'What a lovely name. I love lovely names. Mine's Peggy Ollerenshaw. It's not lovely but it's got a kind of rugged charm. Are you old friends?'

'I thought we were – at least acquaintances,' purred Cardew, 'but it seems I was wrong.'

'Oh? How'd that happen?' asked Peggy, spooning gooey stuff into her mouth.

'I thought we'd – encountered each other before. On the Isle of Wight. Five summers ago. But Mr Binns has informed me that he spends every summer here.'

'So he does,' agreed Peggy. 'Yes, but hang on. You did miss one summer, Charley. Everyone noticed it. That's right. It was five years ago.'

'Really?' said Cardew, with an amused expression. He turned to the senior camper. 'So we could have met on the Isle of Wight, after all?'

The senior camper shook his head positively.

'I was abroad that year. In Portugal.'

'Portugal? Really? Odd that you didn't mention it.'

'Slipped my mind. Just for a moment.'

'Where was it,' Peggy asked Cardew as she scraped up the last of her fudge sauce, 'you thought you'd met? On the Isle of Wight?'

'Actually,' explained Cardew, 'it was also at a kind of camp.'

'A holiday camp? Like Maplin's?' asked Peggy, saucer-eyed.

'Not quite like Maplin's, no,' said Cardew. 'For one thing, there weren't so many amusements. And it was for men only.'

Peggy shuddered.

'A holiday camp for men only! Doesn't sound much fun. Did you have holiday prince competitions? Ooh, I was forgetting. I'm supposed to be at the pool. In case one of the yellowcoats gets heat stroke. I can step into her coat. It could be my big chance. Ta ra.'

And, with a last lick of her now-shiny spoon, the chalet maid jumped to her feet and dashed out of the Laughing Cow Milk Bar. There was silence for some time after her departure. The senior camper began to roll another cigarette.

'Suppose,' he remarked thoughtfully after a while, 'I was the bloke you thought you'd met at the Isle of Wight and suppose I didn't want people – say people like Peggy – to know about it, what would you want me to do?'

Cardew smiled complacently. Then he leaned towards the other.

'Oh, nothing very much. Introduce me to some of your friends –'

For the next quarter of an hour or so, Cardew outlined some of the projects he had in mind and the senior camper listened attentively. From the distance came intermittent storms of applause as the holiday princesses displayed their curvaceous charms for the approval of the campers. At the end of Cardew's outline, Charley Binns said:

'You're in luck.'

'Really?' asked Cardew. 'You mean, you'll help?'

'I will. I'll tell you that you haven't a hope.'

Cardew frowned.

'Why is that?' he asked.

'For that stuff to work you'd need to be dealing with innocent, simple people –'

'Exactly. And there are several thousand of them in this camp.'

'True. The campers. But what about the staff?'

'What about them?'

'They'd never stand for it. At the first whiff of competition they'd run you out of here so fast you wouldn't have time to say "this is your lucky day, sir".'

'Competition? What are you talking about?'

'Practised villains all of them. Fly as fishermen. They've all got their own private fiddles.'

'Utter rubbish.'

'Is it? I know this camp. Let me tell you a little story –'

'I really haven't got –'

'Settle down. Get yourself a coffee with a side order of pistachio nuts and listen. This place makes the West End of London seem like a convent.'

Cardew glanced irritably at his expensive wrist-watch.

'Yes but –'

'Look, if you still feel you want to go into partnership when you've heard the sordid truth, we'll talk further. But I wouldn't dream of having dealings with someone who didn't know the grim facts.'

'Oh, very well,' conceded Cardew with ill grace. 'Get on with it.'

Now this account revolves around the spot of bother Ted Bovis had with his ex-wife a few weeks ago. I don't know how familiar you are with the staff so I'd better give you brief descriptions of them as I mention them. Ted is the short, fat little man whose official job is camp host and unofficial one is fleecing the campers by a variety of ingenious methods. He's a superb singer and he tells the best blue jokes of anyone on the boards but those talents are nothing to his finesse with the fiddles. A good place for me to start is with the announcement that came over Radio Maplin, just before the storm broke for Ted, by our lovely, talented Gladys Pugh, who has an enchanting Welsh lilt, as you've probably heard several times already during your stay here, and a nifty line in extracting gifts from the campers.

'Hallo campers,' carolled Gladys, after she had struck the chimes on her xylophone that commanded attention throughout the whole of Maplin's, 'Hi-de-hi.'

Then she paused to listen and even through the sound-insulation of her little broadcasting booth came the muffled answering roar:

'Ho-de-ho.'

With a faint smile of satisfaction, Gladys began to speak.

'This is Gladys Pugh, your Radio Maplin announcer, and I'm feeling rather sad. It's Friday, the last day of your holiday at sunny Maplin's. Oh dear, I'm going to miss every one of you! Haven't the entertainments staff worked hard for your enjoyment? Well, it's not really work. It's a pleasure. So let's give them a big round of applause.'

To stimulate the applause, Gladys clapped a few times into her microphone and then listened. From all over the camp, came the muffled sound of campers clapping in response. Gladys continued:

'May I remind you of the strict rule that no tipping of the entertainments staff is allowed. Mind you, if you want to express your appreciation with some little gift, how can we possibly stop you? You know what my little weakness is, don't you? It's chocolates. I can't resist them – and perfume, of course. Every girl likes to smell nice. Anyway,

I'll be back on the air in half an hour with a list of the day's events. Until then, Hi-de-hi!'

Amongst those listening to the dulcet tones of the senior yellowcoat, which is the position Gladys enjoys in the camp, were Mr Partridge and Fred Quilly. Partridge is the camp Punch-and-Judy man, a notorious lush and bad-tempered with it. Fred leads out the sorry string of superannuated nags that pass for riding horses here in the camp. He was once a star of the turf but was struck off the jockey's register for some misdemeanour that has never, to my knowledge anyhow, come to life; for all I know he nobbled horses or fixed the tote. During Gladys' begging announcement, Partridge was laying on his bed listening with a grim and knowing smile. Just as it was ending, Fred pushed open the chalet door and entered. He was wearing the mackintosh which serves him for, amongst other things, a dressing-gown and he had a towel slung over his shoulder.

'Did you hear that silly cow?' grunted Partridge to his chalet mate. 'Blatant. She might just as well go round with a collection box.' At this point Partridge wrinkled his nose in disgust and exclaimed, 'You smell of horses.'

'How can I smell of horses?' asked Fred indignantly. 'I've just had a bath.'

Partridge chuckled evilly.

'That's right. You smell like a horse who's just had a bath.'

Fred shook his head in disgust.

'No wonder nobody ever gives you any presents,' he said feelingly. 'You're eaten up with hatred. You're riddled with it. You hate kids. You hate horses. And you hate people.'

'That's right,' agreed Partridge cheerfully. 'Three eights are twenty-four!'

And he laughed so heartily at this feeble joke that Fred suspected, quite correctly, that he'd been at the juice again. He contented himself with remarking:

'You're riddled with old jokes as well. You'd better hurry up and get out of the sack. It's pay day.'

Many of the other members of the entertainments staff had already collected their pay packets and had repaired to the Laughing Cow Milk Bar, as was their custom, to celebrate. Ted was there and also his disciple and assistant, Spike Dixon, the camp comic whom you may have seen about the place dressed as a gangster or burglar or something else sinister. The three gorgeous, but grasping, yellowcoats, Sylvia, Betty and Tracey, were with the two boys, eager to gold-dig and get what they could out of them. Spying Peggy, about the only good-hearted person on the staff, seated alone, they all went over and joined her, hoping, perhaps, that some of her goodness would rub off on their evil selves.

'All want coffee, girls?' Ted asked, as they neared Peggy's table. The girls all signified that they did and Ted shouted to the waitress, 'Five coffees, please, Mavis, and Club wafers all round. I'll have an orange one. Fancy a coffee, Peggy?'

The chalet maid answered with a friendly smile.

'No thanks, Ted, I've just ordered a banana sundae with a side serving of ice-cream with double-fudge sauce.'

'Right,' said Ted and then shouted at the waitress, 'I'll pay for Peggy's order.'

'Oh thanks, Ted,' acknowledged Peggy.

Ted took his pay packet out of his jacket pocket, tore off the end and tipped its contents onto the table. Spike watched this operation with cynical dismay.

'That's typical of you, Ted,' he remonstrated. 'No sooner do we get paid than you start treating everyone.'

'Well, they're my friends, aren't they?' said Ted expansively.

Meanwhile all the others at the table were checking their pay packets.

'That's a bit thick,' grumbled Betty, the petite yellowcoat. 'They've deducted ten shillings for those tennis shorts I split when we were playing the mixed doubles.'

'Reached for a low ball, did you?' grinned Ted. But his smile evaporated when he checked the amount on the table in front of him. 'Look at this, they've taken off two quid for chalet damages.'

Peggy knew why.

‘That was when you had that fry-up and the chip pan caught fire.’

‘You didn’t have to report it,’ Ted reproached her.

‘I couldn’t help it,’ said Peggy apologetically. ‘Miss Cathcart caught me trying to scrape it off the wall.’

Spike exclaimed crossly:

‘They’ve charged me the same – and I wasn’t even there!’ He gazed reproachfully at his chalet mate. ‘You know you’re not supposed to cook in the chalet, Ted.’

‘Don’t start nagging,’ Ted reproved him. ‘You sound like my ex-wife.’

Sylvia, the refined yellowcoat, looked at him curiously.

‘You never talk much about her, Ted,’ she observed. ‘What’s she like?’

Ted looked soulful.

‘Well,’ he said tenderly, ‘you know that picture of the Mona Lisa in the Louvre?’

‘Oh yes,’ exclaimed Sylvia. ‘It’s beautiful.’

‘My wife looks like the attendant who guards it,’ concluded Ted with a grimace.

At this point, Mavis arrived with a tray groaning under the various orders. As she set them in front of the various staff members present, she said:

‘That’ll be four and threepence please, Ted.’

Ted pushed two half-crowns towards her carelessly.

‘Five bob,’ he said expansively. ‘Keep the change.’

Spike sighed.

‘There you go again, Ted. You just can’t wait to get rid of it.’

As Ted spooned sugar into his coffee, he muttered:

‘Nag, nag, nag, nag, nag, nag!’

While this binge was going on in the Laughing Cow Milk Bar, Jeff Fairbrother was reading a letter in his little office. I have to say that Jeff Fairbrother is completely straight. He wouldn’t have any part in the monkey business that his staff get up to and if he knew of the various rackets and confidence tricks that went on under his nose he’d take vigorous action to stop it. But Jeff is new to the game of supervising a bunch of rogues. This is his first season at

Maplin's. Before that, he was an important professor at Cambridge University in charge of examining mummies and bones and things that teams of diggers keep digging up in Egypt and other unwholesome places. He is therefore a bit vague like all professors and so his staff can get away with murder, except they don't usually go that far. Jeff is separated from his wife which is good news for Gladys because she dotes on him but he is a gentleman which is bad news for Gladys because he stays faithful to his estranged wife. While he was reading his letter, Gladys bounced into his office.

'Oh,' she exclaimed, frowning slightly when she saw what he was doing, 'you got your letter then? I left it on the desk for you. It looks very thick.'

Jeff nodded wearily. He is a good-looking bloke with that indefinable something which shows he is from the upper crust and comes out of the top drawer. But he has a slightly twisted mouth which sometimes makes him look very sad. This look of his twists Gladys' heartstrings. He did it now and she felt her heartstrings twisting.

'It's from my solicitor,' he explained. 'He keeps going on about me suing my wife for restitution of conjugal rights.'

Gladys blinked at these tidings.

'I don't like the sound of that,' she said feelingly. 'You don't want them back, do you?'

Jeff smiled reassuringly.

'It's only a formality, Gladys,' he explained. 'Nobody actually does anything.' He held up the sheaf of papers that had come out of the envelope. 'Look at that. Five boring, expensive pages, probably about a guinea a page. I wish he'd hurry up and settle it.'

Gladys is very shrewd and snorted.

'Of course he won't hurry. That's how solicitors earn their money, writing you letters telling you what you know already and then charging you for it. How many of those have you had?'

'I shudder to think.'

'This could cost you hundreds.'

'Oh, that's probably modest. Let's see, it's been going on since –'

At this point, there was a knock at the door and Jeff broke off to call:

'Come in.'

In came Yvonne and Barry Stuart-Hargreaves. These two are the professional ballroom dancing instructors. They give themselves airs but, as you will learn, they are not above tapping the campers when they get a chance. They both look very prissy and refined but some people suspect they are not married at all although they share a chalet and a name. The other thing about them which is common knowledge is that they are always moaning. Some people in fact refer to them as 'The Two Minnies'.

'Can we have a moment of your time, please, Mr Fairbrother?' asked Yvonne primly. 'I know you must think that Barry and I are always in your office, bringing up little points, but we're rather concerned about our professional image, aren't we, Barry?'

Barry nodded agreement at his wife. He looked wilting, as he always does, but he said firmly enough:

'To be blunt, Mr Fairbrother, Yvonne and I do not like greeting the new intake of campers every Saturday and helping to carry their luggage.'

Gladys, who cannot abide the airs the two dancers give themselves, asked coldly:

'What makes you think you're any different from the other members of the entertainments staff?'

Yvonne favoured her with a pained smile.

'We feel that as Star Ballroom Champions we should preserve a certain aura of mystery and elegance.'

Barry offered an even more vapid smile.

'And we can hardly do that if we're humping their tatty cases and brown paper parcels.'

Jeff nodded understandingly and told them:

'I do sympathise with you. On the other hand, I don't make the rules.'

Gladys pointed out indignantly:

'Mr Fairbrother doesn't mind helping out. Do you consider yourself better than what he is?'

Jeff, trying to make light of the whole thing, gave a little twisted laugh and said:

'As a matter of fact, quite a few of them try to give me tips.'

Barry drew himself up like a camel searching the horizon for an oasis and said:

'No one ever offers us anything.'

Gladys said roughly:

'That's because you're supercilious and look down your noses at them. Mr Fairbrother is always charming to all classes, like the Duke of Edinburgh when he opens things and visits factories.'

Barry nodded patiently and pointed out:

'But the Duke doesn't have to hump brown paper parcels, dear, does he?'

Gladys looked nonplussed for a moment but then she rallied.

'Well, he sometimes carries the Queen's bouquets.'

'I think,' said Jeff gently, 'we're veering a little away from the point.'

'I quite agree,' contributed Yvonne firmly. 'Perhaps we can discuss this later when you're alone, Mr Fairbrother.' She gave Gladys a superior glance. 'Come along, Barry.'

As soon as the door had shut behind them, Gladys said bitterly:

'Troublemakers! They're always whingeing. Whinge, whinge, whinge, whinge, whinge!'

Jeff shook his head sadly.

'I can't help feeling a little sorry for them,' he confessed. 'After all, what do they have to look forward to? Their championship days are over and if Joe Maplin didn't employ them, who would?'

'I suppose you're right,' conceded Gladys grudgingly. 'Once their looks have gone, they're finished.'

'Precisely,' said Jeff. 'After all, if *you* get bags under your eyes and a double chin, who cares?'

This was not a speech calculated to make Gladys, who is

always hoping Jeff will see her as a radiant princess, too chuffed. She said huffily:

'I haven't got bags under my eyes and a double chin. What are you getting at?'

'Nothing,' Jeff assured her. 'What I meant was that if you did get bags under your eyes and a double chin, I wouldn't mind.'

Gladys chose to interpret this speech as a touching declaration of affection. She looked at him tenderly and breathed:

'Wouldn't you really, Jeff?'

Jeff was slightly alarmed by this reaction. Mercifully, while he was striving to think of an answer that wouldn't commit him in either direction, there was a knock at the door and he hastily looked towards it and called:

'Come in.'

A stranger entered. It was a woman, stout, blonde and quite attractive. She appeared to be in her early forties. She smiled and asked:

'Is this the entertainments manager's office?'

Jeff nodded.

'Yes, I'm Jeffrey Fairbrother. Can I help you?'

Gladys amplified:

'Mr Fairbrother is the entertainments manager.'

The fair-haired woman smiled and announced:

'I'm Hilary Bovis.'

'Ted's wife?' asked Gladys with great interest.

'Ex-wife,' corrected Hilary.

'How very nice to meet you,' said Jeff warmly. 'Won't you sit down?'

Hilary did not accept the invitation. She seemed a little abstracted and nervous.

'Is Ted expecting you?' asked Gladys.

'Is he on the camp?' asked Hilary in return.

'Of course he is,' Jeff assured her.

'Then,' said Hilary firmly, 'he's not expecting me.' She glanced from one to the other of them and sat down. 'What are you staring at?' she asked defensively.

'I'm sorry,' Jeff apologised. 'It's just that Ted has told me so much about you.'

'I bet he has,' nodded Hilary, a trifle grimly. 'But there's two sides to every story, you know. A comedian's wife runs a close second to his mother-in-law.'

Jeff demurred.

'But I'm sure your mother is charming.'

Hilary shook her head.

'No, she isn't. She's a cow. He got that bit right.'

Just then there was a tap at the door which caused Hilary to tense visibly. Hard upon the tap came Ted himself. He advanced towards Jeff saying:

'Eh, Jeff, I wanted to talk to you about –'

At that point, he noticed Hilary seated to one side of the desk. Without any pause in speech and describing a fluent curve, Ted headed back towards the door, remarking, 'It's all right. I'll come back later.'

But before he had quite reached the door, Hilary said quietly:

'Come here, Ted.'

Again, without any break in his demeanour, Ted swung beaming to face his wife.

'Hello, Hilary,' he exclaimed with apparent enthusiasm. 'You're looking bonny. How are you keeping?'

Hilary contented herself with a one-word reply.

'Poor,' she said.

Ted frowned sympathetically.

'Sorry to hear that. Sciatica bothering you again?'

Hilary shook her head with a wan smile.

'No. I haven't got any money.'

Ted nodded sagely.

'A lot of people in that situation. That fellow Macmillan keeps saying we've never had it so good – totally out of touch.'

'Ted,' said Hilary, with a trace of bitterness in her tone. 'I've not had a penny from you for three months.'

Ted recoiled in well-simulated amazement.

'What are you talking about?' he asked incredulously. 'I sent you a money order only last – er – um – now wait a minute – who did I give it to to post?'

Hilary sighed wearily and shook her head.

'Ted, it's me you're talking to. Time's up.'

With which, puzzling everyone present, she moved rapidly to the office door. But she did not make an exit. Instead she pulled the door open and nodded, apparently at someone outside. This proved to be the case for a large, ugly man wearing a bowler hat and mackintosh promptly entered. Hilary pointed firmly at Ted and said, 'There he is.'

The man approached Ted and asked, in an official-sounding voice, 'Are you Edward Bovis?'

Ted smiled winningly and pointed out, 'My friends always call me Ted.'

But friendship didn't seem to be on the bowler-hatted man's mind. He swiftly produced an envelope from an inside pocket and planted it in Ted's hand.'

'Take this please, sir,' he instructed the comedian.

'He's a bailiff, Ted,' Hilary clarified the situation.

Jeff looked embarrassed and rose to his feet.

'Er, would you like us to go?' he asked courteously.

'It's a bit late for that,' Ted grunted. Then he looked the bailiff up and down and said, 'I wondered what you were doing in the staff room. I thought you'd come to audition as a comic.'

'It's a Court Order, Ted,' Hilary pursued. 'You've got a week to cough up fifty quid. I'll be down next Friday to collect it, and if you don't divvy up you'll be in the nick.'

Ted looked shocked.

'Hilary!' he exclaimed reproachfully.

'It's the law, ducky,' Hilary pointed out. Then she and the bailiff turned and left the office.

'What are you going to do, Ted?' asked Gladys.

But the comedian was, for once, bereft of words. He simply shook his head dumbly and followed his old lady out of the office. He made his way to his chalet where he found his protégé, Spike Dixon, the camp comic, mending his funny chef's outfit.

'You look like you told three belters and never raised a single laugh,' observed Spike.

'No laughing matter,' sighed Ted and he told his chalet-mate about the rude intrusion of his former wife.

'What are you going to do?' asked Spike at the conclusion of the tale.

'Nothing I can do,' grunted Ted morosely.

'This is serious, you know, Ted,' Spike urged. 'If you don't come up with that fifty quid next Friday, you'll be inside.'

Ted shrugged.

'She's always sending summonses,' he muttered.

'This one's different. It's the real thing.'

'That's women for you,' offered Ted bitterly. 'One minute they're promising to love, honour and obey and the next minute they're shoving you in clink.'

'You'll have to –'

'It's hopeless. I haven't got fifty quid.'

Spike abandoned his funny chef outfit and approached Ted.

'Show us your pay packet,' he ordered.

'There's not fifty quid in there, Spike,' Ted said earnestly but he pulled it out of his pocket. Spike seized it from him. 'What are you doing?'

Spike did not reply. He tipped the money out of the envelope and counted it. Then he said, 'Right, eleven pounds, ten. I'll keep the eleven pounds and there's ten-bob pocket money for you.'

And he coolly handed Ted a ten-shilling note. Ted looked shocked.

'What are you talking about?' he exclaimed indignantly.

But Spike was busy. He fished out his own pay packet and tipped the money out of that. He said:

'And there's nine quid from me which I'm lending you – because I'm an idiot. So that makes twenty pounds.'

Ted shook his head in astonishment.

'Spike, I don't know what to say,' he said.

'Don't say anything,' ordered Spike. 'Just think how you're going to raise the extra thirty pounds.'

Ted frowned.

'Well, tomorrow's Saturday, so I suppose I could work the spare chalet trick.'

Spike looked puzzled.

'What's that?' he asked.

Ted got briskly to his feet and made for the door.

'Come with me,' he instructed. Then, just before he reached the door, he turned back to Spike. 'Before we go, I just want to say one thing.'

Spike said expansively:

'Don't start thanking me.'

'No, it's not that,' protested Ted. 'It's just that – could I have another quid for beer money?'

Spike nodded and then realised what Ted had said. With a sigh of exasperation, he pointed firmly at the door.

'Out!' he commanded.

Ted obediently turned but remonstrated sulkily, 'Spike, don't start getting rough just because you're in a position of power.'

Spike followed Ted along the chalet lines for some distance until they reached Peggy's store chalet where she keeps her yellow soap and scrubbing brushes and stuff. Peggy was, in fact, popping in and out, loading a trolley with cleaning materials in preparation for a swoop on grease and grime.

'Hallo, Ted,' she carolled when the two comedians hove into view. 'Hi-de-hi!'

'Peggy,' said Ted earnestly. 'I want to borrow your store chalet for the day.'

'What for?' asked Peggy, surprised.

Ted glanced about conspiratorially and whispered:

'It's a secret. Come inside.'

And the three of them pressed into the chalet. Now there are those who have compared the chalets at Joe Maplin's unfavourably with the Ritz Hotel and it is true that they do not boast room service or even, in most cases, a strip of carpet but I have always found them very snug once you've settled in. But Peggy's store chalet was definitely not in the three-star bracket. It had a cracked wash-basin and was full of shelves holding cleaning materials. Brooms, mops and other such items were stashed against the walls. Peggy had made an attempt to brighten up her citadel with some pictures of film stars, torn from Sunday newspapers, pasted to the walls but these somehow failed to generate a sense of luxury and glamour.

'Nobody's allowed in here, you know, Ted,' Peggy remonstrated with the comedian. 'This is my holy of holies.'

Ted nodded.

'I know it is. That's why I want to borrow it for the day.'

Now Peggy is, as I have said, a good-hearted girl but she is not so innocent that she doesn't know the chicanery that goes on all around her. She shook her finger at Ted and said, 'It's no good thinking you can flog any of this stuff, Ted, because Miss Cathcart's got it all inventoried. If I'm as much as one tin of Vim short it's deducted from my wages.'

Spike looked from Peggy to Ted with a dawning light of suspicion in his eyes.

'You're not thinking of anything like that, Ted, are you?' he asked incredulously. 'Are you, Ted?'

Ted waved the preposterous suggestion away.

'Of course I'm not. Why I'd put my hand in the fire before I saw Peggy exploited in any way.'

Peggy, a softie for compliments, beamed:

'Would you really, Ted?'

'Certainly. Now listen, Peggy, I want you to shift all this stuff out of here. Tidy it up a bit and move in a bunk bed.'

'But what for?' asked Peggy baffled.

Ted glanced around as if he feared the place might be bugged. He spoke softly.

'Well, there's this poor little orphan and he's not had a holiday for fourteen years, so I'm going to sneak him in here and give him the time of his life before he takes his eleven plus.'

'If he's fourteen,' Peggy asked reasonably, 'why is he taking his eleven plus?'

Ted sighed impatiently.

'Because he's not very bright. So I just want to borrow this chalet for the day.'

‘You mean,’ said Peggy, ‘he’s only getting one day’s holiday after all that time?’

Ted shook his head feelingly.

‘When you’ve not had a holiday for fourteen years, one day seems like a lifetime. He’s a lovely little kid.’

‘Oh Ted,’ said Peggy tenderly, ‘I’ll get on to it straight away.’

And she departed to search for a spare bunk bed.

‘What was all that rubbish, Ted?’ asked Spike suspiciously.

‘Look,’ said Ted urgently, ‘I’ve got to raise thirty pounds by next Friday, and this is one of the ways I’m going to do it. Now supposing you came here for your holiday with your lovely young bride for your nuptials and you were shown into this chalet with a torn curtain and broken window, what would you do?’

Spike glanced towards the window.

‘It hasn’t got a torn curtain and broken window.’

Ted sighed irritably, stalked to the window, seized the curtain and ripped it nearly in half. He then took up a broom and thrust the handle through the pane making a cheerful sound of tinkling glass. He turned back to Spike.

‘As I was saying, what would you do?’

‘I’d complain very strongly,’ Spike maintained.

Ted smiled.

‘Ah, but supposing you’d come down here with a piece of skirt for a bit of naughty nookie and you registered as “Mr and Mrs Smith” – you wouldn’t complain quite so loudly, would you? I mean, you wouldn’t want to draw attention to yourself. Isn’t that true, Spike?’

Spike shook his head helplessly.

‘I suppose so. I wouldn’t really know. I’ve never done that sort of thing.’

‘Take my word for it, Spike. This is where I’m going to make a few bob.’

‘Well, tell me how,’ insisted Spike.

So Ted told him and Spike was horrified.

The next day was changeover day. One bunch of campers departed and a new one arrived. In the space of a few hours this whole mighty camp, buzzing like a small town, turned into a kind of ghost camp, empty chalets, empty ballroom, empty everything, except, of course, for the staff and me. And then, a few hours later, a flock of charabancs arrived with the new intake, thousands of pale ghosts waiting to be turned, during the course of the next week, into lobster-red, fun-filled, Maplin's campers. I've seen this happen innumerable times and it never fails to inspire in me thoughts too deep for tears. But there is another side to it. It is a dark side which has nothing to do with spreading happiness and laughs. It is the display of greed and dishonesty which is made possible when thousands of innocents are led into the clutches of a small group of ruthless and avaricious criminals. I refer to the so-called entertainments staff. For, take my word for it, Ted Bovis was not the only one standing in the sunlight near the main gate who had designs on the new arrivals' purses.

Even Gladys, the curvaceous, dark-haired Welsh beauty, a girl who is not lost to all decency, even she had her plans well-laid. Although you would never have guessed it if you could have eavesdropped on her conversation with the one incorruptible man in the whole place, the entertainments manager himself, Jeff Fairbrother.

'How,' asked Gladys earnestly, 'did you spend Saturday mornings when you were at Cambridge, Jeff?'

Jeff smiled reminiscently.

'It was rather civilised actually. Four or five of my students would come into my rooms and we'd have a cup of coffee or maybe a glass of sherry, and talk about the week's work.'

'You mean mummies and things?' asked Gladys curiously.

Jeff sighed.

'There's rather more to archeology than that, Gladys,' he said gently.

Gladys sniffed faintly.

'Did you talk about girls?' she asked.

'Very seldom.'

'Must have been a bit different from meeting a lot of campers off a charabanc.'

'It was,' admitted Jeff drily.

Meanwhile Ted was finalising his plans with Spike.

'You've got the key to Peggy's store chalet?' he asked. Spike whipped the key from his pocket and showed it to his boss. 'And you're sure you know what to do?'

Spike shook his head unhappily.

'I've been thinking, Ted,' he confessed. 'You'll have to do it on your own. I just can't fiddle the campers. I just wouldn't be any good at it.'

Ted was outraged.

'They're not being fiddled. They're just paying the price for their immorality. Knowing what a misery martin you are, you should be pleased.'

But Spike wasn't having any.

'I don't want anything to do with it.'

'Look, Spike,' Ted remonstrated, 'you know very well all the entertainments staff have their own little fiddles for changeover day. That's how they get their beer money.'

But Spike was immovable.

'Sorry, Ted.'

'Oh, all right then. Just carry the bags. You don't want to see me go to prison, do you?'

'I'm not sure sometimes,' Spike admitted. 'All right, I'll carry the bags and nothing else.'

'Thanks very much,' said Ted bitterly.

With a reproachful glance at his chalet mate, Ted moved to where Jeff and Gladys were chatting.

'Do me a favour, Jeff,' he appealed when he reached the entertainments manager, 'and greet the campers for me. I've got a relaxed throat. It's the tension, you know. All this business about my ex-wife.'

Good-natured Jeff never hesitated.

'Don't worry, Ted,' he assured the camp host, 'I'll do it.'

'Ta. You're a pal,' enthused Ted who then moved back to his former place.

Gladys looked after him with suspicious eyes.

'Relaxed throat, my foot,' she remarked. 'What's he up to now?'

'Oh, I don't mind doing it, Gladys,' Jeff assured his right-hand girl. 'Actually, I really feel I'm beginning to communicate with the campers. The more I do, the better I get.'

Gladys, thinking of a quite different activity that Jeff, as far as she knew, was badly out of practice at, murmured,

'It's like that with a lot of things, isn't it?'

And then her attention was taken by the sight they were all waiting for. The coaches came round the bend of the coast road and trundled towards the camp. Gladys seized her microphone and called:

'Right, here they come. Big smiles, girls. Sylvia, take your hands out of your pockets.'

Everyone spruced themselves up and, with smiles from which they tried to remove all trace of avarice, edged towards the place where the first coach would grind to a halt. They watched as the big buses rolled in through the gates and stopped. They closed in on the new arrivals as they began to descend from the machines. And Jeff's voice began to crackle from the microphone. Now Jeff is undoubtedly more at home with elegant and sophisticated undergraduates than he is with the rough-and-ready mob you get at a place like this. But he has a go even though he has not yet acquired, and probably never will, the true common touch.

'Hallo campers,' his Cambridge drawl echoed forth. 'Welcome to Maplin's. Hi-de-hi!'

But he said his 'Hi-de-hi' so feebly that no one paid a blind bit of attention.

'Er, can I have your attention, please?' Jeff requested. 'We have a sort of custom – well, something like a tradition – here. When we shout 'Hi-de-hi' you shout back 'ho-de-ho' and if you don't, we do things to you like chucking you in the pool and – er – other things like that. Most amusing. Ha, ha. Shall we try again? Hi-de-hi.'

But apart from Gladys, who loyally bawled 'ho-de-ho', Jeff again failed to mobilise the great roar that Ted always extracts from the campers. He abandoned the quest and continued with his welcome speech.

'Now then – er folks – this is where your holiday starts right here. And while you're waiting for your luggage I thought I might regale you – er tell you quite an amusing story I recently heard. It appears that there was once this Scotsman going on holiday to some island or another. Well he got down to the jetty and he saw the ferry about six feet out and he said, "Hoots, man", because he was a Scotsman, you see, "Hoots, man, I'm not going to miss the ferry, och aye." So he took a flying leap and managed to jump onto the boat. He found a sailor nearby and said to him, "Hoots, you thought I'd missed it, didn't you?" And the sailor replied: "Arrh" – you'll gather that he was West Country. "Arrh," he replied, "what do you mean missed it? We're just coming in!" Awfully good, I thought. Yes, well, I want to say on behalf of the entire entertainments staff –'

Ted, meanwhile, was scanning the new intake with a practised eye. Suddenly he nudged Spike.

'There's our quarry,' he hissed. 'See how furtive they're looking? Come on.'

Spike followed his gaze and saw a young couple who did, in fact, look a trifle ill at ease. The girl was red-haired and quite pretty. The boy had his hair brilliantined into a slick and was feeling at the collar of his tight shirt. They kept glancing about them as if from fear of being recognised. Ted bore down on them and Spike, with a guilty shake of the head, followed him.

'Welcome to Maplin's,' said Ted heartily, seizing the young man's hand and shaking it. He looked at the labels on their luggage. 'Mr and Mrs Brown, isn't it?'

The boy nodded uneasily.

'Yeah, that's right. This is my – er – wife.'

'How do you do?' said the girl, smiling nervously.

'You look tired out,' purred Ted sympathetically. 'I tell you what. To save you queueing up, I'll go and collect your chalet key while you wait here. Now you can either listen to him up there telling the jokes, or Spike here will do some impersonations.'

And, as Spike gave him a startled look, Ted hurried away to the reception counter. When he got there, he spoke urgently to the receptionist.

'Have you got Mr and Mrs Brown there?' Without waiting for a reply, Ted consulted the list of new arrivals. 'Yes, here it is – Brown, chalet 217. Give us the key, will you? I'll see to them.'

The receptionist, having no reason to doubt Ted's motives, handed over the key with a smile and Ted raced away back to the reception area where he found Spike trying to entertain the young couple in his absence. Spike was singing to them and they were standing looking embarrassed and glancing about self-consciously.

'It's all right, Spike. You can knock off now,' said Ted cheerfully. 'I've got the key.' And then to the couple, 'You're in chalet number 17. I expect that's the bridal chalet. Let's get along there and give it the once-over. Bring the bags, Spike.'

And whistling cheerfully, Ted led the way past the ballroom and along the chalet lines until they reached Peggy's store chalet.

'Oh dear, it's got a broken window,' he said, as they stopped outside the door. 'Oh well, a piece of cardboard will keep the wind out. But I bet the interior is luxurious. Let's see.'

And taking the key which Spike secretively slipped him, he opened the chalet door and led the young couple inside. The interior, as Ted had intended, looked very uninviting. Peggy's cleaning materials were gone but in their place was a battered iron bunk bed. The place was bleak and tatty.

'Is this it?' asked 'Mr Brown' in obvious dismay.

'Lionel,' exclaimed 'Mrs Brown', 'it's got bunks!'

Ted gazed around slowly as if in appalled amazement. Then he said feelingly:

'Fancy giving you this! It's a disgrace. You've got to admit that, Spike. It's a disgrace, isn't it?'

'Lionel,' whined 'Mrs Brown', 'you said you asked for a double bed.'

‘ ’Course I asked for a double bed,’ said ‘Mr Brown’ shuffling his feet miserably.

‘All right,’ said Ted, turning to them earnestly. ‘There’s two ways to handle this. We can all go back to Reception right now and you can bang on the desk and shout at the top of your voice: ‘I’m Mr Brown and this is Mrs Brown, and we ordered a double bed. We have been treated disgracefully.’ Now if you did that you’d be completely justified and I’d back you up. On the other hand, if you prefer not to make a fuss, I can put you in Chalet 217. That’s the VIP chalet, beautiful, double bed, nice bit of carpet, tooth mug, everything. Jewel and Warris were going to have it but they had to cancel the show so they’re not coming. So it’s your decision. If you don’t want to make a fuss, I can put you in there.’

The boy shook his head.

‘No, we don’t want to make a fuss.’

And the girl added:

‘That’s right, Lionel, we don’t want to make a fuss.’

‘Right,’ said Ted firmly. ‘That settles it. Let’s go. Oh, there’s just one thing. I’ll have to square it with Security. They’ll see the lights on. It’ll cost a quid. They’re as bent as corkscrews.’

‘It’s worth it, Lionel,’ urged the girl.

The boy withdrew his wallet from his pocket and fumbled in it.

‘Here you are then,’ he said, handing Ted a pound.

‘There’s two security men,’ said Ted, noting the contents of the wallet.

The boy handed over another pound. As he was doing so, Peggy came beaming into the chalet, with a lolly in her hand.

‘Has that little orphan boy arrived yet, Ted?’ she asked eagerly.

‘No,’ said Ted, waving her away. ‘These are the foster parents, come to see if everything’s all right.’

‘I’ll be back later then,’ promised Peggy and she skipped away with her lolly.

‘What foster parents?’ asked ‘Mr Brown’ suspiciously.

Ted smiled and winked.

'She's potty. Lives in a dream world. Right, 217 here we come. Pick the bags up Spike.' Ted grinned mischievously. 'You haven't got much to say for yourself, Spike? Cat got your tongue?'

Spike contented himself, as he lifted the case, with a reproachful look. Then the whole party moved out and along the chalet lines once more until they reached chalet 217 which was the one the 'Browns' had been booked into in the first place. Ted flung open the door dramatically as if he were an estate agent displaying a stately home to a titled buyer.

'Well, what do you think of it?' he asked.

The girl could not restrain from clapping her hands lightly.

'It's lovely, Lionel,' she breathed, her eyes on the big, comfortable-looking double bed.

'Yeah, great,' admitted the boy.

He reached into his pocket and pulled out half a crown which he handed to Spike.

'For carrying the cases,' he said gratefully.

Ted promptly shot out a hand and seized the coin.

'Yellowcoats aren't allowed to accept tips,' he explained to the surprised boy. 'I'll see it goes to the staff benevolent fund.'

Whereupon he and Spike left the contented young couple and hastened back to the reception area to seek out another young couple that looked nervous and self-conscious and easy victims for an unscrupulous confidence man.

And meanwhile, what were the rest of the entertainments staff up to? It's enough to curl your hair. Let me concede straight away that Jeff Fairbrother was up to nothing more vicious than doing his best, in his boring way, to welcome the campers. But the others –

Well, let's start with Peggy. Yes, I know I have praised her several times. I have said she was good-hearted and so she is on ordinary occasions. But somehow the gold-lust that gripped the entire entertainments staff on changeover day even reached out to corrupt good-hearted Peggy. Like everyone else, she was engaged in helping campers with their luggage and showing them to their chalets. And when she reached the chalet and installed the campers, did she turn with a smile and depart? She did not. She glanced around nervously to make sure that Miss Cathcart was nowhere within earshot and then she said earnestly:

'Before I go, I'd just like to remind you that I'm in charge of your personal valeting service. So if you want any private washing done, just let me know. The charge is very moderate. Hi-de-hi.'

And, blushing faintly, because she is not a hardened criminal, Peggy skipped away for the next batch. And so it went with all of them. Barry and Yvonne Stuart-Hargreaves arrived at a chalet with a middle-aged couple. They were dressed to the nines in their ballroom dancing gear. Barry said amiably:

'This is your chalet. We hope you'll be very comfortable.'

'Thank you very much,' said the male camper.

'Oh, by the way,' remarked Yvonne as if it was just an idea that had come to her out of the blue, 'there's just one thing. My partner and I are the star ballroom champions here. We won the European Cup twice.'

Whereupon Barry, taking up the routine they had practised so often, continued smoothly:

'Not to mention the Gold Slipper Award at the Locarno, Streatham.'

Yvonne's turn.

'As well as giving demonstrations every day, we also give private tuition to certain selected couples.'

While Barry supplied:

'And we just have one vacancy left. Are you interested?'

The clincher from Yvonne:

'Two guineas for four lessons.'

The victim, of course, reached helplessly for his wallet.

They were all at it. Somewhere else, Partridge, the Punch-and-Judy man, normally too sozzled for conversation, was sharp as a tack.

'This is your chalet. I'm Uncle Willy, the Punch-and-Judy man. I do five shows a day – all different. It's good, clean fun, no sex or violence, except for hitting the baby with a rolling pin. Now if your little lad would like a reserved cushion in the front row, it will only cost you ten bob for the week.'

With a wry glance at his wife, the indulgent father reached into his pocket.

Sylvia and Tracey, the two charming yellowcoats, were not without a sideline. Approaching a chalet with a very fat man and his wife, Sylvia was enthusing:

'The food here is excellent, but there's only one snag, they don't give you very big portions.'

'This is your chalet,' intruded Tracey with a charming smile and she put the key in the door and opened it as her henchwoman continued:

'Fortunately, we have got friends in the kitchen and if you give us a pound we'll square things so you get second helpings.'

The fat man anxiously reached for his wallet.

'There's two of them,' remarked Tracey, taking the pound note he held out.

Fred was flogging horse manure. Betty was hawking a supposed 'Special Exhibition Swimsuit' to help a daughter win the Holiday Princess Competition and sad to confess, even delightful, responsible Gladys was flogging off old tennis balls. A sorry catalogue of crime and exploitation.

But of all of them, no one hustled like Ted hustled. And not only on changeover day. All through the week Ted practised the various bent schemes he had long ago dreamed up for fleecing the campers. And at the end of the week, he and Spike sat once more on their beds in their chalet. Spike counted the loot. He sighed.

'However I count it, Ted,' he said sadly, 'I can't make it more than forty quid. She'll be here tomorrow to collect and you're still ten quid short.'

Ted shook his head in resignation.

'Well, I can't think of anything else,' he said. 'I've done the lot – the chalets, the raffle, bingo and the chewing-gum up the paying-out slot of the fruit machine.'

Spike stuck his fingers in his ears and said virtuously:

'I don't want to hear the details, Ted. I'm just looking after the money for you, because I don't want to see you go to jail.'

'Tell you what,' said Ted thoughtfully. 'I know a dead cert in the two-thirty. Give me a fiver of the money and I'll –'

'No, Ted,' said Spike firmly. 'I'm not letting go of this money until I hand it over to your wife tomorrow.'

'You're a hard man, Spike,' sighed bent Ted.

'You'll just have to think of something else.'

'Well, give us a quid and I'll buy you a drink in the Dutch bar while we're working it out.'

'No, Ted.'

Ted shook his head reproachfully and rose to his feet.

'Well, there's only one thing for it. I'll have to go down to the office and throw myself on Jeff's mercy.'

Little did Ted know, as he set off wearily from his chalet, that Jeff was, at that very moment, discussing his plight with Gladys.

'As far as I can gather,' he was saying, 'Ted's still a long way short of his target.'

Gladys tossed her head indifferently.

'Well, he's only got himself to blame. You lent him five pounds yesterday and what did he do? He put it straight on a horse.'

Jeff shook his head sadly.

'I must confess he's a pretty hopeless case. He's just got no idea of money.'

At that moment there was a knock at the door and, after Jeff had called 'come in', the subject of their discussion shuffled in looking distinctly deflated.

'Spare a moment, Jeff?' he asked forlornly.

'Of course,' said the kindly entertainments manager, with a glance at Gladys.

Ted slumped into a chair, held up his hands in an expressive gesture and said:

'Very nearly raised that money. Not far short. Only ten quid.'

'Before you say another word, Ted,' Gladys cautioned

the camp host, 'Mr Fairbrother is not going to lend you a single penny.'

Ted made a face expressive of outraged innocence.

'Who said anything about lending?' he asked plaintively. 'Did I say anything about lending? I just want an advance on my salary.'

Jeff said unhappily:

'Ted, you know as well as I do, there's an absolutely unbreakable rule at Maplin's – no advances on salary.'

Ted managed again to sound deeply aggrieved.

'Who said anything about Maplin's? Did I say anything about Maplin's? I just thought you personally might give me an advance on my salary.'

'I lent you five pounds yesterday,' pointed out Jeff, 'and what happened? You blew the lot on a horse. No, I'm sorry, Ted. It would just put you deeper into debt.'

Ted shrugged bitterly.

'Very well. I came in here with an ordinary, straightforward business proposition, and what do I get? A lecture!'

He rose to his feet and shuffled towards the door, turned and gave a slight, ironical bow. He left, pulling the door shut after him.

'Oh dear,' said Jeff.

'Now don't go getting upset,' Gladys urged him. 'You did the right thing.'

'But what's going to happen to him? I'm very fond of Ted.'

'He's got to learn to stand on his own feet and face up to reality like everyone else.'

'I suppose so.'

And that was Ted's last attempt to raise the extra money. Spike was astonished at his calm and kept urging him to new efforts but Ted seemed resigned to his fate and, the next day, at the time his wife was due to collect, Ted was to be found lying on his bed and sorting out a pathetic bunch of fag ends in a tin box. He finally found one that had a bit of smoking left in it, stuck it in his mouth and lit it. Then, like a condemned man waiting for the guard to come and lead him to execution, he lay back and puffed thoughtfully. Before long the door opened and a woman came in. It was not, however, Hilary Bovis but Peggy, the good-hearted, if slightly bent, chalet maid. She stood for a moment gazing at the forlorn figure on the bed.

'I hear you're in trouble, Ted,' she said gently, at length.

Ted sighed and nodded.

'Too true,' he admitted.

Peggy shook her head reproachfully.

'You didn't have to tell me that cock-and-bull story about the orphan. I'd have helped you anyway.'

'Sorry, Peggy,' said Ted with a faint, remote smile, as if he were already beyond earthly concerns. 'I got carried away.'

'Look,' said Peggy earnestly, trying to shake him from this sinister lethargy. 'I've had a good week, what with the washing and one thing and another, and – well – here's a pound.'

And she quickly put a crisp pound note into the doomed man's hand. Ted contemplated the offering with a sad, grateful smile. Then he shook his head and handed it back to the chalet maid.

'It's very nice of you, Peggy, but it won't make any difference.'

'Oh Ted. Every little helps and you're very welcome.'

Ted shook his head again.

'If I need it, I know where to come.'

But he spoke like a man who was not concerned with trifles like money any more. Peggy could hardly restrain herself from weeping seeing him brought so low but she didn't want to give way for fear of discouraging him even further.

'Well, it's there if you want it,' she said. 'And, Ted, if you do go to jail, I'll come and visit you.'

Ted looked up at her with a brave smile. He was still capable of a jest.

'Thanks, Peggy. You can bring me a pork pie with a file in it.'

'I'll do that, Ted,' she promised. 'A whole tool kit. Oh, Ted!'

And with a stifled sob she turned and rushed out of that chalet of grief. Ted did not stir. He finished his pathetic fag end and did not even bother to search for another. He just lay staring at the ceiling of the place where he had had so many good times. Would he ever see it again? Finally came the footsteps on the walk outside and Spike came into the chalet like a grave harbinger of misfortune.

'Your wife's here, Ted,' he announced sombrely.

'Bring her in,' ordered the supine man bravely. 'Let's get this thing over with.'

Even before he had finished speaking, a shadow darkened the door and Hilary Bovis, looking unrelenting, entered the chalet. She wasted no time in preliminaries.

'Right, Ted,' she said roughly. 'Where is it?'

Ted smiled enigmatically.

'I've got it, Mrs Bovis,' said Spike diffidently. 'There's ten quid short I'm afraid. Ted has tried ever so hard.'

And Spike handed her the money. Then with a look at Ted which said louder than words 'nothing more I can do, old son – I'm afraid you're on your own now' Spike hurried from the chalet. For a long moment there was silence as the two old adversaries contemplated each other. Hilary spoke first.

'What's going to happen about the other ten pounds, Ted?' she asked sternly.

Ted shrugged indifferently.

'That's all there is. You've got the lot. I've not even had a drink this week.'

For another long moment there was silence. Ted wondered idly if, upon a sign from her, blue-uniformed men would storm into the peaceful chalet and drag him away in chains. Then Hilary nodded in acquiescence.

'All right, Ted, I'll settle for this. To tell you the truth it's more than I expected. I'll tell them you paid in full. You'll not go to jail this time.'

Ted looked at her in surprise. He hadn't expected such magnanimity.

'Thanks, Hil,' he said meaningfully. 'I'm glad you've still got a soft spot for me.'

But his wife shook her head firmly.

'I haven't,' she said baldly. 'I'm just being practical.' She looked distastefully around the rude chalet. 'So this is it, eh? You were going to be the big man – Rolls-Royces, penthouse flats in Park Lane – and look at you – smoking dog ends. It's pathetic.'

Ted shrugged.

'Have you done?' he asked quietly.

'It's your ego,' his ex-wife continued harshly. 'You just wanted to get up on a stage and be admired. Have a lot of people cheering you instead of getting a decent job and doing some proper work like everyone else.'

At this point, there was a tap at the door and immediately afterwards the shy, concerned face of Jeff Fairbrother peered round it.

'Er, may I come in?' he asked.

Ted nodded.

'Yes. Hilary's just leaving.'

Jeff looked at Hilary Bovis and then back at Ted.

'I wanted to see your wife as a matter of fact,' he explained. He turned to her. 'Look, Mrs Bovis, I know that Ted was ten pounds short, so here's a cheque on my personal account to make up the balance. Ted and I will sort it out later.'

Hilary took the cheque and contemplated it thoughtfully for a moment. She did not deign to thank the entertainments manager nor, for that matter, her ex-husband. She just said to him, with faint, reluctant admiration:

'You're a jammy devil, Ted. You're a liar, a twister and a con-man, but you always find someone who's a soft touch to help you out. I'll be back.'

And she turned to the door and, with an impressive swing of her powerful haunch, marched out of the chalet and the camp. Jeff shook his head and said:

'Glad I got here in time.'

He looked at Ted anticipating a word of gratitude. But Ted looked far from grateful. He swung off the bed, marched to the chalet door and peered out along the lines to make sure that Hilary was out of earshot. Then he turned on the entertainments manager reproachfully.

'What did you want to go and do that for?' he asked indignantly.

Jeff frowned faintly.

'How about saying "thank-you", Ted?' he suggested.

'Thank you, my eye. I'd just done a deal with her. She'd accepted forty quid. Now I owe you a tenner.'

Jeff nodded agreement.

'You do – and God knows when I'm going to get it back.'

'You're going to get it back right now,' said Ted, to Jeff's astonishment.

And Ted extracted from his pocket an astounding, and very fat, roll of fivers, peeled two off and handed them to Jeff. The entertainments manager gaped at the bank-roll.

'Where did you get that?' he asked faintly.

'The fiver you lent me – as you know, I put it on a horse.'

'But I thought it lost!'

'Who said it lost?' asked Ted irritably. 'Did I say it lost? Did I?'

Jeff looked from the money to Ted and back at the money. Slowly an expression of reproach, verging on anger, crystallised on his face. Finally he turned on his heel and stalked out of the chalet. Ted shook his head in disbelief and rushed after him.

'Jeff,' he called urgently, 'why are you walking out? What's the matter with you? I'm the one that's out of pocket. I'm the injured party. Jeff!'

But the entertainments manager stalked on with a grim expression.

Having concluded his tale, the senior camper leaned towards his auditor and tapped him on the arm.

'And you know why, don't you?' he asked.

Mr Walter Cardew started slightly at the contact, almost as if he had been dozing.

'Hm? What?' he asked.

'You know why Jeff reacted like that?'

'Erm – no, not really.'
'It was his first inkling.'
'Inkling?'
'His first dawning suspicion of the depravity and corruption rampant amongst his staff. Well, in fact, as I said they're a fly bunch and since then they've managed to win their way back into Jeff's confidence. But he has no idea that every time there's a changeover – yes, and in between times too for some of them – criminal conspiracies are formed and practised upon the innocent campers. Anyway, now you know what you're up against.'
Mr Cardew eyed the senior camper narrowly.
'Let me get this straight –'
'That's what I've been trying to help you to do.'
'You're suggesting that these pathetic little fiddles are serious competition?'
'Seems serious to me.'
'I'm talking about a fully-professional operation.'
'They'd be on to you. They wouldn't like it.'
Mr Cardew grinned wolfishly.
'They wouldn't know what hit them. We could clean out this place under their noses.'
'We?'
'Oh let's drop the pretence. We both know who the other is. We'll start this evening in one of the bars. I suggest we kick off with the race-horse lark. You can –'
'Hang on, hang on,' urged the senior camper, holding up one hand warningly. 'I don't know what you're talking about.'
The other shook his head sadly.
'If you want to make it hard for yourself – well, I'd better get over to the pool and have a word with that dotty chalet maid.'
Mr Cardew began to rise to his feet. The senior camper shrugged.
'If you want. She's not a very good conversationalist. But I'll tell you something – if I was this bloke – the one you met on the Isle of Wight, do you know what I'd have done?

I mean when I first spotted you getting out of the taxi here last Saturday?'

Cardew stood for a moment, looking down at Charley Binns. Then he seated himself once more and, fixing the other with a questioning gaze, asked:

'What would you have done?'

'Well, I'd have asked myself what a middle-grade fraudsman out of the Smoke was doing here in Maplin's? I'd have figured that it wasn't lust for gain that brought him so far from his native pastures but that perhaps those pastures had got a bit hot for him. So then I'd have contacted one or two people I know down South and perhaps I'd have learned that the Chelsea police were very interested in establishing the whereabouts of this geezer – something to do with a property-development swindle that went wrong. After that I'd have had a word with Mickey Branlis.'

'Who's Mickey Branlis?'

'Nice fellow. Completely straight now. He's the camp photographer, you know, goes around taking candid shots of the families and the loving couples and then tries to flog them the results. Mickey did a short stretch in Parkhurst a few years ago – five I think it was – but he's been straight ever since. I'd have asked Mickey to do me a favour and he'd have done it.'

'What kind of favour,' asked Cardew tightly.

'Get a few candid snaps – something like these.'

And the senior camper reached into his jacket pocket and withdrew a few prints which he scattered carelessly on the table in front of him.

'Came out well, didn't they?' he asked warmly. 'Like the flared collar – makes you look even more distinguished than the outfit you're wearing at present. I'm sure Inspector Tonks of the Chelsea CID would be delighted to receive a few holiday snaps like these.'

'You're playing with fire, my son,' said Cardew evenly. 'Two can play at that game.'

'But why should they play at all? You see if I was this bloke – the one from the Isle of Wight – and I'd got myself dug in cosily at Maplin's with lots of friends and three months every year to prepare for the fray and get my strength back, all I'd want is to be left alone. So I'd explain that situation to the fraudsman from the Smoke and suggest that we parted affably. In fact, I'd go further than that. I'd book a taxi for him to be waiting at the main gates at precisely half-past four and carry him away to greener pastures elsewhere. Live and let live.'

For a long moment, Mr Cardew glared at the senior camper who occupied himself in rolling a new little cigarette. Then Mr Cardew smiled and finally chuckled:

'Neat,' he said. 'Your set. Don't think much of this patch in any case. But we may meet again somewhere – sometime – and finish the match.'

'We may,' nodded Charley Binns. 'But it's a big world.'

Cardew rose to his feet once more.

'I'll be off then,' he said.

'No, no,' protested the senior camper. 'Half-past four, he'd have ordered the taxi for. It's only twenty to now. Take you ten minutes to pack and get to the main gates. Leaves half an hour. Just long enough for me to tell you the strange tale of Mr Partridge, the grumpy old Punch-and-Judy man, and his encounter with –'

'Go to hell,' said Cardew feelingly. 'I've listened to enough of your guff.'

'No, you haven't,' returned the senior camper, sounding hurt. 'My stories are famous around here. Everyone loves them. You shouldn't have come to Maplin's if you didn't want to hear them.' The senior camper reached for the snapshots scattered on the table, shuffled them into a little pack and tapped it meaningfully on the table top. 'Sit down,' he said pleasantly.

There was a moment's pause and then Walter Cardew sighed deeply and sat down.

'Good,' said Charley Binns, 'now this story began one cold and dreary day –'

Maplin Intercontinental

The senior camper read the telegram carefully three times and then started to pack. The telegram was signed 'Uncle Henry' and it was quite long. It explained that the sender was planning a little fishing trip, that he had learned of a stream filled with very fat fish and that he hoped his friend, Charley Binns, would be able to join him on the trip. 'Uncle Henry' planned to set out on his fishing trip the following day and if Charley Binns cared to accompany him the latter would have to be at 'Uncle Henry's' place by six in the evening.

The senior camper's first impulse was to ignore the telegram. It was only Monday and he was not due to leave Maplin's until the following Saturday. He was reluctant to lose five whole days of his annual holiday even though that holiday lasted for three months every year. But then he reflected that it was, in any case, nearly time to resume his working life, that 'Uncle Henry' had an excellent nose for big fish and that, in any case, the weather had taken a turn for the worse. He would leave by the 11.45 train the following morning. There was no address on the telegram but the senior camper knew that he would find his 'Uncle Henry' in a small room above a corner shop in a back street in Leicester. From there they would set off on their fishing expedition which might, previous experience suggested, take them anywhere in England and possibly beyond it.

When asked about his profession Charley Binns normally contented himself with declaring that he was self-employed. If pressed about it, he specified that he was an insurance broker. It was certainly true that insurance companies were the ultimate source of his income but his relationship with them was devious and unofficial. There had been a time when Charley Binns had dreamed of a different profession. He had been raised in a Barnardo's home and had never known either his mother or his father. He had, at

Barnardo's, revealed a considerable talent for painting. When of age, he had set up as a painter in London and had even had a few one-man shows and decent reviews. But he had never sold enough paintings to live on and he had ultimately met someone, not unlike 'Uncle Henry', who had taken him under his wing and directed him into his present line of work. It was not bad work, Charley Binns reflected, in that it was exciting, challenging, interesting and, at its best, highly-profitable. But it did carry certain risks to dignity and even liberty and, twice in his life, Charley Binns had found himself compulsorily resident in an institution where he would not have been from his own choice.

Early in his second career, Charley Binns had decided that he needed to have, once a year, a complete separation from it. He had hit upon the idea of his long annual holiday at Maplin's where, over the years, he had become an institution. Amongst his colleagues outside the camp, only 'Uncle Henry' knew of the senior camper's annual retreat and this was, in fact, the first time that 'Uncle Henry' had ever contacted him there. This too was a factor in persuading the senior camper to abbreviate his holiday. Only a big project would have induced 'Uncle Henry' to breach the senior camper's stern injunction that he must not be disturbed during the summer months.

Intrigued though he was by the telegram, the senior camper was nonetheless a trifle heavy of heart at having to leave his beloved Maplin's five days early. Having finished his packing the senior camper went to the door of his chalet, opened it and looked out at the day. It was, in fact, just ending and large, dark clouds, laden with rain and night, were scudding above the chalet-lines. Fierce gusts of wind, carrying a fine spray of rain-drops, periodically shook the trees and brought down the first of the dead leaves. The senior camper smiled. He was glad of the weather. It meant that most of the campers would be indoors and he would be able to take a last, nostalgic walk in reasonable solitude.

Half an hour later, having visited all his favourite spots, like the kiddies' paddling pool, the skating rink, the fishing pool and the horses' meadow, Charley Binns entered the Dutch bar for his last drinking session of the summer. It was still relatively early and the place was only about half full. The senior camper bought himself a pint of best bitter and looked round for an empty table. There was none but at one table the only occupant was a young woman. Charley Binns made his way to it and asked politely:

'May I join you?'

The young woman glanced at him, shrugged and glanced away. Charley Binns chose to interpret the gesture as an assent and he seated himself. The young woman, he noticed, had no drink in front of her. With a shrewd glance, as he seated himself, Charley Binns noticed that she was about twenty-one or twenty-two, shabbily dressed, thin and that she was gnawing her lower lip. She looked somehow detached from the place as if she were not fully participating in the endless fun-and-games. Perhaps, reflected the senior camper, she needed cheering up with a rousing tale of camp life.

'Can I get you a drink?' he asked, by way of striking up an acquaintance.

She looked at him vaguely and said:

'What?'

'You seem preoccupied, my daughter,' the senior camper remarked.

'Oh, go to hell,' muttered the girl ungraciously.

'You shouldn't be rude to strangers,' the senior camper chided her. Then he noticed that her eyes were red-rimmed and that her mascara had run. 'You've been crying,' he said.

'So what?'

'Have you got a problem?'

'Yes. I can't decide whether to gas myself or drown myself.'

The senior camper was shocked. This was far from the spirit of Maplin's.

'You're joking, my daughter,' he said without conviction.

'Am I?' asked the girl, favouring him with a hard stare.

The senior camper decided that she was in earnest.

'No, you're not. What's happened? Had a tiff with your boy-friend?'

'No. I haven't got a boy-friend. That's what I came here for – to get a boy-friend and now – now –'

The girl looked away. For a moment, she gazed straight ahead and then, as tears began visibly to roll down her cheeks, she covered her face with her hands.

The senior camper reached out a comforting hand but, the instant it made contact with the girl's shoulder, she shuddered violently and hissed:

'Leave me alone.'

'As you wish. But it often helps to talk about things.'

The senior camper took a swig of his beer. He noticed that several people had noticed the girl's distressed condition and were glancing at them. After a while the girl said, through sobs:

'What's there to talk about? Talking won't get it back.'

'Get what back?'

'My purse.'

'Is that it? You've lost your purse?'

'Yes, that's bleeding it,' said the girl, removing her hands from her eyes and looking hard at the senior camper. Her eyes were, by now, even more ravaged but her glance was direct. Charley Binns had been somewhat shocked by her use of the word 'bleeding' because otherwise her way of speech had struck him as dignified and pleasant.

The girl sniffed and wiped her nose with a handkerchief.

'Sorry about this,' she said grimly. 'If you meant it, I wouldn't mind a drink – gin and lime.'

'Certainly,' said Charley Binns cheerfully.

The service was slow and it took the senior camper the best part of ten minutes to get the order. When he returned to the table, the girl was more composed and had, moreover, cleaned up her face somewhat. It was, Charley Binns decided, a pleasant face, if thin.

'Here we are,' said the senior camper and deposited the gin and lime on the table in front of her. She took up the glass and sipped thoughtfully.

'Better tell me about it,' suggested the senior camper.

The girl shrugged.

'What's to tell? My purse was in my bag – this bag –' and she indicated a brown, mock-leather affair on her lap. 'And now it's not.'

'When did you notice it was missing?'

'I had a drink in here earlier. When I got back to my chalet, I opened my bag to get out my lipstick and found my purse was gone.'

'Have you told Security?'

'Of course I have. First thing I did.'

'And what did they say?'

'Said all they could do was wait and see if anyone handed it in. Likely, isn't it? Around here. Some good, honest soul finds a purse with fifty-three quid in it and –'

'How much?' asked the senior camper, astonished.

'Fifty-three quid.'

'That's a lot of money, my daughter.'

'Every penny I had in the world. Took me a year to save it. Now it's gone.' The girl smiled faintly as if the humorous side of it had only just struck her. Then she stopped smiling and Charley Binns wondered if he had ever seen a face that looked quite so cheerless.

'When did you last have it? For certain?'

'Here, of course.' The girl pointed at the bar. 'I bought a gin and lime there, so I must have had it then. But I've asked the barman – same barman that served me and he never saw it – or claims he didn't. I was sitting at this table. If I'd dropped it, it should be here. Do you see it?'

Charley Binns glanced about on the floor around the table. Then he stopped. The girl would, of course, have made a thorough search. It wasn't likely her purse would be just laying around.

'Still,' he said encouragingly, 'no need to take it so hard. It's only money.'

'That's right,' said the girl. 'Only money. Only it's the only money I had. Without it, I haven't got a penny to spend here during my holiday. I can't buy the clothes I was going to buy, any make-up or even a cup of bleeding tea.'

'Can't you phone home for some more?'

'My cat doesn't speak English.'

'What?'

'I haven't got any home. Just a bed-sitter with a cat in it. The landlady likes cats so she's agreed to feed it while I'm away. But she doesn't like single girls so she wouldn't send me any money.'

'Live alone, do you?'

'Apart from the cat, yes.'

'But you've got a mother and father?'

'My mother's dead – been dead for eight years. I've got a father but he ran off when I was nine. He wouldn't even recognise me even if he did ever want to see me again in which case he wouldn't know how to set about it. I haven't got anyone, not anyone.'

'Still,' said Charley Binns striving to find some consolation, 'you've paid for your week here in Maplin's, I take it?'

The girl nodded.

'Well then, you can still have a holiday.'

'I didn't come here for a holiday.'

'No?'

'No. You know how I spent today?'

'I am no mind-reader, my daughter.'

'Window shopping. Look at me. I look like some kind of slum girl out of an old film. I decided I'd wait till I'd got here and seen what the place was like and then buy some clothes to match it. So today, in town, I saw this stunning sack dress – electric blue – perfect for me because I look good in sacks.'

'You can have fun without new clothes.'

'I didn't come here to have fun. I came here to find a fellow. Shameless, aren't I? Well, I haven't got any shame left. It's been burned out of me by loneliness. I'll go mad if I have to go on being alone much longer. So I came here to find a husband – or just a rotten seducing lover – just some fellow that'll have me. You fancy my chances, dressed like this?'

'Some men –'

‘Pull the other. You were going to say some men don’t care about glamour and stuff? I’ve never met them. Now It’ll take me another year to save up and I don’t think I can wait that long.’

‘What do you do? For a living?’

‘Work in a cake shop.’

‘You’ll see. By the time the week’s up, you may have found a – a companion.’

‘I’m not staying. I’ll be off tomorrow. I’m not going to moon around here in my rags. You know, I think gas might be best. It’s slow but I just don’t fancy drowning.’

‘Are you serious?’

‘I don’t know. Have to find out when I get back to the bed-sitter and the cat. One good thing, there’s plenty of gas in my room. Gas fire and gas ring, so I won’t have much problem.’

‘You’ve had a disappointment –’

The girl laughed harshly. The senior camper continued:

‘But you’re not the only one, my daughter. Everyone has small disappointments and a lot of people have big ones. And life has to go on. Do you know Peggy, the chalet maid?’

The girl looked puzzled and then nodded.

‘The one with glasses and an overblown figure?’

‘Could be Peggy.’

‘She’s always singing while she works.’

‘You’ve said it, my daughter. Well Peggy recently – about three weeks ago, had a disappointment that makes yours look like dropping a tanner down a plug-hole. She wasn’t the only one. It was a season of disappointments. Tracey, the upper-crust yellowcoat, she also had a disappointment. Not as big as yours but real to her. Both those girls have come through just as you have to come through, my daughter. Would you like to hear about their problems?’

The girl put her elbow on the table and her face on the palm of her propped up hand. She looked sideways at the senior camper and said humorously:

‘Gee, I just love a good story.’

‘You’ve come to the right place, my daughter.

It all started in Jeff Fairbrother's office. Jeff, as you may know, is the entertainments manager of the camp and a very honourable bloke. He was once a famous professor at Cambridge but he found that nursing mummies all day made him get out of touch with reality. So he accepted a job here in Maplin's to meet real people, rather than embalmed ones, and he has been doing a good job. He was talking to Ted Bovis. That's the camp host, little round fellow with a big voice and a strong line in naughty jokes. Ted was saying:

'Let's get this straight, Jeff, are you giving me a bit of advice? Jeffrey Fairbrother, my friend, whom I have bent over backwards to help and to keep out of trouble? Or are you telling me off, from the other side of that desk, in your official capacity?'

Jeff, who hates to be pompous and formal but sometimes has to take a firm line with rascals like Ted, cleared his throat and said hesitantly:

'Well, actually I'm speaking to you with my entertainments manager's hat on.'

Ted snorted with wry mirth and returned cheekily:

'I've got news for you. You're not wearing it. You're talking through it.'

This impertinence angered Gladys Pugh who was present at the meeting as she usually is. Gladys is the raven-haired yellowcoat who leads us in sporting activities and makes those musical announcements over Radio Maplin in her charming Welsh lilt. Gladys adores Jeff and would do anything for him and she tries to protect him from cheeky staff members. Now she said:

'You've no right to say that to Mr Fairbrother. He's a very warm-hearted man. You don't think he likes having you on the carpet.'

Ted, seizing the opportunity for one of his famous innuendos, returned slyly:

'I've no idea who he likes having on the carpet.'

As Gladys tensed for a furious retort, Jeff said hastily:

'Look, we're wandering away from the point. The fact remains that I've had this complaint from Admin. that

Peggy can't get into your chalet, Ted, until 9 o'clock because you don't go to breakfast with the others.'

Ted sighed and shook his head wearily.

'Jeff, put yourself in my position,' he urged. 'I'm winding up them campers till half-past twelve at night. When I get back to my chalet my mind's in a turmoil. I can't just turn it off. You won't believe this but I go through my whole act again. I relive every nuance.'

Gladys saw her chance.

'Yes, all those dirty jokes!'

Ted glanced at her bleakly and appealed to Jeff.

'Does she have to be here?'

'I do feel for you, Ted,' said Jeff, prudently ignoring the query. 'My mind is very often desperately overloaded. I have a sort of technique for dealing with it. It goes like this. I sip my cocoa in bed, then I turn out the light and do what I used to do when I was a little boy.'

At this admission, both Gladys and Ted stared at him in astonishment. But Jeff, oblivious of their concern, explained what he meant.

'I imagine I'm climbing into a flowerpot and there's nice soft moss in the bottom with a faint, soporific smell. I curl up in the moss and snuggle down and listen to the rain, which I don't mind because I'm all dry and warm. Then I imagine myself getting smaller and smaller and I drop off.'

Ted nodded ironically.

'I'll try that tonight,' he promised. He glanced at his watch. 'Meanwhile, it's ten o'clock. Are you going to get yourself back to normal size and take the staff meeting, or shall I go next door and tell 'em all to buzz off?'

'No, no,' said Jeff hastily. 'Tell them I'm just coming.'

Ted hoisted himself to his feet, asking:

'Is that all you've got for me then?'

'Yes, but some time today I'd like you to tell me about the Most Popular Girl Yellowcoat of the Year Competition.'

'That old thing,' muttered Ted.

'We have to do it this week,' Jeff pointed out.

'I dunno why you bother,' said Ted. 'Gladys here has won it for the last five years. See you in a minute.' He waddled to the door but, just as he reached it, turned back with a frown on his face. 'There's just one thing, Jeff. How d'you stop the rain from coming through the hole in the flowerpot?'

'Oh, that's no problem,' Jeff assured him with a smile. 'The flowerpot is in the conservatory.'

Ted nodded.

'Of course. I forgot. You grew up in a big house.'

Whereupon Ted rolled through the door into the staff room. There he found most of the entertainments staff waiting impatiently. Mr Partridge was absent. He's the grumpy bloke that does the Punch-and-Judy for the kiddies. And Peggy, the chalet maid, who is not strictly entertainments staff but hangs around with them, was also missing.

Spike Dixon, the camp comedian, who you may have seen around looking like a bottle of OK sauce or a giant radish, and who is Ted's student in mirth, said testily:

'You were a long time, Ted. What have you been up to?'

Ted grinned.

'I've been having a chat with a little man that big who sleeps in a flowerpot,' and he held up two fingers about an inch apart.

'You what?' asked Spike, puzzled.

But before Ted could clarify his meaning, the office door opened and Jeff and Gladys came into the staff room.

'Good morning, everybody,' said Jeff cordially.

Then, before he could open the meeting proper, Yvonne Stuart-Hargreaves, as usual, began to moan. Yvonne is the partner of Barry Stuart-Hargreaves. The two of them are those dancing beanpoles you may have seen demonstrating fancy steps in the ballroom. They think highly of themselves and do a lot of complaining.

'Mr Fairbrother,' fluted Yvonne in her phoney upper-crust accent, 'before we start, there is just one small thing I want to get off my chest.'

Ted chuckled and commented softly:

'If it's on your chest it must be a small thing.'

Yvonne shot him a venomous look and continued:

'As you know, I'm not the sort of person to complain but last night, just as I was going to bed, I saw this awful face leering at me through my chalet window.'

Barry, her partner, sighed deeply and explained:

'It was, needless to say, Mr Partridge.'

'He was looking through all the windows,' Ted commented. 'He's been hitting the sauce. He was legless.'

'But I was in my nightdress,' screeched Yvonne.

Fred, the one-time ace jockey who now looks after the nags here, unwisely tried to match Ted's talent for wisecracking.

'That's probably what sobered him up,' he murmured.

But Fred, a decent sort of bloke, is vulnerable on one count and that should keep him from being insulting about others. This weakness of his was now exploited by Barry who wrinkled his nose, and remarked:

'There's an awful smell of horses around here. I wonder where it's coming from.'

Once again, Jeff hastened to intervene and keep the meeting from degenerating into a free-for-all.

'I'll have a word with Mr Partridge,' he assured Yvonne. 'Actually he has been much better lately. Now I'll just read out the alterations to Thursday's events.'

He took up a paper from his desk-top, cleared his throat but was halted by Partridge stumbling, red-faced and bleary-eyed, into the room.

'Sorry I'm late, Mr Fairbrother,' he apologised. 'I had a terrible night. Couldn't get to sleep. I was going through my Punch-and-Judy show again and again. Every time I closed my eyes I got 'orrible visions. I'll have to get some sleeping pills.'

'You don't need those,' Ted assured him. He looked at Jeff and went on, 'Tell him about the flowerpot, Jeff.'

At which point, Peggy, the chalet maid, bustled breathlessly into the staff room. She gasped with relief to see that the meeting was still in progess.

'Oh, I'm glad you're all here,' she explained. 'I thought I might miss you. I've just come from the Admin. block. There's a letter for you, Mr Fairbrother, and it's from Joe.'

Gladys gave her a steely look.

'Mr Maplin to you, Peggy,' she rebuked the informal girl. 'Give the letter to Mr Fairbrother.'

Peggy did so and Jeff began to open it immediately. As he was doing so, he remarked, 'I expect Mr Maplin will want me to read it out straight away. Normally I like to glance through it first – so please excuse any hesitations.' Jeff withdrew the letter from its envelope, unfolded it and began to read it aloud. ' "It's getting bigger and bigger my empire. That boring Chancellor of the Exchequer says we need to export, so I'm exporting Maplin fun and larking about. I'm starting up a venue for Yank holiday-makers on an island at Bahamas called San Martin. I've asked the Queen if I can change the name by deed pole to San Maplin. The locals are a lot of banana-eating layabouts who sit around all day doing sweet you-know-what. So I'm shipping in my best girl from each camp." ' At this point a stir went through the room and all the girls present murmured and glanced at each other speculatively. Jeff went on, ' "Whoever wins the Most Popular Girl Yellowcoat Contest will find herself hi-de-hiying under a palm tree in two weeks flat." '

'Wow!' exclaimed Tracey, who is small and comes from a more classy background than the other yellowcoat girls. 'Just think of all that sun and sand! Blue seas, white surf and waving palms.'

Betty, a cheerful yellowcoat, said, 'Anyway it's an improvement on last year's prize.'

'What was that?' asked Tracey, who wasn't here then.

Sylvia, the tall yellowcoat, explained: 'A three-quid voucher at the hairdressers for a permanent wave.'

'Which costs five quid,' amplified Betty.

Gary, one of the boy yellowcoats, piped up:

'I don't think it's fair.'

'Yeah,' agreed Bruce, another boy yellowcoat. 'Why don't we have a competition for the most popular boy yellowcoat?'

Jeff once more oiled the troubled waters.

'I expect Mr Maplin thinks the campers prefer to look at pretty girls.'

'Excuse me, Mr Fairbrother,' burst out Peggy excitedly. 'If one of the girls is going to the Bananas –' Peggy is not too strong on vocabulary '– there'll be a vacancy for a yellowcoat, won't there?'

Jeff nodded.

'I expect there will.'

'Can I be considered, please? I don't want to be pushy but I've done lots of little things for you around the camp and, well, I just think I ought to be considered.'

Now I should explain that it has been Peggy's dream for many years to become a yellowcoat. She would rather achieve that ambition than become Princess of Wales although I have no doubt that once she became a yellowcoat she'd be quite willing to marry the prince as well. She has got near her goal many times and has sometimes stood in for real yellowcoats in emergencies but she has always had to go back to her mop and pails and producing the cleanest plug-holes in Maplin's. But this seemed at last to be her chance and she was in seventh heaven when everyone in the room set up a chorus of approval. She gazed around at her friends and supporters and, in a choked voice, exclaimed:

'Oh! Oh, thanks! I don't know what to say. I'm going to cry. I'll have to go.'

And, overcome by emotion, she skipped out of the staff room. Jeff turned to his trusty girl Friday and said, 'Gladys, tell Peggy later that I'll definitely put her up for it.' He glanced at his watch. 'Time seems to be getting on. We'd better leave the rest of the points until tomorrow. So, Hi-de-hi!'

Gladys loyally returned 'Ho-de-ho' but the rest of the entertainments staff merely glanced at their boss morosely and began to shuffle out. As they went, Spike said to his chalet mate:

'This is exciting news, isn't is, Ted? Do you suppose they'll give any of us a chance to go out there?'

Ted nodded thoughtfully.

'They might do. Mind you, in your case, for American audiences you'll need a totally different style. I mean – forget funny vicars and chickens – you've got to think in terms of Bob Hope, George Burns and Jack Benny.'

'And Al Jolson?'

'I don't think you need go quite that far. Hey up, let's have a jar. I'll buy you a rum and Coca-Cola.'

Jeff and Gladys Pugh had returned to Jeff's little office. Jeff went straight to the window and gazed out thoughtfully for a while. Then he turned and said, 'A season in the Bahamas could add a whole new dimension to your life, Gladys.'

Gladys shook her head doubtfully.

'I'm not sure that I want to go in for the competition this year. There's so many things to keep me here. There's family obligations, emotional ties, expectations. No, I won't go in for it this year. It's only fair for me to give the other girls a chance now and then.'

This was, for anyone who knew Gladys Pugh, a strange and baffling speech for her to make. In the first place her idea of being fair to the girls under her was to bully them day and night. In the second place, she was a keen competitor who liked to win at anything she entered. In the third place, she was just as attracted as the other girls by the idea of a tropical paradise. But there was one important consideration behind her decision. Gladys Pugh was in love with Jeff Fairbrother and to give the girl her due would have followed him to a Maplin's camp on a glacier in Iceland, except that Joe Maplin would have too much horse sense to build one there, rather than go without him to the most heavenly spot on earth. But she could not say this outright. Jeff knew of her passion for him but Jeff was married, though separated, and felt himself unable to reciprocate. Therefore Gladys had to pretend that she had got over it and was basing her decision on quite different things.

Before Jeff could reply, the phone rang and he answered it.

'Jeffrey Fairbrother,' then his voice perked up. 'Oh, good

morning, Mr Maplin. How unusual to speak to you in person. I've just been reading your letter to the entertainments staff.' He listened for a moment and then rolled his eyes comically for Gladys. 'No, no, I didn't posh it up, Mr Maplin. I read it just as you wrote it. Word for word. Yes. Yes. Who, me? How exciting! Well, I'm overwhelmed and rather honoured. Thank you for letting me know. Goodbye.'

He put the receiver down and stood stock-still for a moment, obviously musing heavily. Gladys tapped her foot impatiently and then could stand the suspense no longer.

'What was all that about?' she demanded.

Jeff looked at her thoughtfully.

'It was Joe Maplin in person.'

'I know that,' said Gladys irritably. 'But what did he say?'

Jeff smiled and gave a little modest shrug.

'It's about this new camp,' he explained. 'He's going to send an Englishman out as entertainments manager. I'm on the short list.'

Gladys gaped at him.

'You're joking,' she protested.

Jeff shook his head. He was amused.

'Why would I be joking? In fact, it's a very short, short list. It's between me and Dick Meadows from Camber Sands.'

Gladys stared at him with a faintly-anguished expression. Then she said, 'Well, you'll get it for sure. It'll be a walkover. Dick Meadows is common as muck!'

She stood for a moment longer in thought. Then she squared her shoulders, turned and headed towards the door.

'Where are you going?' asked Jeff in surprise.

Gladys stopped and turned to explain, her manner glowing with purpose.

'I'm going to get to work on those campers. I'm going to win that competition.'

'But I thought you didn't want to go?'

Gladys smiled faintly and in her smile was all the mystery of the female sex.

'Well, I've changed my mind, haven't I?' she said softly. 'It's a woman's privilege. Women don't get many privileges around here.'

And she set off to win votes.

As you might expect, for the next few days practically the only topic of conversation amongst the entertainments staff was the new camp in the Bahamas. Over drinks in the Jolly Roger bar, which featured a plastic Long John Silver with a plastic parrot on his shoulder waving his crutch at a plastic Captain Kidd, Yvonne said to Barry:

'You know I've been thinking. I'm going to enter for the most popular girl yellowcoat competition.'

Barry did a mild double take and then pointed out:

'But you're not a yellowcoat, dear.'

'I do many of the boring yellowcoat duties,' Yvonne said a trifle sharply, 'thanks to you not reading our contract properly in 1956.'

Barry sighed delicately.

'It wasn't my fault. Our agent was supposed to read it. I couldn't read it. I didn't have my glasses with me when we signed it.'

'Yes, you did,' snapped Yvonne, with unaccustomed severity. 'They were in your top pocket. You were too vain to put them on.'

Barry did not reply to this allegation. He simply said:

'You wouldn't stand an earthly competing with all those young girls.'

'But all they have is youth,' protested Yvonne. 'I have charm, sophistication, experience and breeding. The Americans love that sort of thing. That's why they have English butlers.'

Barry looked a trifle crestfallen.

'Well, supposing by some fluke of chance you did manage to scrape home and win. What am I supposed to do while you're lolling around in the Bahamas with all those American millionaires and their English butlers?'

But Yvonne was not open to such appeals.

'You can get yourself another partner until I get back,' she snapped.

Barry rolled his eyes to heaven.

'Charming,' he said feelingly. 'And after all I've done for you.'

Yvonne's eyes glinted dangerously.

'After all you've done for me? May I remind you that when I first took you up you were a third-rate chorus boy. I taught you everything. I taught you how to dress. How to speak. How to stand up when a lady enters the room. I stopped you holding your tableknife like a pen. I even allowed you to use my name. My family name, Stuart-Hargreaves.'

'And what a mouthful it is,' murmured Barry. 'Yvonne and Barry Stuart-Hargreaves. Compères never get it right when they introduce us. On the posters it won't even go on one line.'

Yvonne smiled with silken rebuke.

'And just how far do you think you would have got in this profession with a name like Bert Pratt?'

At this, Barry glanced about anxiously.

'That's right,' he reproached her mournfully. 'Tell the whole camp.'

'You don't like to remember about Bert Pratt, do you?' went on Yvonne remorselessly.

'Please, keep your voice down.'

Observing this scene from a nearby table were Fred Quilly and old Partridge. They could not hear the actual conversation but they grasped the tone of it.

'Look at 'em,' said Partridge. 'They're hissing at each other like a couple of vipers.'

'They'd fit right in in the Bahamas,' pointed out Fred. 'You'd have the palms waving, the surf roaring and them moaning.'

Patridge looked reflective as he downed his whisky at a gulp.

'I'd go well out there, you know. I'd be a novelty for them American kids.'

Fred looked incredulous.

'Punch-and-Judy? It's too corny.'

'I'd adapt my act to suit the audience. I'd dress Punch up as a gangster – instead of sausages I'd have hamburgers and instead of a policeman I'd have an American cop.'

'Well, I wouldn't go if they asked me,' proclaimed Fred. 'My horses just couldn't stand the trip.'

Partridge laughed nastily.

'They wouldn't take them old horses,' he jeered. 'They'd have new American horses.'

Fred shook his head positively.

'I can't start getting to know new foreign horses at my time of life.'

'You'd have to train them to –'

But at that point there was an interruption. Looking dishevelled and yet ecstatic, Peggy flew into the bar, crying:

'Yvonne, Barry, Fred, it's happened! I'm going to be a yellowcoat. My dream has come true.'

Fred failed to get excited by these tidings.

'A bit sudden, wasn't it?' he asked mildly.

Peggy rushed over to him.

'Mr Fairbrother did it,' she gabbled. 'He rung up Head Office to ask about a replacement for the girl who is going to the Boheemers and they said it was up to him. So he's given it to me. Oh, he's a lovely man.'

Fred smiled faintly and rose to: 'Well done, Peggy. You deserve it, all right.'

'Oh, thanks. Will you have a drink, Fred? No, everyone's got to have a drink. Highballs all round. I'm paying.' Peggy rummaged in her bag and emerged from it looking a little nonplussed. 'Hang on, I've only got half a crown. Could you lend me a pound, Fred?'

Meanwhile, in the chalet he shared with Ted Bovis, Spike was behaving somewhat peculiarly. He was seated on a chair with a violin on his lap. On his head he wore a snap-brimmed hat and in his left hand he held a giant cigar. To the empty chalet, and in an excruciating American accent, he proclaimed: 'Greetings, Ladies and Gentlemen. A funny thing happened to me as I was on the way to the theatre tonight and I would like to play you a little music on my violin while I tell you about it.'

During the latter part of this effort, Ted entered the chalet, paused and listened critically to what his protégé was doing.

'What's up, Spike?' he asked, when it was over.

Spike winked at him.

'I'm doing what you told me. I'm making my act American in case we get a chance to go to the Bahamas.'

'I see. You don't mind if I make a suggestion?'

'Feel free.'

Ted seated himself on his bed.

'Well, "Ladies and Gentlemen's" a bit formal for Americans. How about "Good evening, folks?" '

Spike shook his head ruefully.

'Of course. Why didn't I think of that.'

'And, Spike, you never told me you could play the violin?'

'I can't Ted. I just go as if to play it and then I stop to tell the gag so I never get around to playing it, see?'

'Knockout,' said Ted. 'Let's have the gag.'

Spike cleared his throat.

'Well, folks, I'd sure like to play you a little music on my violin while I tell you about it.' Here, Spike stuck the huge cigar in his mouth and looked as if he was about to play. But he went on talking instead. 'As I got off the bus and stepped on to the pavement an old tramp came up to me.'

'Just a minute, Spike,' Ted helpfully but irritatingly interrupted again. 'I don't want to criticise, but I can't hear a word you're saying for that cigar.'

'Right,' agreed Spike. 'I'll have to take it out before I start talking.'

'Is it going to be lit?'

'Of course it is.'

'Well, you don't mind me saying, do you? When you go to use your bow, you'll burn your arm.'

Spike sighed.

'I'll have it on the other side of my mouth.'

'Then you'll burn your violin, won't you? I'm afraid it's either the violin or the cigar, Spike.'

'I'll have the cigar.'

'Continue.'

'As I stepped off the bus on to the pavement an old tramp came up to me.'

'Hang on a minute, Spike. It's not a bus in America, it's a streetcar. It's not a pavement. It's a sidewalk – and they don't have tramps, they have bums.'

Spike put down his violin and stood up. He went morosely to the tiny window of the chalet and looked out. He turned.

'It's not going to work, is it, Ted?' he asked hopelessly.

' 'Course it is. Tell you what, we'll work up a Fred Astaire and Ginger Rogers routine. You can be Ginger Rogers.'

'Bum,' said Spike feelingly.

Preparations for the great night of the competition went on, and soon it was time to draw lots for the sponsors. Jeff had two piles of small slips of paper on his desk. The papers in one pile held the names of the competitors and the papers in the other pile held the names of the sponsors. Gladys entered holding two boxes about ten inches square. Peggy was with her. Gladys glanced about and said testily:

'Isn't Ted here yet? I want to get this done before the staff meeting.'

'Oh,' said Peggy helpfully, 'he may be a minute late. I had to shake him to wake him.' She brightened up. 'I won't be doing that much longer, will I? I went down to the town yesterday tea time to try on my yellowcoat. I'm having one specially made, you know.'

'Well never mind about that now,' Gladys admonished her. Then she asked Jeff, 'Have you got the girls' names?'

Jeff nodded and indicated one of the piles of slips in front of him.

'They're in that pile and the sponsors are in the other.'

Gladys started putting the two piles in separate boxes. Jeff continued, 'Now, Gladys, please explain to me how all this works.'

Gladys shrugged.

'It's the same at every camp. The host – that's Ted – presents the show in the ballroom. The girl yellowcoats come on one at a time and are introduced by different members of the staff, who give them a sort of build-up. You see, they're the sponsors.'

'I see,' said Jeff. 'But –'

At this point, Ted breezed into the office.

'Evenin' all,' he greeted them.

'Come on, Ted,' urged Jeff. 'You're late, as usual.'

'Ah, but it's all your fault,' said Ted firmly. 'I couldn't get to sleep last night. So I crept into that flowerpot like you said. I snuggled down on the moss and listened to the rain. Suddenly this huge beetle the size of a horse came straight for me and before I knew where I was I was fighting for my life. I didn't get a wink after that.'

Peggy exclaimed in wonder:

'Oh, do you use a flowerpot too, Ted? How funny. I've always done that when I couldn't sleep. I shan't do it any more now you've told me about that beetle.'

'Do be quiet, Peggy,' snapped Gladys. 'Can we all proceed with the matter in hand?'

'Yes, of course,' Jeff promised. He looked at Ted. 'I'm sorry about the beetle.'

Gladys ignored all this chatter about flowerpots and beetles and instructed them. 'Now we pick the names out of the boxes to make sure everything's fair and above board. We have to be especially careful this year with the winner going to the Bahamas.'

Ted spoke to his boss.

'Any news about you getting the job, Jeff?'

Jeff shook his head.

'No, I haven't heard a thing.'

'You're bound to get it,' Gladys said positively. 'Now, draw the first yellowcoat, Peggy.'

Peggy made a big thing of it. She screwed up her eyes like a child playing a party game, stretched out her hand, fumbled about for the box, found it, dipped her hand in and drew out a folded slip. Then she opened her eyes and peered at it.

'I can't see,' she exclaimed. 'My glasses have steamed up. It's the excitement.'

'Give me that,' said Ted and whipped the bit of paper from her hands. He read the name. 'Betty.'

At this, Gladys drew a slip from the other box and said, 'Her sponsor is Fred Quilly.'

Peggy drew another name and peered at it.

'Ooh, my glasses have cleared now. It's Tracey.'

Gladys drew a slip.

'Her sponsor is Mr Partridge.'

She looked expectantly at Peggy. But Peggy, as happens to her very easily, had got sidetracked. She burbled:

'I wish they had a competition for the most popular boy yellowcoat. I'd sponsor Gary. When he looks at me my knees go to jelly. Mind you, he doesn't look at me very often.'

Jeff tapped on the desk-top.

'The next name, please, Peggy.'

'Oh sorry,' said Peggy, drawing another slip. 'It's Sylvia.'

'She's drawn Spike,' said Gladys. She sniffed, 'He's going to have a job making her sound attractive.'

'Yvonne,' said Peggy.

'Barry,' said Gladys.

'Serve them both right,' said Ted feelingly.

'Gladys,' said Peggy.

Gladys drew a slip. She looked at Jeff with a rueful smile.

'You're going to have to do me, Jeff,' she said softly.

Jeff smiled at her.

'Let's hope you win it again, Gladys,' he said encouragingly.

'Don't worry,' returned Gladys. 'I'm taking no chances. We'll just see who's the most popular girl yellowcoat in the camp.'

'Oh, Gladys,' said Peggy, 'I've been meaning to ask you. Can I follow you round and take notes? I want to learn all I can.'

Gladys smiled patronisingly at the yellowcoat-to-be.

'Help yourself, Peggy. It'll be quite an education for you. Those girls won't see my heels for dust.'

And so, for the few remaining days before the competition, Peggy followed Gladys around learning how to be a champion yellowcoat. It was an impressive course. Peggy watched Gladys hand out sickly sweets to small children, wearing an even sicklier smile. She watched Gladys helping old ladies up and down steps. She watched Gladys bobbing for apples and laughing heartily at the circle of campers around her when her hair got wet. She watched Gladys doing a hundred things to endear her to the campers. Of course, the other girl yellowcoats were engaged in the same kind of canvassing for votes but there seemed little doubt to Peggy, agog with admiration, that Gladys moved twice as fast and three times as successfully as the rest.

At last the great night came. The ballroom was packed. It had been beautifully decorated for the occasion with plastic flowers and garlands. Coloured lights played over the scene. Waitresses circulated with trays of drinks and the atmosphere was festive.

The earlier part of the evening was devoted to songs and instrumental music performed by talented boy yellowcoats and a display of Viennese waltzing by Barry and Yvonne. After the dancing, Yvonne hurried off to change into her yellowcoat outfit and Stanley, a boy yellowcoat, did a Mario Lanza impersonation. At its conclusion, and after the enthusiastic applause, Ted came out onto the stage. There was a fanfare and a drum roll and a spotlight picked out his rotund figure. Ted gazed around for a moment as if overcome by the occasion and then roared:

'Hi-de-hi!'

'Ho-de-ho!' roared the campers back at him.

'And now,' said Ted, 'the moment you've all been waiting for – the most popular girl yellowcoat of the season contest.' There was an even longer and more impressive fanfare and then Ted continued. 'Now you've all got your voting papers. When you've seen all the girls, put a cross on the one of your choice.' Here Ted made a little joke. He pointed towards a dark corner and said sternly, 'No, sir, not on the girl, on the voting paper. That's better.

When you've all voted Peggy will collect your slips in her secret ballot box.'

Peggy, not yet a yellowcoat but becomingly attired in a flowery summer dress, held out the ballot box for all to see.

Ted resumed:

'The first contestant – sponsored by our resident children's entertainer, Uncle Willie, is the delightful pocket-venus, Tracey Bentwood.'

From the wings came Tracey, immaculately groomed and smiling winningly, and grumpy old Partridge, his face fixed, as Gladys had instructed, into a hideous leer which was the closest he could get to a friendly smile. Tracey did a little pirouette and curtsy and then stepped back a pace. Partridge seized the microphone and began:

'Tracey Bentwood is twenty-four. She was born in Stoke Newington. Her vital statistics are thirty-six, twenty-three, thirty-six. Her hobbies are tennis, swimming and stewing.'

Tracey frowned momentarily and hissed under her breath:

'Sewing!'

'Hm? Oh yes, sewing,' amended Partridge. 'I can't see properly with all those bleeding lights in my eyes. Anyway, I think you ought to vote for Tracey because she's a lovely girl who goes around like a ray of sunshine.'

Partridge continued frowning at his script and turning it over to see if there was any more but Ted stepped forwards and smoothly elbowed him to one side.

'Come on, campers,' roared Ted. 'Let's have a big hand for Tracey Bentwood.'

Whereupon wild applause broke out in the great auditorium and all the yellowcoats other than Tracey felt their hearts sink into their pretty boots. Ted went on:

'Next, sponsored by your resident jockey, Fred Quilly, the curvaceous Betty Whistler.'

The campers, quick to take the cue, greeted the attractive yellowcoat with loud and prolonged whistles as well as cheers. Fred Quilly, who had cleaned and scrubbed himself thoroughly and whose close connection with horses was thus only detectable to those standing very close to him, joined her and, when the applause had died down somewhat, spoke into the microphone.

'Betty Whistler is twenty-five, born in 'Arrow-on-the-'Ill. Her vital statistics are forty, twenty-four, thirty-six. Her hobbies are reading Charles Dickens and jujitsu. I think she ought to win because she's a good sport and doesn't use the jujitsu except as a last resort.'

To Fred's surprise, since his little attempts at humour usually went down like a belch at a banquet, the campers laughed uproariously even as Ted said:

'Let's hear it for Betty Whistler!'

And then Betty got a hand which was not far short of Tracey's. Peggy, who had, by now, gravitated into the audience and who was so excited that she couldn't contain herself, bent over a startled camper and babbled:

'I shall be illegible for this competition next year. I'm going to be a yellowcoat to replace the winner. Isn't life wonderful?'

And she pattered away to another table as Ted resumed.

'Next – introduced by our camp comic, Spike Dixon, the girl you all like to whistle at but you can't because your tongue's hanging out – Sylvia Garnsy – known to us all here at Maplin's simply as "Legs". Show it "Legs".'

Whereupon Sylvia, daringly, entered with her skirt held an inch or two above the knee, producing rapturous squeals from the male campers. Spike moved to the microphone.

'Sylvia Garnsy,' he proclaimed, is twenty-five.

This was too much for Gladys who, severe with all her yellowcoats, has always reserved her special criticism for Sylvia, perhaps because she is always having to tell her to take her hands out of her pockets and perhaps for some other reason. In any event, at this statement of Spike's, she turned to Jeff, who was standing beside her at the bar, and said scornfully:

'At the very least.'

Jeff smiled faintly. Spike went on.

'Sylvia was born in Littlehampton. Her vital statistics are thirty-four, twenty-three, thirty-four. She's very sporty and her hobbies are riding, swimming, sailing, running and climbing.'

At which, Gladys said with feigned surprise:

'He's left out the main one.'

'I think,' continued Spike, 'that you ought to vote for her because she's always laughing and joking and fooling around and she makes sure that everybody has a good time.'

Spike retreated and Ted advanced and ordered:

'Give her a big hand, campers.'

And Sylvia too received a rousing ovation. Who was in the lead? It was hard to tell from the amount of applause since all the yellowcoats so far presented had received nearly as deafening a round.

'Next,' said Ted, 'and sponsored by her partner, Barry, I ask you to welcome Yvonne Stuart-Hargreaves.'

Whereupon Yvonne and Barry, looking as if they were about to fling themselves into some wild fandango, minced out onto the stage. This time the applause, although encouraging, was definitely not so wild as it had been for the younger girl yellowcoats. Yvonne smiled in a ladylike way, nevertheless, and her consort, perhaps still a little miffed from her announcement that she was quite prepared to go to the Bahamas without him, presented her in the following terms:

'Yvonne was born in 1914 –' and at this below-the-belt blow Yvonne darted her partner a venomous glance. Barry went on serenely, 'She comes from Southport. Her vital statistics are thirty-two, thirty-two, thirty-two. Her hobbies are advising people, character analysis and witty conversation. I think you ought to vote for her because she's different from all the others.'

Yvonne put a brave face on things and smiled sweetly at the campers but there was a sense of strain in her smile which the audience could not miss.

'Let's hear it for Yvonne,' said Ted and there was a scattering of applause. As the Stuart-Hargreaves left the platform, Ted went on hastily:

'And last, but not least, sponsored by your entertainments manager, Jeffrey Fairbrother, your popular sports organiser – Gladys Pugh.'

A little before the announcement, Jeff and Gladys had stationed themselves in the wings and, as the spotlight swung towards them, they stepped forwards to centre-stage. There was an explosion of applause from the floor and Jeff could only make his presentation in the end by holding up his hand for silence. Then he smiled his slightly twisted smile and began:

'Gladys Pugh is twenty-six –' At this there was an unseemly, but fortunately barely-audible, titter of mirth from the the other yellowcoats now standing amongst the audience, which caused Gladys to direct a vengeful glance in their direction. Jeff continued quickly. 'She was born in Pontypridd. Her measurements are thirty-six, twenty-six, thirty-six' – and at this point Jeff attempted the thing he always attempts but never gets right, a little joke. '– although, of course, I haven't checked them. Ha, ha.'

There was no answering 'ha, ha' and Jeff resumed.

'Her hobbies are looking after children, collecting stray dogs and reading to old people. I think she should win because she's a thoroughly genuine, warm-hearted and good person and we all love her.'

'Thank you, Gladys Pugh,' Ted came in as Jeff retreated from the mike. 'Well, campers, how about a big hand for Gladys?'

And once again the auditorium shook as the campers roared their approval. Surely Gladys had the edge? Yes, but Tracey had done well too and so had – no, it was no use. No one listening could have picked a winner from the applause thus far although it did seem likely that poor Yvonne Stuart-Hargreaves was trailing badly.

'You've seen them all,' said Ted, and then couldn't resist, 'although you haven't seen all there is to see of them. But we don't want to be closed down, do we? Well that's it, campers, the rest is up to you. Just put your cross on your voting paper and then place it in the secret ballot box and very soon now you'll know the answer to the big question: who is the most popular girl yellowcoat at Maplin's this year? Is it Tracey or Gladys or any one of the others? Only you can tell. Play, Ramona.'

Whereupon, Ramona struck up on the organ and, a moment later, Ted loosed forth one of his favourite sentimental songs. Jeff collected the secret ballot box and retired to his office to count the votes. The yellowcoats all felt the strain. After all, this was no ordinary annual competition. The winner would be off to the sunny Bahamas. Several of the girls went to the bar to help pass the waiting period with a drink. Peggy capered about amongst the campers confiding in favoured ones the great news that her ambition was soon to be fulfilled.

Ted finished his ballad and started another. After the third, he summoned Gary up on stage to relieve him and, having bowed himself off stage, marched purposefully off towards Jeff's office. The campers, tired of waiting for the results, were starting a slow handclap and poor Gary could hardly make himself heard.

Ted flung open the door to Jeff's office and strode in.

'What are you doing, Jeff?' he asked. 'They're going wild out there.'

Jeff sat, looking miserable and perplexed, in front of his little heaps of ballot papers. He sighed as he looked up at Ted.

'I've done two recounts,' he confessed, 'but it always comes out the same. There's 182 votes for Tracey, 229 for Betty, nine for Yvonne and then the crunch. Gladys and Sylvia have got 345 votes each, a dead heat. The box held one thousand, one hundred and ten marked ballot papers and one spoiled one.'

Ted shook his head reproachfully.

'Well, you'll have to do something, Jeff, and do it soon. Gladys and Sylvia can't both go to the Bahamas.'

'I know,' said Jeff miserably. He picked up a ballot paper which was separate from the rest and peered at it closely. 'This silly ass has put a cross halfway between Sylvia and Gladys. Which one do you think he meant to win?'

Ted took the paper and studied it. He shrugged.

'Who knows? You'll just have to make up your mind which name is nearest the cross.'

Jeff took the paper back.

'It could be either –'

'Well, you can't delay any longer. Listen to that clapping.'

They both listened and heard distinctly the distant thud of the dreaded slow handclap.

'I don't know what to do, Ted,' the harassed entertainments manager confessed.

'Look, Jeff,' said Ted in an exasperated voice. 'Just for once in your life, you're going to have to make a decision.'

For a moment, they gazed at each other. Then Jeff stood up.

'Right,' he said. 'I have.'

'That's the stuff,' said Ted approvingly. 'I'll get back there and announce you.'

A few moments later, Ted was back on the rostrum with the microphone firmly in his grasp.

'Sorry to have kept you waiting, campers,' he said, as the slow handclap grudgingly abated, 'but for the last hour Mr Fairbrother has been incarcerated in his office and that's a nasty thing to happen to anybody. He's been counting the votes. And now here with the winner is your popular entertainments manager, Jeffrey Fairbrother.'

Jeff did his best to beam at the campers but, as always, he did not do it very convincingly.

'Well, ladies and gentlemen,' he announced, 'it's been a close run thing. I've had to re-count the votes several times.'

Gladys could bear the suspense no longer. She was now standing next to Ted and she whispered to him:

'Who won?'

Ted shrugged.

'I don't know. Jeff had to give the casting vote.'

And Jeff continued.

'The winner of the 1959 Most Popular Girl yellowcoat Contest is Sylvia Garnsy.'

The audience burst into a perfect storm of applause as Sylvia, practically jumping up and down with delight, came forwards to receive her sash. True, a few of the less polite campers, disappointed that their favourites had lost, booed a little but generally speaking the occasion was not marred by loutish behaviour. Ted reverently placed the winner's sash around Sylvia's neck and the band played 'For She's a Jolly Good Fellow'. Jeff edged his way off stage and joined Gladys Pugh who was looking faintly stunned by the result.

'So,' she said quietly although her voice throbbed with deep reproach, 'you've got me out of your hair. I know you had to give the casting vote.'

'True,' agreed Jeff.

'And now you'll be taking Sylvia to the Bahamas with you.'

Jeff looked her full in the face and smiled his little, shy smile. He shook his head.

'I'm not going, Gladys,' he informed her. 'There was a telegram this morning.'

Gladys gazed at him in wonder. She looked like one of those druids when the sun comes up over Stonehenge, full of joy and praise.

'Oh, Jeff,' she breathed. 'You gave her the vote so that we could stay together.'

Jeff nodded.

'I had to, Gladys. I couldn't run the place without you. You're a damn good right-hand man.'

Just for an instant the rapturous look on Gladys' face wavered but then she decided that the news was too good not to appreciate and it returned in full force.

'Oh Jeff,' she whispered.

The next day, at lunchtime, the entire entertainments staff gathered in the Jolly Roger bar, under Long John Silver's upraised crutch, for a little celebration. Sylvia was, naturally, the centre of attention. Jeff raised his glass to her and said:

'Here's to you, Sylvia.'

There were murmurs of 'hear! hear!' from many of those present and everyone raised his or her glass and quaffed.

'Are you packed yet?' Ted asked the lucky winner. 'Just think, ten more days and you'll be soaking up all that sun.'

Gladys smiled benevolently at the girl who had snatched the prize from under her nose and said feelingly:

'I'm glad for you. I really am.'

'I expect,' surmised Ted, 'you'll be buying some fancy gear in London to take with you?'

'Well, no,' said Sylvia, looking starry-eyed. 'I'm going via New York. The clothes there are great.'

Partridge frowned.

'You want to watch yourself in New York,' he cautioned gruffly. 'It's full of muggers and hoods – a bit like Kilburn.'

Barry Stuart-Hargreaves edged up to the camp comedian and whispered:

'Ted, I never asked, how many votes did Yvonne get?'

Ted cleared his throat diplomatically, noticing that Yvonne herself was within earshot, and said:

'It was very close.'

Yvonne swung round and confronted him.

'How close?' she asked eagerly.

Ted sighed.

'Well, let's put it like this. If your fan club hadn't got himself locked in the toilet, you might have got into double figures.'

Barry smiled faintly causing Yvonne to round on him.

'What are you smirking about?'

'Pure relief, my dear, that I'm not going to lose you,' breathed Barry hastily.

There was a stir as the second 'winner' came bustling into the Jolly Roger bar. Peggy had, as everyone noticed, a brown paper parcel tucked under her arm: She looked radiant. She went straight up to Jeff.

'Mr Fairbrother,' she babbled breathlessly, 'as Sylvia's going Wednesday week, can I take over the ballroom on Tuesday night?'

Jeff smiled graciously.

'Yes, of course you can, Peggy,' he assured her.

Spike approached the new yellowcoat and tapped her brown paper parcel.

'Is that your coat?' he asked her.

'Ooh yes,' admitted Peggy. 'I've just collected it. It's a lovely fit. Even the man in the shop said it was one of the best fits he'd ever seen.'

'Put it on,' urged Fred Quilly gruffly.

Peggy blushed and looked around at all of them.

'Shall I?' she asked hopefully.

There was a chorus of approval.

'Well, turn your backs,' said Peggy.

'What for?' asked Partridge. 'It's not knickers. It's a coat.'

'You're right,' said Peggy. 'It's just that I feel so self-conscious. Like Cinderella, you know. But she didn't turn her back when the mice turned into pumpkins, did she? Here goes.'

Peggy began to undo the parcel. Because of her nervousness it took her some time but finally she drew out a brand-new canary yellow coat and held it up for all to admire. Then, like a queen pulling on her coronation robe, she put the garment on. There were murmurs from all present and a scattering of applause.

'Oh, it's such lovely stuff,' gasped Peggy. 'I can hardly believe it. It's like a dream.'

'Let me get you a drink, Peggy?' said Jeff pleasantly. 'To celebrate.'

'Ooh, thank you,' squealed Peggy. 'But I shouldn't drink on duty, should I?'

'You're not on duty yet,' Jeff assured her.

'Well, in that case,' said Peggy. 'I'll have a small sherry.'

'Sweet or dry?' asked Jeff.

'Ooh, wet, please,' said Peggy, stroking her coat.

Jeff grinned and turned to the barman. Then he stopped and a slight frown appeared on his face. He was gazing hard at the television set behind the bar which was on and showing some pictures of what looked like a tropical storm. There were mountainous waves lashing a shore where palm trees waved madly. There were flattened buildings and cars which had been blown onto their sides and people stumbling about amidst wreckage. Jeff said to the barman:

'Turn up the sound, would you?'

Spike glanced at the picture and said:

'What's up, Jeff? It's only the news.'

But by then the barman had reached up and increased the volume. As the announcer's voice blared out, everyone turned and looked at the set.

'At 4.30 yesterday afternoon hurricane Angela hit the island of San Martin. Most of the island escaped serious damage but the North tip received the full force. This is the location of the new Maplin Holiday Camp which took over two years to construct. It was completely destroyed in two hours. From his home in Hampstead Mr Maplin said "Fate's clobbered me and that's a fact. I never had none of this at Camber Sands". Cricket. At Lord's today England gave the Indian bowlers a run for their –'

'Turn it off,' ordered Jeff quietly and the barman reached up and switched off the set. A profound silence reigned amongst the entertainments staff as everyone took in the significance of the amazing tidings they had just heard. Then, with almost a single thought, they all turned and gazed at Sylvia. She reached up and covered her eyes and said 'Boohoo', but they could tell she wasn't really crying.

'Oh, Sylvia, how awful,' said Betty.

'I think I knew something like this would happen,' said Sylvia sadly. 'When I was a little girl my dad promised to buy me a pony for my birthday. The week before he was transferred to a new office and we had to live in Birmingham.'

'I wonder what you'll get as an alternative prize?' said Yvonne and the secret satisfaction in her voice was apparent to all.

'A voucher to have my nails manicured, I should think,' said Sylvia sadly.

'I wouldn't worry,' said Fred in a kindly way. 'Joe Maplin will rebuild it. He won't be beaten.'

'But it'll take another two years at least,' pointed out Spike.

'And I might not win next time,' said Sylvia.

'What about Peggy?' exclaimed Ted, remembering the

other girl whose hopes would have been blasted by the big wind in the Bahamas. He looked around and said, 'Where is she?'

'She was here a second ago,' said Spike. 'Look!'

He pointed to an object on the floor near where Peggy had been last seen. They all stared at it in silence. It was the yellow coat.

For the next week Peggy slunk about the camp radiating gloom. Whenever one of the entertainments staff happened to pass her and greet her, she would reply with no more than a sad smile. There was no bounce left in her. She'd been a chalet maid for a long time and it was obvious that she felt now that there wasn't much hope of her ever being anything else. She gave up eating knickerbocker glories with double-whipped-cream, extra thick fudge sauce and a side helping of pistachio nuts and instead took to knocking back white ladies in the Dutch bar at night until she was a little unsteady on her feet. It reached the stage where Miss Cathcart complained about her work to Jeff and he promised to have a word with her.

It was about a week after the devastating news of the hurricane that Jeff went searching along the chalet lines, having steeled himself to perform a duty he hated – reprimanding Peggy Ollerenshaw whom everyone loved in spite of her scatty ways. He was hoping, indeed, that he wouldn't find her but, after a few minutes, he saw her issue from a chalet, carrying a duster, and move away towards her holy of holies, the cleaning chalet.

As she approached her little citadel, a group of campers came out of a side path and moved towards her. As they passed, they said cheerfully:

'Hello, Peggy! Hi-de-hi! How's our favourite maid?' and similar things. But poor Peggy didn't respond.

The campers shrugged and moved on. But a moment later something happened which surprised and delighted Jeff. Peggy turned and called after their retreating forms:

'Ho-de-ho! I'll make it. I'll be all right. Hi-de-hi!'

She hadn't seen Jeff who was concealed by some shrubs. The campers she had addressed turned and looked after her with smiles as she turned back on her path and skipped away towards her cleaning chalet shouting at the top of her voice:

'Hi-de-hi! Hi-de-hi! Hi-de-hi!'

Jeff watched her go, smiling his strange little smile, and then turned and headed back towards his office. He knew that she had come through.

'So you see, my daughter,' the senior camper addressed the girl who had lost her purse, 'you can survive disappointments. You just have to find the spirit. Now where's your spirit?'

'In Dexter's.'

'Dexter's?' asked the senior camper, puzzled.

'The dress shop in town. That's where my electric blue sack dress is. Oh, god, I wish I'd bought it today.'

'Why didn't you?'

'Because it was twenty-three pounds and I've never spent that much on a dress in my life. I decided I'd think it over for one more day but really I knew I was going to have it. Now, I'm not, am I?'

'Peggy never got to wear her yellow jacket. But, as you said yourself, she goes around singing.'

'I can't sing.'

'But you can dance. They have dances here every day. You'll meet a good bloke.'

The girl smiled.

'I already have.'

The senior camper looked puzzled.

'But I thought –' then he took her meaning and grinned. 'Not a father-figure, my daughter. A bloke your own age.'

'I'll tell you what –' said the girl.

'What?'

'I'll stay if you buy me a drink every evening and tell me another story. How's that?'

Charley Binns smiled.

'You're what I've been looking for all summer. But I'm afraid it's too late.'

'Why?'

'I'm leaving tomorrow.'

The girl's face fell.

'But tomorrow's Tuesday. People don't leave on Tuesday. They leave on Saturday.'

The senior camper sighed.

'I know. But I've got to cut short my holiday. Work.'

'What do you do?'

'I'm self-employed – to do with insurance –'

'Where?'

'I travel, my daughter. All over England.'

'Well, I'm not staying without you. I don't know a soul here.'

'You will. You're a pretty girl.'

'Not without make-up. I'm practically out of that. Even if I could patch up some of my rotten old clothes.'

'Here,' said Charley Binns, taking a big, white fiver out of his wallet and holding it out to her. 'That's just on account.'

'What do you mean "on account"?' asked the girl looking hard at the note but not reaching for it.

'On account of your fifty-three quid which I'm going to get back for you.'

The girl nodded ironically.

'Oh, I am glad. Just how are you going to do that?'

'My name's Charley Binns – what's yours incidentally?'

'Mo Thompson.'

'Mo?'

'Maureen, then. The other girls in the shop call me "Mo".'

'Well then, Maureen, I'm the senior camper. I know more about this place than anyone. I spend three months here every year. If your purse is still in the camp, I'll find it.'

'And if you don't?'

'Then you can owe me the fiver. Give me it next summer.'

'I may not come next summer.'

'You will. Everyone comes back to Maplin's. Now then, what's your chalet number?'

'Two hundred and five.'

'And it was a brown purse with fifty-three pounds in it. What kind of notes?'

'Ten fives and three ones.'

'Old or new?'

'Brand new. They always pay us in new notes. And the purse wasn't brown. It was green.'

'Got it. Green purse with ten fives and three ones, all new notes. I'll just go and prowl about a bit. If I get lucky you'll see me again this year – if not, next.'

The following morning, at half-past nine, there was a knock at Maureen's chalet door. She went to the door and opened it. Charley Binns stood there, grinning at her.

'What time does Dexter's open?' he asked.

She gaped at him.

'You're not saying –'

The senior camper drew from his pocket a small, shabby green purse and held it out to her.

'Better get down there,' he urged, 'before someone else snaffles up the dress.'

Maureen seized the purse and opened it. Inside was a fat bundle of new notes. She counted them.

'There's a fiver short,' said the senior camper apologetically. 'It's the fiver I lent you last night. You don't need a loan now, do you?'

Maureen threw her arms around his neck and kissed him fervently on the neck and cheeks.

'How did you do it?' she gasped. 'Where did you find it?'

Charley Binns shrugged.

'Matter of fact, I haven't done anything. Except collect it from Security. Someone handed it in this morning, just before I called there to see if there was any news. Just as well because my inquiries had not proved fruitful as they say in the law reports.'

'You've been good to me – lending me that fiver, and you didn't know if you'd get it back.'

'Glad it's all turned out well. You'll have a good week

now. I happened to notice, a lot of fine young men came in on Saturday. You won't be short of company.'

'Bet they can't tell stories like you.'

'They'll have other qualities, my daughter.'

Maureen sighed.

'Still, I'm going to miss you. Do you have to go?'

''Fraid so.' The senior camper glanced at his watch. 'Matter of fact, my taxi'll be at the main gate in quarter of an hour. I'd better get my things.'

'Hang on –' said Maureen urgently, as Charley Binns turned towards the door of the chalet.

Charley Binns turned back. The girl was gazing at him hard.

'How about –' said Maureen, gulping faintly. 'How about if I came with you?'

The senior camper gazed at her in surprise.

'Do what?' he asked.

'You're alone, aren't you? Like me?'

The senior camper was indeed alone. He had long ago decided that it was better that way. He didn't want to subject a wife, and possibly a family, to the risks of separation that his work necessarily entailed. He had friends, in different parts of the country, who were hospitable to him when he visited them but he had no commitments, no durable relationships, with any women.

'I travel light,' said the senior camper.

'Well, I'm tired of travelling light. I wouldn't mind travelling heavy for a while, perhaps for the rest of my life. I'd be good to you. I've got a very kind nature, really I have. And when I'm dressed up right, you wouldn't be ashamed of me.'

Charley Binns tried to visualise Maureen Thompson in her electric blue sack dress. He failed but he didn't really need to. She was a little pale and a little shabby but he could see that she had the makings of a stunner. She had a pretty oval face and a flawless figure. Dressed up at night, in certain clubs and other places of entertainment he knew in London and other big cities, she'd be an eye-catcher. It would be elegant and delightful to travel with such a girl.

And he was a pretty good judge of character. He believed her when she said she had a kind nature. She would be good to him. And he felt sure that they'd make a good team.

'Well?' asked Maureen.

But she must be twenty years, at least, younger than he was. He was strongly tempted but he knew that he hadn't the right. He smiled eagerly.

'Do you mean it?' he asked, taking her hand and stroking it.

'I mean it,' she said quietly.

'You wouldn't be sorry,' he said fervently. 'And you wouldn't have any trouble with the old woman.'

'With who?' asked Maureen withdrawing her hand.

'My old woman.'

'You're married?'

'Who isn't?' asked Charley Binns, rolling his eyes comically.

'But you said you were alone.'

'I am now. She went home last week because she had one of her turns. My eldest daughter took her. She's about your age. You'd get on a treat together. You could both take turns nursing the old woman when she's down with her back or her head – it's always one or the other. She's a little odd at the best of times but she's deaf as a post – which would be all right for us, wouldn't it?'

Maureen gazed at him in dismay.

'But –' she began.

'I know what you're thinking,' Charley hurried on. 'How could we get away with it? Nothing easier. I've been telling her my work's getting on top of me and that I've got to train up an assistant. You're the new assistant. You'd be able to come with me on some of my trips – maybe once a month. The rest of the time you'd be quite snug in our house in Bethnal Green. You'd have to get a job, of course, but there's lots of shops in the neighbourhood. It would be a real home for you. And, in addition, we'd have our little trips now and then, wouldn't we?'

The senior camper winked very suggestively. Maureen hung her head.

'Right,' Charley Binns said positively. 'There's not much time if we're to catch the train. I'll drop you at Bethnal Green, introduce you to the family, and then I'll be off for a week or two while you settle in. Get packed and join me at the main gate in twenty minutes or so. But don't be late. I won't be able to wait if you are. Understood?'

Maureen nodded slightly. Charley Binns grabbed her hand again, pulled her towards him and kissed her on the lips while his hands roved fervently for a moment over her body. Maureen bore it patiently.

'See you very soon – my darling!' said Charley Binns amorously. He turned and hurried out of the chalet.

Maureen Thompson sat down on her bed. A few tears started from her eyes and trickled down her cheeks. She sniffed, reached up and brushed them away. Oh well, she'd got her money back. She thought of the sack dress and the thought cheered her up. She was lucky really. She might have gone with him and found all that out when it was too late. At least now she had her holiday in front of her. Then a thought struck her. Suppose when she didn't turn up at the main gate, he decided that he really wanted her? He'd come looking for her. She'd better clear out of the chalet until he was safely out of Maplin's. She never wanted to see that one again.

She hastily smoothed herself up and left the chalet. She took her money with her. There was the back entrance to the camp. She'd go out that way, walk along the sea-front to the town, and get her dress. By the time she got back he'd certainly have left – and if he hadn't, she could take care of herself. She'd just tell him that she'd changed her mind.

As she was making her way to the main gate, she passed the building where the security office was. And it suddenly occurred to her that she ought to find out who had so honestly handed in her purse. Whoever it was they deserved thanks and perhaps a box of chocolates or a bunch of flowers. She turned into the building and went up a flight of stairs to the security office. She knocked on the door and a voice called, 'Come in.' She entered and saw the same young security man she had consulted about her loss the day before. When he saw her he smiled sympathetically.

'Hello,' said Maureen. 'It's about my purse. I'd like to know who handed it in?'

The young man nodded.

'I'll have a look in the book,' he said, bringing out a small notebook from a drawer. 'Sorry about the money,' he added.

'What?' asked Maureen, a sudden pang tightening her chest.

He shrugged sadly.

'I suppose whoever first found it nicked the money and just dropped the purse. Big temptation, fifty-three quid. Let's see, here it is: "Mrs Amanda Wiles, Chalet 236". She found the empty purse this morning outside the dining room and handed it in at eight forty-seven. Charley Binns collected it for you at just after nine and I assume he's returned it to you?'

Maureen nodded mechanically. Something else occurred to her.

'He's very kind, isn't he?' she said. 'Charley Binns?'

'The best,' said the young man.

'And his wife – what's she like?'

The young man looked puzzled.

'Has he got a wife? Never seen him with her and I've seen him every summer for the past six years. Hang on, don't you want to take down –'

But Maureen had an urgent appointment. She wanted to travel all over England with the kindest, most generous, most entertaining man she had ever met, even if he was old enough to be her father. So she ran as fast as she could. She ran towards the main gate, past the staff chalet lines and the ballroom, along the path lined with flowering shrubs, past the reception hall and hairdressing salon, dodging amongst campers and occasionally bumping them in her flight, on past the 'Olympic-sized swimming pool' which was when she saw him. He was at the main gate fifty yards or so ahead of her and he was just stepping into a taxi. She called as she ran, 'Charley! Charley! Wait for me! Charley! I'm coming with you! Charley!'

He heard her and stopped. He looked over the open door of the taxi at her. He smiled. She was close enough now to see what a warm smile he had under the thatch of iron-grey hair. He raised a hand and blew her a little kiss and then, in a trice, he was in the taxi. She ran harder and she knew it was no use. She saw the little puff of smoke issue from the car's exhaust and then it started rolling. She was almost level with it. Charley Binns was looking at her and, still smiling but with something very sad in his countenance, he was shaking his head. And then the machine, with the senior camper inside, picked up speed and moved out of the gates and away up the coast road.